Josh's Garden
Worlds of War Away

By Shelley Rae

Summary: Young Josh is sent away at an early age to find a long
lost paradise and must fight the Law and the enemy to keep them
from finding the paradise that his father sent him to find. He
finds his betrothed unbeknownst to him, at the time, and they
initially live happily ever after.

ISBN: 978-0-9973863-0-1 Paperback
Library of Congress Copyright Registration #: TX 8-190-225

Acknowledgements

Kevin Edminster for his understanding and compassion while I wrote 24/7.

Greg Forkum of Sooner Printing, Inc., Miami, OK for his help with printing and setting up the cover and the trimming of the pages. My deepest gratitude for his help to get me started on my first publishing.

Dedicated to my son Christopher whom, without his teenage-ness in my life, at the time of this writing, and his encouragement throughout the years to finish and publish this book, it would not have happened.

PROLOGUE

She waited. In the cold dark hours of the early morning, as the sun rose late in the ice blue sky, she waited. For what purpose; was there a dark secret to this mystery woman that no one knew? She had come to the small town once before, but that seemed like generations ago.

She was a ravishing blonde with deep green eyes. She didn't fit in here: she had fine jewelry and beautiful clothes. She came to the small town for the first time, that long ago day, with a fine man on her arm. He had dark hair and those same mysterious green eyes. He wore the finest that money could buy. But, why were they here then?

Why was she here now, alone? Were they hiding some deep dark secret, that they felt they could not share with anyone? Was she still hiding the same secret, or did she just wait? Why would she stay here alone?

They were the only people left in the small town who had a car, only they never rode in theirs. They had a horse, and that was their mode of transportation. They never left the small town. All of their necessities were purchased in the small, expensive local store.

She still used the horse for transportation. She held a secret that only the love of her life knew, and she would stay right there and wait for him. He would come to her again. He had always returned to her. This time it was an unspoken promise. She had the same feeling now that she'd had all the other times. She would just wait; her and the baby she carried inside of her.

CHAPTER ONE

"Josh, can you give me a hand here? There is a storm due in at the end of the week and we must get these hides where we can work on them," His father's voice was strong, but kind. "As soon as we are done then I need you and your sisters to go to the store for double supplies. They are predicting a bad one this time." You could see the disgust in his eyes. It seemed as if he hated the storms now but it had not always been this way. The storms had changed since the war had started in the outer worlds and Naihu, Josh's father, was unsure if this was a changed storm or if it would be an ordinary period of white.

Josh was but seven seasons when his father had called him that day. They ran a hide business in a small town on the world SuKhan, a town that had not seen the sights of war or enemies for many, many turns of the sun.

His father's father started the business when he was not much older than Josh. They had plenty to live on. Josh never wanted for anything, except to make his father and mother proud of him. He worked hard for his father and

1

never seemed to complain that he never had time to play. Their family had worked hard for many generations to get where they were, and Josh knew how important it was.

He longed for only one other thing in his life. He wanted to know that there was a woman out there, somewhere. One that was as kind, smart, strong, and beautiful as his mother. When he turned seven seasons his body and his mind started changing. He began to think more like an adult and not so much like a child.

Josh was the oldest of six children. His sisters helped with the business since his youngest and newest twin brothers arrived not long ago. His mother spent all of her time with them and his other brother, who was only a few season older than they. She was able to help when they rested in the late mornings and afternoons. Sometimes she rested herself, but only when there was little to do.

Josh's mother was a stunning woman. Her long golden hair with light streaks of auburn red throughout was tied in a high knot on the back of her rounded head. He had only seen it down a few times. Her eyes were almost as golden as her hair with a squint of green speckled around the inner eye. She was a gentle being and no matter how tough things got she always had a simple solution to make things seem not so tough.

Josh spent all of his time with his father or with his good friend when time permitted. Josh had not heard the birds and animals that morning, so he knew his father was right. His father was a wise man. He knew the storms were coming before anyone else. He had seen many seasons of storms, but he had always said, 'They are good for the trees and animals. They are important because, they provide the nourishment to the land. If there weren't storms, there would be nothing'. Until recently, they had begun to disgust him. He knew more about them than anyone. There was a time when it seemed as if he wanted them to come. Now, there was an uneasy tone in his words and Josh could hear it loud and clear.

His father told him, "There's a place, somewhere, where the days are long and hot and the sun raises high and stays there somehow. Someday, my children, we will go to find this place, this 'land of Naru'. Until then, we must prepare the hides for market." Naihu would sit back in his chair and watch the amazement on his children's faces. They always seemed to enjoy the stories that he told.

Their house was very large. It had three floors; one was the 'work' room. That is where all the hides were prepared for market. Josh's mother and two sisters worked the hides, in the season of no storms, out on the ground. But when the storms were due, the hides were taken into the work room through the large wooden doorway. Everyone would work the hides in the storm season since there was little else to do. The long flat iron would smooth the inside of the hide and make it feel like downy. This also stretched and shaped it. Once the hide was shaped then it was hung to cure. After that, patterns were drawn on them with a stick from the warming fire that had been cooled quickly in water. Josh's mother would then cut each piece and help sew them together with the threads that were stripped from the inside of the hide.

The middle floor was where the cook fire and warming fire were, a place where the family gathered daily, in the cool hours, to talk of dreams and business, to tell stories of long ago. Josh's mother prepared all the meals there.

When the business and the two younger boys took all of her time, she hired a woman from town to prepare meals. Her name was Marhya, and she was a wonderful person.

The top floor was where everyone slept. Each space was divided from the other with thick hides hung from the ceiling. Their beds were piles of rich, thick, soft hides. Every season these hides were taken to the work floor and turned into materials to be worn by the family or sold at the local market. New hides from the previous season replaced these. Each space had a trunk in it for materials and personal things, each of those with a removable drawer on the top.

Josh, being the oldest, had a space to himself. His two younger sisters shared the same space and his three brothers stayed in the space with his mother and father. They were still quite young and to keep them from waking the others in the cool hours, his mother kept them close to her.

Their house was one of the largest in the small town, though; Josh's father had told him one time that there was some that made theirs look small. Josh could only think of two others, the storekeeper's and his best friend's. But those two did not make this one look small. Theirs had always seemed to be the best.

Their work floor was made of large stones, like most of the houses in the town. It went half way under the land. The rest of the house was built from the large trees that covered the land. Josh's house had many windows in it, unlike most of the small houses, which had only one or two. The light was needed during the storms to prepare the hides.

Josh had always lived here, a place where the sun only reaches the horizon. Then, after a while, it would raise high in the sky. He had been told by his best friend that there were places that the sun left for many hours. There was total blackness, like taking all the furs on the sleep surface and putting them on your eyes. His friend was from another place, somewhere very far away. Maybe he knew of the 'land of Naru' that his father spoke about from time to time.

He had moved to the town when Josh was small, like his brothers. And, unlike most of the strangers, his family stayed for many seasons. Josh could remember the time that the boys met for the first time. It was at the storekeeper's. Josh had noticed the difference of the boy's clothing. They had not lived here long and were in to buy supplies and proper clothing.

Josh remembers commenting to his father, "Why does he have that kind of clothes?"

His father would just tell him, "There is more to life than the style of material that you put on your back. You will learn this, my son, when you are older."

Josh was not sure what his father meant most of the time. It was always something he would learn when he got older. Sometimes he wanted to be older just to be able to truly understand his father.

Marhya was Josh's best friend's mother. She was a very polite woman, just a few seasons younger than Josh's own mother. They had lots of money and a car. They seemed to drive it everywhere, even to the store, though it was only half a day's ride, by horse, to their house.

Ran told him, "It only takes a short time this way, and you have the rest of the day to play." Ran seemed to

5

have more time on his hands for play than most of the kids Josh knew. But they seemed to find enough time together to become the best of friends in a short while. Marhya would bring Ran with her when she prepared meals for Josh's mother.

Until Josh was old enough to help his father, the two boys spent many hours playing. Sometimes they would go to the running water and catch the animals, only to set them free again and start all over. It was a game that Josh enjoyed playing with his father, until his father became so busy with the business.

"What kind of games do you like to play?" He would ask Ran from time to time.

"I like to look to the horizon and wonder where the sun goes."

"The sun doesn't go anywhere, it just shrinks. If you wake up in the middle of the cool hours you can see what is left of it. I have only seen it a few times."

That is when Ran told him of the place where it goes away for many hours.

"Where does it go?" Josh inquired.

"How should I know? It just goes. Why does your sun shrink?" He teased.

Josh and Ran spent the long days playing together. Sometimes they helped Josh's father. They would take the white, after a storm, and make things like castles. Ran taught this game to Josh. He had learned to make it from the ground, though, not white.

"Josh, if you are done with your daydream, I could sure use your help here."

Josh did not hear his father. He was lost in his daydreaming. Josh did not see much of his friend anymore.

He spent most of his time with his father, taking care of the business. His father would catch him daydreaming almost every day.

Ran would come with his mother soon to help her prepare the meals, but he did not like the hard work of preparing hides, so he would help Josh's mother with the other three boys. They were like one big family. Many times they would all eat together, especially in the storm season. Sometimes they would have to spend the night because of the storms.

"Josh!" His father's voice was stern this time.

"Yes, father. I am sorry, it's just that..."

"You will have plenty of time later in the week to check on Ran. Now, we must get these hides in. At this rate it will take us two days." His father was teasing. The two of them would have the hides on the sled in plenty of time for Josh to ride to the store and be back shortly before the cool hours began.

They piled the hides on the sled and pushed the sled to the door of the work floor. While Josh emptied the sled for the next run, his father skinned another one. Josh was learning to skin, but he was not fast like his father, yet. He knew the time would come, and his father could spend his days doing the light work and Josh could take over the heavier work.

They finished with the hides just as Marhya and Ran drove up.

She greeted Josh's father and ruffled the dark hair on Josh's head. "How is everything this fine day? Are the storms getting closer?" Marhya asked. She could see they had taken the hides to the work floor.

"Yes, they are due at the end of the week."

7

"Father, may I take Ran to the store with me?" Josh asked with so much excitement in his voice, his father could hardly say no.

"If it is okay with his mother it is okay with me. Just don't doddle and lose track of the time. It will take you some time to get there and I want you back before the cool hours. Ran may not want to take the ride with you; however, he has never done it by horse." He glanced at Marhya and winked, knowing that Ran would jump at the opportunity.

"Yes, it is fine, if he wants to." Her voice teased.

The two boys ran to the horse jumping and screaming for joy. This would be the first time in a few seasons that the boys would have almost half a day together. Who cared if they were only going to the store? For them it was just another adventure.

"Josh, remember, double supplies. And, pick up some of the good tanning threads. I have some important hides to prepare this season and I want them to be of the finest quality," his father called to him as they rode off through the trees.

The ride was more fun this time. Maybe it was because it gave the boys a chance to catch up. Josh showed Ran a small house, close up. Ran had only seen them from a distance as they whizzed by in their car. They were similar to their own large houses, but small. The bottom floor was made of stone, but only a fraction the size of the boys' bottom floors. They only had one other floor, though.

"Where do they sleep in the cool hours?" Ran questioned his friend.

"In front of the warming fire, on the floor," Josh replied, thinking of his own space that would take up most of the small house. They both shuddered to think of having no space at all. Ran's space was quite a bit smaller than Josh's. But he had no sisters, and only one brother, who stayed with his mother still. He knew that in a few seasons he would have to share his space, but for now it was all his.

"Josh, why are you so quiet?" Ran was concerned that Josh might be keeping something from him, and they kept no secrets. None.

"I am just thinking of what my father said as we rode off. Why does he want special tanning threads? We usually make our own, and they are fine for what these people need around here." Josh was confused.

He had helped his father now for three seasons, and only one other time did he want this type of thread. Josh could not remember what his father had done with those hides, but he could remember the storms that year. They were some of the worst he had seen. One time, it took his father nearly three days to tunnel the family out. He remembers, because they all stayed at the storekeeper's until the white disappeared that season. He did not see much of his father that season. The men would come and get supplies, and then, they would be gone again.

"Josh, do you like the hide business?" Ran questioned him, again.

"Yes, it's okay, but sometimes, especially now, I wish I had more time to spend with you. We always had such fun. My father always told me 'when you are older, you will understand.' I always wanted to be older, so that I could understand. Now that I am older, I don't want to be. I miss the times of being able to play." He seemed to grow older even as he spoke. He had a lot of responsibility, and he admired his father. "We had better get moving, or we will surely freeze to death in the cool hours." He kicked the horse and made it go faster.

Ran had become older, too. He did not have the responsibility of helping in a business, but he had a much bigger one. His father was not home much. He worked somewhere in a place Ran referred to as the old world. Ran was the family caretaker. He took on the responsibilities of his father while he was away. Josh considered this one of the biggest responsibilities that existed. Though Ran never had to work to pay for their supplies, he still had to keep track of what was there and how much was needed.

As they came into a clearing, there was the store. A man sat on a bench outside, reading the daily reports. "Hey, Josh, how's the business?" He asked.

"Busy, we are preparing for the storm season. Can I have my father place an order for you?" Josh was a business man. He could sell a hide to just about anyone.

"No, I placed my order a few days ago. Your mother and sisters probably have it almost finished. I will stop before the storm hits and pick them up, he replied.

The boys thanked the man and went inside. Josh knew that double supplies would take a while to load and he wanted to get started. "My father says we need double today. He says they are predicting a big one this time. Also, I need some of that special tanning thread that you have." Josh busied himself with loading the supplies into the satchels on the horse.

"Is your father planning a trip, young man?" The storekeeper asked as he followed Josh out to help with the last of the list. The storekeeper was as curious about the thread as Josh.

"Not that I know of, he has a special order to fill for someone." The special order was not out of the ordinary, but they always used the tanning threads that they made themselves.

"Okay, Josh, here are the rest of your supplies and your threads. Ran, do you have enough supplies for your family, in case this storm hits sooner than planned?" The storekeeper knew that Ran and his family had only been in a few days ago, but they were not predicting the storms to start then.

"Yes, sir, we have plenty, thank you," replied Ran, as he jogged the list through his head of things that they may need.

"Well, we are loaded and ready to go. We will be back before the cool hours begin, if we get going now." Josh was anxious to get back. He did not like being out in the cool hours. It was very hard to warm up again, and they only had enough material on to keep them warm while the sun was high.

The boys returned just in time to have a hot plate by the warming fire. It was a nice evening, and Josh was happy to have his friend beside him. They would not be able to stay. The storms were on the horizon and would be here late the next day. Ran needed to finish preparing his home for the season.

Marhya had prepared enough meals to last Josh's family a week. This would give his mother time to fix the work floor up for the season, and she would not have to prepare meals at the same time. After the hot plates had been cleaned up, Marhya and Ran gathered their things and prepared to leave. Josh hated to see him go. They still had so much to say to each other.

"I will see you this season, won't I?" Josh quizzed his friend as if he would never see him again.

"Yes, if you think that you can pull yourself away for a few hours of castle building." Ran loved to make the castles in white.

"I will make every effort to do that at least once this season." They hugged like brothers and said good bye.

CHAPTER TWO

Josh's father had gone to the work floor to continue with the special order after he finished his hot plate. He had been down there for a long time. Josh went to tell him it was time to sleep, only to find that his father had most of the order complete and was holding it up checking the quality of his work.

"Who is this order for, Father? I do not remember anyone coming in for this one." Josh was always curious, especially about the business.

"This one, my son, is for you and the other for your friend." He was serene, almost sad. Josh had not seen this side of his father. "You will be eight seasons when this one is over. I need you to go and find the place that my father told me about, the 'land of Naru,' that I have told all of you children about. I am getting along in my age, and I do not want to spend my relaxing days digging and messing with white.

"My father told me when I took the business from him, 'Do not let your boys take this business. It is time for this family to see more than just hides'. I made him a promise that we would work the business until you were old enough to find the 'land of Naru'. I have been working with some large businesses in the last few seasons and in a few more seasons from now we will be able to turn the business knowledge over to them and they will pay us just for the knowledge. We will never have to work again. We will be able to let our children play all day, just like Marhya does with her children." He made it sound so wonderful: a time to sit and relax, work if you want, but not because you have to.

Josh knew that his father would have this talk with him. He knew of the arrangement with his grandfather, but the way he understood it they would all go together in search of this wonderful place. It was starting to sound like Josh would have to travel alone. This frightened him. He had never left the confines of the small town.

"The storms are predicted to be the worst they have ever been this year. It will be a tough time for you, but I know that you will find what we are looking for and you will return when you find it. I cannot leave the business yet."

His father did not explain any further though Josh knew there was more. Why would he send him off alone? What did his father know? Was it something he had seen, or maybe something that the elders from another time had told him when he was just a boy?

"Father, where will I go to look for this place? Ran has told me of a world that the sun leaves from and comes back many hours later. Would this be the 'land of Naru' that I am looking for?" Josh had so many questions. "How will I get to these places? I will not be able to take the horse. You will need it."

"Son," his father's voice had changed, "you will have no problem getting to where you need to go. Sit down. There are some things that I must tell you."

He became very serious, a side of his father that Josh had only seen when he spoke of the business accounts with his mother. "There is a war in the outer worlds. It started a few seasons ago, and now seems to be getting bigger and closer to this world." The tone in his voice had anger in it.

"Why do people have to fight? There is plenty for everyone if they would learn to share." This angered Josh too - he did not like to see people fight.

"They fight for the lands. The storms are changing; there are more and more places that have lost all of their trees. They have no animals. The enemy has destroyed them. And now they want other places to destroy with their use. If we don't stop the enemy this time, there will not be any people left either.

"The time will come for you to soldier and fight for the lands that we hold near to our hearts. Your great grandfather remembered a time when the people warred for the lands. They were so far away, but the news was everywhere. That was when he told your grandfather the same story that I have told you many times. You must not tell anyone of the wars. The people who know are the only ones who need to. The rest will find out in time.

"This season you will help me prepare work for the following season. When the season is over, you will go to look for the 'land of Naru'"

He had completed his lecture, without telling Josh anything that would help him find what he was looking for. Josh helped his father clean up, and headed for sleep. His father checked that everything was in order and made sure the secret door to the lower floors was covered well. He would check on the progress of the wars another time.

Naihu, had abilities that Josh shared with him. It was a trait that they had acquired through their ancestors. Josh would learn about one of these abilities in the next few days. Naihu did not want to teach them all to him at once, though with this change in plans he would have to teach him more than he had planned, and in a hurry. He would be better off not knowing them all at his young age. Some of them would only confuse him, and Naihu needed him to be strong.

If this new storm season brought what the elders predicted, there would be disease on this land as well.

When Josh awoke the sun was high. It looked like any other day.

Josh's father had gotten up early to prepare the horse for hunting. This would be the first time that Josh had gone hunting. All the other seasons he was told that he was still not old enough. Josh scurried into his materials and raced for the horse, stopping only long enough on the cook floor for a biscuit hot off the fire. He did not want his father to go without him. The excitement showed all over him.

Josh remembered the conversation with his father from the night before. There were so many questions that Josh needed to have answered before he left on his endless journey. Naihu would teach him the basics and nothing more. He would learn all that he needed to when he arrived at the new world that he would be sent out to find.

"Why didn't you wake me? I could have helped you prepare the horse." He seemed angry with his father.

16

"I thought after last evening's discussion, you might need a few more minutes to clear your head this morning." Naihu spoke quietly so he would not wake the others, but everyone, except the younger boys, was already awake.

Josh remembered the conversation with his father. It seemed to be the only thing on his mind since he had sat with him. "I have so many questions for you. Will you teach me all that I will need to know, before I go? Will I have time to learn it all? How will I get there? Will I..." He stopped.

His father gave him a look that made Josh feel at ease. It was the same look that he was given when he started to learn the business and had so many questions.

"You will learn what you need to and the rest you will pick up along the way. I will not have time to teach you everything. There just is not enough time. Now, let's go do some learning."

The first place they headed was the ridge. You can see as far as your eyes will let you from the ridge.

"This is where I learned about the storms." His father stopped the horse and pointed at the edge of the land for Josh to see what he was talking about. Naihu knew what Josh could see and now Josh would know also.

The storm could be seen at the edge of the horizon. It looked similar to a puff of smoke from the cook stove, but much, much larger. It covered the whole horizon. It made the cool blue sky look gray on the edge. It was the same gray that covers the whole sky during the storm season.

"If you stand still, you can see the storm move. The more you practice this the better you will be at predicting the storm's arrival."

The two men stood on the ridge for quite a while. The gray seemed to grow thicker on the horizon the longer they watched.

"Father, this one seems to be moving fast. Will we have time to hunt before it gets here?" Josh had caught on fast to this new lesson.

"There will just barely be enough time and certainly not if we stand here and watch much longer. There are very few people who have eyes for the storms. You were born with yours like I was with mine, among other abilities that you will learn about later. The green color seems to be the key. It makes your eyes able to focus on things that are far away, unlike most eyes that can only focus for a short period of time at these distances." His father climbed back on the horse and headed away from the storm.

Josh kept his eyes on it. He could see the dark gray growing thicker on the horizon, even though they moved away from it.

"How can you tell how bad a storm will be?" he inquired, hoping that his father had an answer, and not one of those 'as you get older' replies.

"The darker the gray, usually the bigger the storm," his father started. "You will get used to them as you get older."

Josh knew that was coming. It always did when his father was teaching him.

They rode for another hour. Josh watched the storm the whole time. He could see the movement, even without standing still. Why? Were his eyes better than those of his ancestors? Or was it his imagination? Maybe it was something that he acquired from his mother.

The horse came to a clearing and stopped. There was enough meat and extra hide in this field to feed the whole town. The animals did not stir; they were preparing their stomachs for the long season ahead.

As his father got off the horse, one looked in their direction, and then went back to feeding.

"You must remember, only take what you will need to eat. Leave the rest for someone else that might need it." His father's voice was barely a whisper.

He took the arrows from the pouch on the side of the horse and drew one up.

"Whoosh" was the only sound heard. The animal fell, but it didn't disturb the rest of the herd.

His father took another arrow and handed it to Josh, "Now, aim for the shoulder or neck. You must make it a clean shot or you will scare them off and we will have to find another herd somewhere else."

Josh pulled the arrow back and whoosh, the animal fell, not disturbing the others.

"You are a quick study. At this rate we will be done in no time at all."

They only took two more. This would be enough to keep the family fed until the next season. The animals were small; they had very tiny front feet and long heavy back legs. Each one had enough meat on it for many meals.

Josh helped his father clean the insides out and sheer the hides. These were the hides they would use for their beds. Their clothes were made from the hides of the old bed furs. They did not use the hides of the business for their own use. As they finished, the gray had grown thick enough it could now be seen over the trees.

"We should get going, Father. The gray..." he stopped. His father had been watching, also. "Father, do you have to be standing still to see the storms moving?"

Josh had become concerned that he could watch the storm move, even though he moved.

"I don't know what you are talking about, Josh. I have already told you that you must stand very still. If you cannot listen and learn from these lessons, then maybe it is not time for you to learn yet." Naihu was strong with his answer. He needed Josh to be ready before the wars hit this world.

The enemy would surely want him on their side if they found out about his ability.

"But, Father, I see the storm moving when I am moving." Josh was glad that he had asked the question even though his father had scolded him for not paying attention.

"Are you sure, Josh?" Naihu waited with anticipation for his son's answer.

"I am very sure, Father. It moves with great vigor toward the trees. I can see that it is moving at about an inch a minute across the sky." Josh watched as they moved toward the ridge, again.

"Yes, it will be a big, heavy one this time. Come, we will need to get this meat to your mother. Do not tell her that your ability is much keener than mine. She is not happy that you were chosen when you were born to go in search of our ancestry. It will only make her unhappy that you will be going soon."

They arrived just in time to unload their catch and get in before the white started to fall.

This storm was different. Josh could feel it. The white fell for many hours. It became darker as the day turned colder, darker than Josh could ever remember.

Naihu stood by the window in the space of the sleeping room. He could see the white starting to cover everything in sight. This made him uneasy. He had not seen white like this in many seasons, since the time he was a small boy and nearly all the town had been buried. That was the season that the men got together and made the chimneys stronger, and taller. They put in special vents to keep air flowing so the fires would not go out.

So many people had died that season, mostly from the cold, some from the disease. The white covered their chimneys and put out their fires. With no air from the outside, the fires would not start again. The people would huddle together in a corner until the white was gone or they froze. It was a devastating year. He remembered it well.

Many people and friends had passed on that season, not from cold, but from disease. It had spread through the town like the white spread over the ground. Quickly! It took all of a person's strength and left them with no will. He shuddered at the thought. He had not seen the disease since that season, but he had not seen a season like that either.

Naihu only hoped that the disease would not come with the storms this season. He had heard that the enemy was causing disease in many other worlds. The enemy had caused the last disease that fell on the worlds.

The belief was that there would be disease with this season. The ancestors had predicted it for many generations.

Before the white filled all the windows, Naihu went to the work floor. He had to make contact with the elders. There was definitely a difference in this storm. Naihu would find out if the enemy was close. Would Josh be able to finish the season before he had to leave? Naihu felt that he would probably leave as soon as this storm was finished.

Naihu was born to this world but his ancestry was from the place that Josh needed to find.

If the enemy had discovered how to change the disease, it would threaten all that Naihu's name stood for. His grandfather had come from another world to help the lost tribe of Shahi with the wars from his time. Without the ability to contact the elders, he had lost his way to the other world. He foolishly left without a contact.

The Shahi tribe had perished, except for the young children who were left to carry on the name. When the children grew old enough they left the world they occupied and found one that would never cause them harm again. They had lost most of their families, either to disease or to death by the enemy's hand.

The white continued to fall. Soon the windows on the work floor were covered.

The hides had to be moved to the sleeping floor for the light. After several days, the windows on the cooking floor were covered also.

And still the white continued to fall. It was as if the sky had opened and was dumping everything it held all at once.

Josh's father finally came away from the window.

The family had been indoors with no contact from anyone for over a week. The windows were completely covered now, so there was very little work done. Josh's mother would sit by the warming fire and tan the hides, but the faint light made it difficult.

The children were getting restless. They had never seen storms this big. They did not like the windows covered. Josh kept mostly to himself thinking of his conversation with his father. He knew that the time to leave was getting closer.

"Josh, I will need your help when the storm is done." His father was quiet.

He had just come from the work floor. He had not seen this kind of devastation since he was younger than Josh. "When the white stops falling, we must get you out of here. It is time for you to go. I was hoping that you could stay until the season was over. There is so much you will have to learn on your own now."

His father drifted in and out of conversation and thought. He ran over the list of things Josh would need to begin his journeys. "The white will soon stop falling, but it will be some time before we will be able to dig the tunnel through."

Tunnel? Josh remembered his father doing a tunnel when he was smaller than his brothers were now. He couldn't remember how it was done. He had not given it any thought, even as the windows had become covered. He spent most of the storm thinking of what his father had told and taught him in the previous hours. It seemed like forever since he and his father spoke in the work room that cold evening and yet it had only been a few days.

How were they going to dig a tunnel? White was like feathers, fluffy. All you had to do was blow on it and it would flow through the air and settle in a new spot. If you wet it, though, it made great castles. Josh had no idea that this is what his father had in mind.

It had been since Josh was very small, only a season or two, when his father dug his last tunnel. The white just didn't fall that heavy anymore.

"In the work room there is a flat plate, made of material like the cook pans. Next to it is a small machine with a hose on it, and a can of fuel. When the time is right, I will need you to get those things out for me. I hope this stuff is done soon."

Josh could hear the distaste in his father's voice. He hated white.

After this storm it was easy for Josh to hate the white just as much, if not more than his father. It was dark, like Ran had told him about the place where the sun goes away. He could hardly see his hands in front of his eyes.

He wanted the sun to come high in the sky again. He wanted to see his friend Ran. He ached to build the castles of white. They would be able to build a very large castle after this storm; maybe even one large enough for them to live in.

"Josh, the white has stopped now. We must get started. Our supplies are getting low."

His father busied himself with a ladder and a saw. He would cut a hole in the ceiling of the sleep room and see how deep the white was above the house. He hoped that it had not gone to the top of the chimney, or he would have to spend time clearing it away before the next storm.

Josh went to get the items that his father had told him about, but he was not sure that he remembered seeing these things before. The metal plate and the machine were right where his father said they would be, in a wooden box with no lid on it. Josh took the whole box. When he returned to the cook room, his father was waiting for him.

He opened the door to the outside only to find white from top to bottom. The air of the door didn't even move the white. It was solid. Josh had never seen it like this.

"It is still very soft and powdery, my son. Don't let this appearance fool you."

His father took his fist and threw it hard against the white. A big puff blew around his hand and as he pulled it out the weight of the rest of it filled the hole in.

"How are we going to build a tunnel, if this stuff is going to..." Josh stopped in mid-sentence. Of course, they would use water to make it hard like he and Ran did for their castles.

"The tunnel cannot go straight up, it must go at a gradual angle or no amount of water will make any difference." His father looked at him to make sure he understood. "We will work in two hour shifts, no more than that at a time. The cold will make you sick otherwise. Your mother and sisters will cook and keep hot plates ready for us. There are not many supplies left, so we will have to do the best we can with what we have." Naihu stopped his monologue long enough to put fuel in the machine and attach the hose. Josh watched him carefully, so that he would know how to do it for himself, if the time ever came that he needed to. He certainly hoped not, but he knew that was a hope that would never come true. His father would do the refueling each time, for now; Josh would watch and learn.

They started at the open door, as they poured the first water near the floor, in minutes it was frozen. The water as it froze carved a hollow spot in a small area. Each time the water was sprayed in a wider circle, acting as a barrier to keep the weight of the white from collapsing.

His father took the first shift of two hours. There would be plenty of time for Josh to get the hang of it. Naihu predicted, by the hole in the roof, that it wouldn't take them more than two days to get out. That was when the real work started for Josh.

The hours seemed to flow into each other, one after the other. Soon they had finished a long enough stretch that a lamp had to be taken to the end so they had light to see. Josh took his turns scooping the white into the bucket on top of the machine, and spraying the liquid on the walls and ceiling of the tunnel with the hose. He didn't mind; it gave him time to think.

He thought mostly of the place his father had spoken to him about. What would it look like? Would there be ground there to build castles, like the ones Ran had told him about? What about girls? He was getting to the age when he liked to think about girls. Most of the ones in his town were too young for him to even give a glance to. There was one who was the same age as Ran, but she was Ran's girl. He could hardly wait to get out now. He worked furiously. He was ready now. So he thought.

After his last shift, he was so exhausted that instead of a hot plate, he took to sleep. His father did one more shift, ate, and he too took to sleep.

They had gone more than half way and it was just the end of the first day.

Josh's mother woke him with hot rolls and butter. "You should get started again. You have slept for nearly two shifts," she whispered lightly in his ear.

That was enough for Josh to jump up, dress and eat, and be down to the end of the tunnel in no time. He didn't realize how worn out he was. The sleep felt good. It had refreshed him enough to work even more vigorously than before. As his shift was finishing, the top of the tunnel was lighter, like the sun was piercing right through it. He turned to head down the tunnel, back to his father, and noticed something else. Little drops of water on the ceiling. Could this mean that they were almost out! He grabbed his supplies and ran to his father. He had to know why the tunnel dripped.

Panting, he asked his father, "Why does the top of the tunnel drip? Does it mean we are close to the end?" the excitement in his voice piercing the silence of the small room.

His father's eyes had fear in them. "Mother, get the boy's sled out and pack it to the hilt. Get the children ready. We will have to finish the tunnel together, all of us."

Josh did not understand. Why would they take everyone into the tunnel? His father repeated to him many times in the last few days, "Only one of us at a time in the tunnel. Do you understand?"

Josh did not understand at all, now.

"Father, why?" Josh's curiosity made him ask the question.

"If the sun gets too hot, the tunnel will collapse from the weight of the frozen white that will turn to water from the heat, we will surely all die of hunger if that happens and we are in the house. There are not enough supplies to keep us for more than one more day." Naihu's voice was strong with fear and desperation.

Josh scrambled to help his family. The last thing that he wanted now was to be stranded in his house any longer. His three brothers were still too young to do much. They usually questioned Josh and their father most of the time, but not this time. They sat and stared at the family bustling about, like they knew they would be in the way if they tried to help.

Josh had his sled and his father' sled; the rest of the family shared a sled with the remaining supplies. There was just enough for all of them to get by until they were rid of the white. More than likely they would stay at the storekeeper's. It had the best roof in town and it already had a ladder from the roof to the floor and a door in it with a hinge on one side. This was always the building they used when the white covered everything. It was the tallest and strongest. The store hadn't been used for white for many seasons though.

"Josh, when we are at the end of the tunnel, you will need to go to your friend and get off of this world. Your health is important and I will not know if the disease comes with this storm." Naihu still had the fear in his expression.

Though the elders had told him that there were no more storms without disease, Josh wondered what he feared so deeply. What disease was his father talking about? It must be something that he remembered from his own childhood. There was no time now for Josh to start questioning his father the incessant way that he did.

"Okay, is everyone set? Josh, you go first. I will follow behind you then mother, sisters and brothers." Naihu took charge of the situation.

"But, father, wouldn't it be better if one of us stayed behind the other children?" Josh's concern for his family showed in his eyes.

"No, they will be fine. Stay close, everyone." Naihu's greatest concern was getting Josh to safety. The rest of the family was strong enough to take care of themselves.

Naihu did not fear the tunnel collapsing. It was too late in the day for the sun to warm too much, but it should not be warming at all. It was the season for cooler temperatures and little sunshine. The storm clouds usually covered the sun for the better part of the storm season. This storm seemed to vanish into thin air as soon as the white stopped falling.

The cool hours had returned and the dripping had stopped for the time being. Josh worked on the end of the tunnel, following his father's directions to the exact word. One more scoop and the opening was clear.

Josh sprayed around the outside to keep the opening from collapsing. His father took the metal plate from him and gave him his sled and a wide pair of over shoes to keep him from falling through the powdery white. Josh looked at him, and knew that this was the time.

"Go now, my son. Get your friend Ran and find the place your grandfather spoke about. Hurry before the wars are any nearer than they already are. I love you, son. Make me proud. You will always have enough money, and you have learned a lot already. Watch the storms. Remember the cool hour stories as I have told you all of your seasons." Naihu spoke with great pride and knowledge in his tone.

"Good bye, Father. Please take care of yourself. I will return with the way to 'land of Naru'." Josh turned and without looking back, walked to his friend's house.

In white, it took him almost a day and a half to get there. When he came to the clearing, he could see the chimney smoke, but that was all. He remembered all that his father had taught him and found the edge of the roof.

The sun had become high and hot already, so he must not waste any time.

"Ran?" He yelled.

"Josh, is that you?" A muffled voice comes from under the white.

"Yes, would you like to build castles today?" he teased his friend.

"No, I would like to get my brother to the storekeeper's. He is sick. I don't know if he will make it. Josh, can you take him there?"

Josh sat on the roof; he knew that he could not take the child. He had a mission from his father. What would he do now?

"I can help you get him out and you can all go to the storekeeper's. My family is headed there now. Did you start a tunnel?" Josh already knew the answer. He wanted to hear the surprise in his friend's voice. "I am going to cut a hole in your roof, so that we can hoist you out of there," he added without pausing for an answer.

"A tunnel? What in this world or any other, would make you ask such a silly question?" Ran was truly astonished.

"Stand back," Josh called to his friend as he made the last cut in the roof, "The idea that I just spent two days digging one with my father. How do you think I got here?"

The hole was cut, and he could see the quizzed looked on Ran's face. It was so funny looking that Josh rolled over with laughter.

"Do you think that we might be able to be serious for a moment? My brother..." The fear and almost anger in Ran's voice shook Josh back to reality.

"Needs help," Josh finished the sentence for his friend and became very serious. "Let's do it, man. Here, tie this rope around the skids of your sled, and I will tie this end to the chimney. In no time at all we will have you out in the wonderful sun again." He joked with his friend in a lighthearted tone, because he knew the fear. He had seen it in his father's eyes, and he had felt it, not long after the white began to fill the windows.

"Where is your mother, Ran?"

"She got ill right after the storm hit. She only lasted a few days. I will come back after the white is gone and my brother is feeling better and take care of her properly." Ran said it with no feeling in his voice at all. He had become older in the last days, much older. However, with no one to look after his brother, he would not be going with Josh, anywhere.

"I am so sorry, my friend." Josh's heart sank. He liked Marhya, she had become a good friend to him and his family. "Have you heard from your father? Do you know when he is returning?"

"I have not heard, but he is due back soon. I suppose he will probably take us back to the old world with him. With mother gone now, he will not want to stay here." Ran was sad. This meant he would never see his friend again. "I will have to write letters to you, so that we can keep up with each other's happenings. I will want to know how the business is and who is preparing the meals."

Josh could not bear to keep the news from his friend any longer. He pulled the sled of supplies through the hole, then Ran.

"Take your brother to the storekeeper. My mother will help you look after him."

"Where are you going to be?" Ran questioned his friend like a common criminal.

"I am on a mission for my father. I must find the place that his father told him about as a boy. There is no white in this place, the sun is always warm, and the trees have fruit on them." Josh could not go any further. He had begun to cry and he didn't want Ran to worry for him. "I was to take you with me, but..." He did not continue. It was not necessary. Ran knew that he could not go. He had his own responsibilities.

"I will keep in touch with your family, and I will find out where you are. When my father returns, maybe he will let me go and find you." Ran hugged his friend and wiped the tears from his cheeks.

The young men embraced, said good bye and headed in opposite directions, possibly never to see each other again.

CHAPTER THREE

Josh did not know the right direction to go. He just walked, mostly the roadways. There wasn't much of the roadway that could be detected, but the heat that came from them made an indentation in the ground showing the outer edges in most places. There were no cars, and the trees were all but covered with white. The people all stayed in the confines of their homes. Some working their way out and others, new to the area, did not know what to do.

Josh supposed he would find something, though he was still not sure what that something was, or where. He was exhausted after tunnel digging and stopped early the first day. The cold would come early because of the storm. He would have to find a shelter for sleep.

He came to a place in the road where it went in both directions. He looked both ways to see which one posed a better place for sleep and shelter from any more storms. There was a rock face one way and trees and clearings the other. The rock would be better, and he would just keep going when the sun came high again.

He found a small opening in the rock on the side away from the road. It was perfect to shelter him, along with the hut sticks and furs that his mother had packed in his sled for him. He had everything: money (more than he would ever need), cook firewood, warming wood, rolls, jerky... there was so much he thought that he might leave some behind, so that his journey would be lighter. He would think about it in sleep, and decide when he awoke.

The hut was dark and warm; Josh opened his eyes and felt the heat on the furs. Why was it so warm? He felt like he had only slept for a few hours. He opened the fur door on the hut to find the sun just coming high.

It must have warmed in the cool hours. But how could that be? There were always a certain number of cool hours, always had been, ever since Josh could remember. What was going on? His father had not spoken of... He had, his father remembered the drip of the tunnel. It had put such a scare in him. He wondered, why? Now he felt like he knew. It scared him as well, and he wasn't even sure why it would. Somehow he knew that it was not good. Though to feel the warmth without a warming fire, he had a hard time thinking it could be that bad. Something was definitely different about this season, one Josh would remember from season to season.

Josh figured he should fix a hot plate and clean up and get a move on. He had no idea how far he had gone, or how far he would eventually have to go. There would be another town soon, he hoped. Josh had never been outside the small town where he lived. He had no idea what the land posed for him. Was it all the same, what would happen when he hit the horizon?

His father had told him once that there was so much land that you could not see all of it, even from a transport.

With the heat coming up before the sun was truly high, the white disappeared quickly. Some of the covered areas, that weren't directly hit by white, were already starting to look like the white never came. Though, there was still no sign of anything in the way of houses or anything. Only the tops of most trees could be seen.

Josh had no way of knowing if there were any people here or not. There was never any need to go from the small town. Everything they needed was there at the storekeeper's. Josh kept thinking about the conversation with his father. There were things that just didn't fit. His thoughts raced with questions, why would he not tell him everything? There was plenty of time. Instead, he sat in front of that stupid window and watched the white. For someone who hated the stuff so much, he was almost obsessed with watching it. Was he looking for signs? Would he ever find out all that he should know? Why did his father not wait until the end of the season? Why did he teach me of the storm watch?

"Why didn't he tell me more? Why?" Josh's thoughts spilled over his lips without even thinking. He had almost yelled the thought as if he wanted his father to hear him.

The day seemed to rush by. He thought, at one time, he saw chimney smoke, but as he cleared the hill, it was...a storm! Josh had to find a house, and fast, he could see the storm move as he walked, then ran. The color of this was different. Lighter. Maybe this one would not be so bad. Still, he would not be caught out in a storm. His father had taught him this when he was very small, before he met Ran.

Above the next hill, Josh saw a distinct chimney. It was not burning, so it was either abandoned or the people were inside. Maybe frozen! Josh ran even faster. He had a hard time keeping his footing the faster he ran. He definitely had too many things with him. He would leave some at the house. That way he could cover more ground while the sun was high.

As he approached the chimney, he could see small puffs of smoke every once in a while. The people were in there and they needed his help. He climbed to the chimney and yelled at the top of his lungs, "Hello! Who's there?"

No answer. Maybe they were afraid. He tried again, louder this time.

"Hello?" came a faint reply. "Can you help us? Our fire will not start. It is starting to get chilly," the voice came, a little louder this time.

"I can help you, but I will have to cut a hole in the roof. Do you have a ladder?" Josh questioned the voice.

"Yes, we have two."

"Stay away from the chimney, I will cut here." The saw buzzed with each stroke. Finally, he was through. He looked in the hole to find a young lady, two small boys, two young girls, and a man.

"Hi," he waved. "When did your supplies run out?"

"We have not run out of supplies. The fire will not start. I don't understand why." The young lady was beautiful. Her dark hair was short, but very neat. He wondered if she had always lived here, and why had Josh never seen her. There must be a town nearby. It was the only explanation that Josh could come up with, as to why he had never seen this beautiful young lady.

Josh looked around the chimney. The air vent had been plugged by white.

"There must have been wind during the storm here. Your air vent is plugged. There, try that." Josh rubbed his mitted hand on the stone of the chimney and cleared the vent that had been covered by white.

"May I come in, now that I have damaged your roof? Not that I can't repair it. I will have to. Another storm is on the far horizon." Josh was very polite, but anxious to get in and fix the hole that he made in the roof. He waited for an invitation to enter.

The faces on the children dropped. He had never seen such sadness in a child's face. He knew that they had been inside for many days and he was sure that they did not want to remain inside any longer than they had to.

"I am sorry; my folks have called me Josh. I am on a mission from my father. You may have heard of him. He is the hide supplier, Naihu," Josh apologized for being rude and not introducing himself right away.

"I have heard of a hide supply not far up the road, maybe a few days." The man spoke with a deep husky voice. He was a kind man, not very tall. Gray had tinged his hair tips; he must be as old as Josh's father. "These are my children, and this is my love." He pointed to the young lady. She could not have been much older than Josh. Maybe twelve seasons at best, he guessed.

"How do you do?" Josh was polite, he had been taught well. "Well, I guess that's hardly the right question is it?" He muffed the hair of one of the children as he jumped to the floor from the rooftop. The lady offered Josh a seat and busied herself with a cook fire.

Josh realized now why he had never met this lady. She already had a husband.

"Where are you from young man, Josh?" The man was inquisitive.

"I am the son of the Hide supply man; I come from the small town just two days up the road." Josh could see by the size of the house and the worn clothing that these people had very little. He was ashamed that he had so much. "Like I said, I am on a mission from my father. I have a long way to travel and I have spotted a storm on the far horizon. I would like to know if there is another town near here." Josh had become the businessman that his father had taught him to be.

He knew when he needed to spit out the words, and when not to say anything at all. Now was the time to spit. He felt uneasy, not afraid; just uneasy.

"Yea, there is a town one and a half days from here. Walkin'."

The man spoke in a different tongue. Josh had never heard 'yea' before.

"May I stay here until the sun comes high? I would like to see what the storm is doing. It seemed to be moving quite quickly, but it was hard to tell the direction as I was running."

The man's eyes lit up, he raised his glass lens above his eyebrows and gazed at Josh's eyes. Josh had never seen anyone take notice of his eyes. "Do you know when the storm will come? I could take you into the town tomorrow, and that way I can get more supplies. Will this one be another confounded big one like the last? 'Bout how long will it last, do you think?" The man threw so many questions at Josh he could not keep up. He had no idea of the answer to some. His father had not taught him everything. He had only learned of this 'talent' a few days ago. However, it was strong. He could almost feel the storm, the power of it. He had a similar feeling during the last storm.

"I will have to look to the horizon to see how fast it is moving before I can tell you when it will come. I don't know how to tell how big they are. I only know that this one is not the same as the last one."

"Well, look out through that hole you made and see how fast it is moving!" He demanded.

Josh did not know what the big deal was. There was always time for preparation around storms. Why did this man have no idea? He climbed the ladder and checked the horizon. He stood very still, as his father had taught him. It didn't seem to be moving very fast. No wait, it had changed direction. Did they do that? He questioned himself.

"Near as I can see, it looks like it won't be here for a few days at best. May not come this direction at all. You see, my father told me of my eyes only a few days before the last storm." He seemed apologetic, though he wasn't sure why.

"That's fine, Josh, sit down. Have a hot plate and we will talk a while." He was kinder all of a sudden like he had known Josh for a long time. He had. His words had changed also, they were more refined and sophisticated, unlike the first few sentences that came out of the man's mouth.

Josh sat and ate quietly. He looked up only once or twice. He did not want to look out of place, even though he already did. His materials were of the finest hide. He wore foot hide clear to his knees and had wide shoes to walk in the white. He had a cap for his head, also made of the finest hide. His father believed, only the best for what you can afford. Josh understood this now. He had never seen anyone with so little. However, their food supply was very healthy. The man probably provided most of it through hunting.

When the meal was finished, the man began with, "I am Zac. I have lived in these parts for as long as I have been alive. Your father and I have known each other for many seasons. I was a young apprentice of your grandfather's before he left. He taught me many things, as well as your father. He told me of you when you came. He was happy that his first born would be the one to travel for his name and the lost tribes. I am sure that is why you are here now. Your father spoke to me of your journeys, not long ago. You had just turned five seasons. I did not expect you until the season was over. Is everything all right at the business?"

Josh was astonished, so much so that he could hardly speak. He had never heard of his father speak of anyone they called Zac. Who was this man? Why had Josh decided to go that direction? He would have to be careful, but he did not know why.

"Everything is fine at the business. When did you speak with my father?" Josh choked the words out.

"I spoke with him on the ridge more than two or three months ago. He could see the first storm, but just a smidgen above the horizon. He told me then that he was sending you, only, not until after the season. He must have had news come about the wa..." He stopped. Did Josh know of the wars? He must have told him.

"The wars? You know of the wars?" Josh quizzed him, carefully, trying to hide his excited tone. He still was not sure of this man. He remembered his father saying; only the ones who need to know of the wars already knew. Josh began to feel a little more at ease. He wanted to sit and talk until the sun came high. Josh wondered if this Zac could teach him anything to help his journeys go smoother. He hoped so.

"He did tell you. Good. I am relieved that I did not spill any unnecessary beans. You will have a lot to learn before your travels are done. I can remember the stories your grandfather told. I would lean back on my arms and take in every word. I knew that I would never have what it takes to travel all of the places, but when your father told me of you I knew that you would. Your grandfather knew it too. It is a shame that you did not get the opportunity to meet him. He was a fine man. He wore the finest clothing, like you do. Your father has taught you well. He was kind and friendly to everyone that came across his path. In those days, there were many, many folks. That was a time before the sickness. A storm came in and with it came something devastating, a sickness that made the folks hot, so hot the water from their insides would seep through the skin; like it was boiling."

Zac stopped.

Josh's expression went blank. He remembered his friend. His brother had the same signs...

"What's the matter? You look like a spirit just walked across your nose. Are you okay? Josh?"

"Huh?" Josh had only heard his name. "My friend, his brother, he had the same kind of water on his skin. I sent them to the storekeeper's. My family was there. I didn't know. What can I do?"

"Don't worry; your father will recognize the signs. There will not be much that can be done, though. Once the water came, it was usually only a matter of time." The man had become sad. His memories from that long ago time came flooding back.

The sleds were filled with supplies and the men would haul them to the houses near the storekeeper's and give them to the people that could not get out of their houses. They worked day and night getting the supplies out and the sick to a place where they could be buried. There were so many sick. If they were found alive the men would take them to a temporary shelter, until they died and could be taken to be buried. There were so many more people then. Some had left the awful place for a better world. The rest perished from the sickness. Only a few remained.

Zac had come to this world just before Josh was born. He knew of the world that Josh's ancestors hoped he would find. He had found his beautiful love, not long after he found that he would not be able to return to the world he came from. They had two children, at first, and then they had the other two. He seemed to cherish them the most.

Zac knew that if there was ever a chance that he would see his beautiful wife and daughter again, he would never have had Sharhi join him for companionship. She knew about his wife. They had kept no secrets from each other. Zac was not much older than Josh when the last disease had come. The disease only struck some and not others. There was no way to make the victims feel better. In fact, it was such a short time before it took them, that they did not suffer long.

"I have to go," Josh jumped to his feet. "I must make sure that I have not caused harm to my family."

"Sit down Josh. You have not caused harm. This is something from the white. It picks out its victims and leaves the rest. If you have not showed signs yet, you will not, especially after being out in it. I will check on your family and make sure that all is okay. Your friend is probably fine also. If he did not show signs, he is probably not going to."

Zac rose to leave the room. His thoughts were surrounded by how much he would have to teach the young Josh, before he sent him out into the world in search of the land that his ancestors told about.

Josh felt bad for Ran. He had lost everything. Now all he had to hope for was for his father to let him come and find Josh. He would probably take him to the old world, and they would never see each other.

"The last time sickness was in these parts, the storms seemed to heat up. They would keep the cool hours warmer than normal, and then before the sun could get high, it was hot, too, hot!" the man began again, interrupting Josh's thoughts. "Has your father told you of the disease?"

"No, I had no idea. However, my father acted differently. I had never seen that kind of fear. He must have known something was not right. He did not have the chance to teach me much. He..." Josh's voice trailed off.

The last memories of his father flooded his mind. Josh did not understand everything yet, but he had a feeling that would soon change at least a little.

Josh had not gone the way he did because he felt it was a better direction for shelter. An inner power had told him it was the way he should go. Zac had been preparing for his arrival. He would be the teacher to the boy that would bring all the tribes back together.

Josh was already starting to understand the fear. How many people had been on this land? Why didn't his father tell him of the disease? Was he not certain that the storm carried it? Josh had to know all there was to know about the enemies' disease. He would stop them, even though it was not a part of his mission. There would be a time when everyone had time to play. Josh was determined to make that happen.

"Your father was one of the last ones to see disease. He was a few seasons younger than you are. He learned the business quickly, and he learned a little of reading the storms, not much more than you were taught, my friend Josh." Zac had interrupted his thoughts. "Can I call you a friend?"

"Yes sir, I mean Zac." He wanted to know all that Zac would tell him, even if it were just a little. A little knowledge was better than none, and he didn't have much more than that right now.

"I was never able to read the storms. My eyes would not focus. Only those that carry the 'green' in their eyes can read the storms; green like the trees, deep and mysterious. Are you sure the storm is moving away from here? It might be a sign of another time long, long ago back when this world was known as 'Harshlands'"

Zac gazed at the hole in the roof. He could still see the sun high. "Why don't I help you patch that up and you can check the progress? I used to love watching your grandfather. He would stand for hours, never move a muscle."

"For sure, I am not very good, though my father thought me a quick study."

Josh stood and climbed the ladder to the rooftop. Zac followed behind him eager to see what the storms were going to bring this season.

Josh's grandfather had taught Zac all the signs, even though he could not see them. Naihu, Josh's father, and Zac had become very good friends. They had a lot of time to do so.

Josh's father was the only son. His grandfather needed at least one other man that would know the ways, and what better person than his son's best friend. And Zac had come to this world to find other members of the lost tribes.

Zac found the Naihu names in the burial grounds that he had come across his first day on this world. He thought that he would be here a great time before he would be able to find the members of the tribes that had disappeared many generations ago. When he found the Naihu name on a bulletin at the storekeeper's, NAIHU HIDE CLOTHING, ORDERS TAKEN DAILY, he knew that he would find the tribes and hopefully find the man betrothed to his beautiful daughter.

Naihu and Zac met at the storekeeper's and became good friends immediately. Naihu and his father would teach him the ways. They were the only part of the tribes that Zac had ever come across. He stayed close and learned the ways of the Naihu tribe. He traveled to other worlds in search of any other tribes that might be out there.

Zac knew the Naihu tribe would be the only one that would finally get him back to his homeland. Zac had to be careful the last few seasons and he stopped his search. The Law had come to keep an eye on things and make sure that there was no trouble from the people in the land. They used Naihu, but Josh didn't know much about that and he didn't need to for the moment.

"The storm has gone in the direction it came in. Is this the way they are supposed to go sometimes? They don't always go in the same direction once they start? Zac, I really hope that you can teach me some of these things." Josh shot questions at Zac so fast he started to laugh.

"Not unlike your father at all, are you?" he teased. "Your grandfather taught me plenty." He became very serious. "The storms that move in and quickly move out, especially after one like that confounded last one, can have signs of tampering. Your grandfather told me of a time when the storms did this. After a great storm, the Harshlands was what was left."

Zac shuddered. He had not seen anything like it, but the stories from the elders would make you want to pack all that you could and leave. There were no trees. The land became a dull gray color. The sun would rise high, but as the normal cooling hours came it would still be warm. There was never a need for the warming fires.

Smaller houses were built at that time. Only after the lands became nourished again did the people put the cook and sleep floors on them. There was never any need before. They cooked and slept in one large room. This was made of the rock hard ground. There was a small opening to the surface, but not much was done there.

Traveling back and forth to the main houses, they would go two and three floors under the ground. Sometimes the elders would talk among themselves of the large work houses, but never loud enough for anyone else to hear unless you were lucky enough to get close without being seen. Even then, the conversations often came to an abrupt halt. They always seemed to know when the wrong ears could be listening.

Zac climbed down the ladder and handed Josh a handful of roof nails. They were long and had grooves all the way up. Josh reapplied the piece of roof he had removed and added a hinge. This would make it easier the next time...Josh stopped. Would there be a next time? Zac had made it sound like there may never be another storm.

"How do you stay in contact with my father?" Josh questioned. "You must have met him on hunting trips on the ridge, right?"

"Most of our communications were done on the ridge," Zac started, "but," he hesitated. He was not sure if Josh would need to know this information yet. "Never mind, I will teach you that also, while you are here."

Zac continued to tell Josh the stories from the elders. He told Josh that most of what he needed to know would come to him as he traveled. Zac had been preparing for Josh's arrival, though he did not expect him quite so soon. His love had come to sit by him on the floor. He smoothed her shiny black hair, reached around her and kissed her. Josh could feel the passion clear across the room. His heart ached to have a woman that he could hold. Would there ever be anyone for him?

Zac had excused himself and seemed to disappear. Josh did not know where he would go. There was only the one room. It had been divided with furs hanging from the ceiling to the floor. Zac had gone behind them, but Josh could not hear or see him. He started to feel uneasy again.

The young lady had repositioned herself closer to Josh. She prepared to take the hides from his feet. Josh assumed that she was readying him for sleep.

Zac returned almost as quietly as he had left. Her beautiful eyes met his, as he looked at her with approval for what she was doing. Zac was not married to the young lady. He kept her for cooking and watching after the children. And, of course, for the sexual companionship that she was always willing to give to him. He loved her, but not like he had loved his wife.

"That will not be necessary right now." He looked at her as if she had done this to all the visitors that came to their house. "Josh, I have some news that you will need to know. Your family is fine. Your friend, Ran, is it?"

"Yes, how do you...?" Josh was more curious now then he had ever been.

"He is fine, also, however, his brother did not make it to the storekeeper's as I suspected. Your father says that the disease has returned. You will only have a few days here, so I must teach you day and night. It will take a lot of strength from you, but I will make sure that you are rested before you continue your journeys." Zac did not seem as serious as Josh's father was when he spoke of learning.

They both ventured behind the hanging furs. Zac lifted a door from the floor and went down the stairs. He motioned for Josh to follow. Josh had never seen anything like this before. There were always stairs to the lower floors, but no one ever hid them. There was no need. Every space in a house was used, especially in the smaller houses that only had the two floors. When he got to the bottom of the stairs, there was another door. It led to another flight of stairs. Did all the small houses have two floors below?

Josh's mind had started to question everything now. What was going on here? Where had Zac disappeared to? Where were they going? Did this have anything to do with the work houses that Zac had told him about earlier?

What would he be able to learn here? How did Zac contact his father? It was nearly three days walking distance. As Josh hit the last step to the bottom floor there was a huge machine against one wall, a microphone, a light, a warming fire, and a cook fire. Only the warming fire was lit. The cook fire did not look like it had been lit in generations.

"This is a communicator. I use it to keep in touch with very important people, like your father. I have spoken to him, and all is well, or, as well as it can be. Your family is fine. Ran's father had already showed up at the storekeeper's when he arrived. They will be leaving for the new world. His father is in need of his help, because of the wars. Your father has asked me to find you a transport that will take you away from this world. So far, no luck."

Zac had started the teaching and Josh would carry it with him. Zac showed Josh how to use the communicator. They listened to reports of the wars. Though Josh had not heard anything about land, he kept hearing things like, "This one would make The Law a lot of money, and still plenty of people on it, too." What were they talking about?

After they had listened for a while, Zac taught Josh all the signs of storms. He would need to remember it all, though most of the storm watchers had no problem remembering. They seemed to have another gift. They could see things with their eyes whether they had seen them before or not. Josh had experienced some of this, but he was sure it was from the stories that his father had told him and his imagination put the pictures in his head. He soon learned that this was not the way it happened. Josh's ability to 'see' was greater than Zac had ever seen in any of the storm watchers that he had met over the seasons. This is why he was the perfect man to take on the journey.

The hours passed by, very slowly, as if time had begun to stand still. Josh learned of the place that his father had told him about. He could see it in his mind, as if it were right in front of him. He could not see the path that led him there, though. This would make it more difficult, but not impossible.

He could see the war transports with the soldiers on them. He could not see where they were going. He would have to practice this new ability, and make it sharp.

Zac told him of the large work houses. The soldiers would not be looking for land. They would be looking for a beautiful rock that lay beneath the surface of some of the worlds. Only the worlds that had storms would have this type of rock under it. That meant, sooner or later they would be headed to his homeland after the trees were gone, and the ground had become solid.

This small house was one of the old work houses from before his great grandfather's time. There was yet another floor below the one with the communicator. It had tunnels leading off in several directions. This is where the 'work' was done.

There were hundreds of these houses on this world. Josh's was one of the main ones. He had never noticed any doors in the floor, though. These were the things that the elders spoke about in their private conversations.

Josh's great grandfather was one of those elders. So was Zac, but Josh did not need to know this now.

Soon the wars would grow stronger, the forces were heavy already. The communicator crackled with conversation as the two men sat and learned all there was to learn.

"Z?" came a noise from the communicator. It was clear. "Z, a non-soldier transport leaves in three days." A voice unfamiliar to Josh came over the communicator. "I will reserve the seat you asked for." The transmission was clear, but there was secrecy in the voice. "J will be the passenger, correct?"

Zac grabbed the microphone. "Correct, make sure there are no soldiers on this transport." He let go of the lever on the microphone. It was important to keep the transmissions short. Otherwise the Enemy would detect the location of the communicator. They already were risking a lot.

"What is the destination?" Zac asked quickly. They were running out of time.

"Destination, New World Jemini." The voice cracked and was gone.

"Jemini," Zac thought aloud. "That is about three worlds from here. It will only take you a short time. This is good."

"Zac, how many worlds are there?" Josh had only heard of the one where his friend was from and Jemini was not it.

"There are literally hundreds." Zac replied.

"How will I find the 'land of Naru', the place that my father spoke of?" Josh did not want to spend a lot of time looking for this place. His desire was to go to it, find a house, return to his family before the soldiers came, and take them away.

"You will have to use your eyes. Every time you get on a transport, look through your mind at all the places you pass. The one you are looking for will show up, someday." He hesitated, as if he had more to say. "There are very few non-soldier transports left. It will be hard for you, but if you find a communicator, you can at least find a transport. If you have to or are forced to, join the soldiers that are on our side. They will be wearing your father's hides for uniforms. It will not be hard to tell them from the others. Now, it is time for you to have a rub down, then sleep. Sharhi will help you."

They both climbed the stairs to the main floor. Sharhi was waiting for Josh. She sat on the edge of the furs with nothing on. Her breasts were full and round, her skin very dark, like she spent all of her time in high sun.

Josh did not know what to do. He did not like the idea of another man's wife in the same bed with him.

"Don't be shy. She is very used to this. Don't worry, we are not married. She is just my lover." Zac turned and went to the door in the floor again. "I have a few more things to prepare for you. Enjoy!" he said as he closed the door in the floor.

Sharhi was very gentle. She took the materials off of Josh's lean body and gently laid him on his back. He could feel the passion in his body, as she gently smoothed her hands over him. She rubbed oils on his dark skin, and then she rolled him over and repeated everything on his back side. She taught him all he would need to know when he found his own love. As she turned him over again, he rose up and met her lips with his. He desired her, but not with love. He ran his fingers through the short dark hair and down her back. He embraced her again, and kissed her rosy lips. She lay down under him and let him make love to her. His passion was deep. She liked the things that he did. He massaged the inside of her legs. Then he kissed her breasts sucking on each one like a small child. This enticed her to keep going. She kissed his whole body, and then his lips, swirling her tongue inside of his mouth, causing his groin to ache with more passion than he had ever felt. They made love over and over again, as if Sharhi were making sure he learned well.

Josh rose after the sun had been high for many hours. He was refreshed, though he could only remember Sharhi rubbing the oils on his skin. He wondered if it had all been a dream. He knew that it was not, when she returned to him with a hot plate. She stood before him naked; her breasts were as beautiful as they had been during the cool hours though he could not remember the hours getting very cool.

He ate, and then made love to her again touching her breasts and caressing the skin on her soft body. He had become a man overnight, and he knew now that he would be able to accomplish his mission with little or no problems.

When they had finished, Zac was standing beside them. "I hope that you have enjoyed this part of your learning. I could not send you out in the world without knowing how to handle a woman," he chuckled.

"I have one more thing to teach you, the disease!"

He did not know exactly how to explain to Josh. "You will see a lot of it. The communicator has informed me that it is on three worlds now. It will destroy what it needs to and then be gone. It is believed to come from the enemy, not the white. It is something that they are able to put in the large storms with their transports. You will not get it, but try to find out all that you can about it. This is how you will contact your father or me if you need to. Remember, though, we do not want to use the communicator very much. If we are detected, they will not even bother looking for the rock. They will just destroy us."

Zac handed Josh a piece of paper with his communicator identifier on it and a place that he could send letters to. "Have a safe journey, my friend. The transport will be ready for you when you get to town. Just follow the road. You will see where you need to go. The white is all but gone now, so you will be in town in less than a day. The transport leaves at the end of the cool hours. Travel safe, and remember all of your abilities will help you. All you have to do is use them."

He shut the door as Josh walked away. He would miss the companionship, but he was ready for the worlds now.

CHAPTER FOUR

Josh left most of his supplies with Zac. He would buy more as he needed them, but he needed to travel as light as possible. It had only taken him half a day to get to the transport site. He found a place to sleep, but sleep would not come.

He had Sharhi on his mind, and all that Zac had taught him. He still wondered why his father had not told him about everything. Why, at least, didn't he tell him of the hides for the soldiers? He could have helped to prepare them. He remembered his father telling him of the people that would pay him for the knowledge. Were these the same people? They had to be. What a fantastic thing for his father and family. They would be able to join him in a few seasons and then there would be time to play.

Josh had never been on a transport. He had never even seen one close up. They were very large. It seemed like he could put his whole house in one and have plenty of room left over.

A man approached him and asked him if he was "J". He did not wait for an answer, as if he already knew.

"Your transport is ready. Z has told me that you can see storms." He carefully looked into Josh's eyes.

"Yes, I can, though I am not good at it yet. I hope to never have to be very good at it." Josh did not like white and after all that had happened in the last storm he did not care to see another storm.

"You must have a pair of lenses. You will not want everyone to know your abilities. It will not be hard to hide, though, with these." He handed Josh a pair of lenses. They were dark colored and when he put them on, it changed the color of everything.

"Try to look at the horizons with them on. That way, others will not be able to tell what you are looking for." The man waited, as if he wanted to see Josh use his ability.

Josh looked to the horizons. He could see the storms, but they were not moving now. When he removed the lenses, they still did not move. This was not a good sign. Zac had told him, "When the storms stop moving, but you can still see them, it usually means that they are not producing white. This will cause all the trees and animals to die. They need the nourishment from white to live."

Josh kept seeing the homeland in his mind. Bare, nothing there but rock and a few large houses. He could even see his own house, but it was different. There were no windows left. Why? It was very hard to make hides with no light from the windows. He desired to speak with his father and family, but he knew the dangers and dismissed the thought from his mind.

The man took Josh's supplies and loaded them on the transport. They would be ready to go soon. Josh had begun to feel uneasy again. This time was different. It was like he had eaten something that did not sit right with him. He dismissed the feeling and climbed aboard.

As they flew above the world, Josh could see more and more of the land. He wondered why he had never ventured away from the small town. His excitement grew as he checked his abilities. By now he could see many worlds. There were some close by, some very far away, but none that he could see in his mind had no white. Would Jemini have white?

He would know soon enough. They were almost there. The vision crowded his mind. He could see nothing but rock. Was this one of the 'Harshlands' that Zac had told him about?

When the transport landed, the same man gave Josh his supplies, sent him to a house, and bade him luck on his journeys.

"You will not need anything more than money and what you carry on your back." the man told Josh. "I have another transport headed for Shurfate in the morning. Do you want to be on that one?" He questioned Josh, as if he knew this was not the place he wanted to be.

"Where is Shurfate?" Josh asked, wondering how far away it was.

"Shurfate is almost twelve worlds away. There are many worlds between here and there, but most of them have been diminished to nothing but rock. I do not know if Shurfate has come to this or not. We only do one transport there a season, but it is always full to the hilt. Mostly supplies though. I can get you on it if you want. Let me know, as soon as you decide. I will have to put you on the list."

"Have you ever been there? Will there be a transport to take me further when I get there?" Josh wanted to make sure that he was not going to the wrong place, or worse, the wrong place with no way to get out.

"I flew a transport there many seasons ago. The place is, or was gorgeous, then. Yes, there are other transports, but most of them are now being used for the wars. From now on it will be difficult to get transports, unless you have one of these." He held up one of Josh's father's special order hides. The man could see, by the expression on Josh's face that he had seen them before.

"As a matter of fact, I have two. My father is the maker and when he sent me on my mission he gave me one, and one for my best friend who was supposed to accompany me on my journey." Josh was proud to see his father's new work.

"Your father is Naihu?!" The man seemed pleased. "I have known him for many seasons. Three or four seasons ago he brought these materials here. He was very businesslike and determined that these were the best materials to survive the after-white. He never went any further, always returned to his own world within a day or so." The excitement showed in the man's face. He should have known the green eyed Josh was relative to Naihu.

"It was three and I remember the order well. My father had bought special tanning threads for these. He said that it would make them stronger, so they would last many, many seasons." Josh was astonished that his father had never mentioned Jemini before.

"Will you be on the transport or not?" the man seemed to be pushing Josh.

"Yes, I suppose that is as good a place as any right now." Josh's mind had gone back to the work room where he and his father had spoken. It seemed so long ago. He remembered the first order of hide and now could remember his father being gone for a few days. This is where he went. It was no wonder he never mentioned Jemini. There was nothing here but transport sites as if it had been made that way, just a stopping point for transports to refuel and be gone again.

The sun was high, and Josh wanted to rest and see what he could of Jemini. He wondered if there was a ridge close by, he wanted to sit and run things through his mind.

"Is there a ridge near here?" he questioned his new friend.

"Yes, the one your father always went to. Just beyond the first hill, you will see it. Your transport leaves after the cool hours. Don't be late. There will not be another one for several seasons, unless you are soldiering."

Josh did not care about the time. He had plenty of seasons to look for the 'land of Naru'. If he were back, he would be on this transport. If not, he would catch the next transport in a few seasons from now. At this time he wanted to explore, his mind and all of the worlds. One by one!

He already knew that this was not the place he was looking for. If it were, his father would have brought them all here long ago. When he reached the ridge he could feel his father's presence and Zac's also. He felt very close to them, as if he could hold a conversation with them. He stood very still for a very long time. He wanted to see all that he could focus on.

He saw houses, large and small, large groups of soldiers all wearing the special hides, but no storms. He started to leave when he heard his father's voice.

"I am sorry, my son. I wish that I could have shown this place to you myself, but there was no time. The transports have started to land here now. They pick up the hides and take them to the other side of this world, where they are given to the soldiers."

Josh could see the silhouette of his father as plain as day. He did not know of this talent. Did he possess it, or was it something that only his father could do?

"My son, you possess many talents. This is one of them, but you will not develop it until you are older, like me. The family is fine. Ran has gone to Shurfate, many worlds from here. If you can get a transport there, go. He will be waiting for you."

The image of his father disappeared as fast as it had come. Josh knew that he must head back to the transport site immediately. It was exciting to know he would soon see his friend again. It had been many weeks now.

It felt like months since he had pulled Ran from his house. He could see his friend's face: the devastation that had been caused by the white, the sadness he felt for the loss of his mother and brother.

He reached the transport site just in time to get aboard and take off for Shurfate. The trip was long. Josh could see many worlds, but the ones that were not solid rock, had white. There were none where he could see fruit on the trees, not any! Where could this land of Naru be?

He drifted in and out of sleep. It seemed like days had passed before the transport finally landed.

"Shurfate, all supplies off," the speaker above his head sounded loudly.

Josh grabbed his supplies, and walked across the transport site. His stomach had begun to churn with excitement. He could feel his friend's presence.

"I am looking for Ran Tis. Do you know where I might find him?" Josh asked a woman behind a counter.

"Tis?" she replied, "They are located at the other side of the city. Take the main road and go to the trees. You will come to a large building. That is where you will find Mr. Tis." She did not even look up as she gave the directions to Josh. It was like she did this for everyone that had ever stopped at this transport site.

Josh picked up his supplies and headed to the other side of the city. There were many big buildings. He could hardly see the tops of them. There were cars, and trucks, and horses, and people everywhere. Josh could not believe his eyes. He had never before seen so many people with so many different materials. No two were the same. He continued to walk though many drivers stopped to see if he needed a ride.

The high sun was very warm, and he enjoyed the solitude. He declined them all, until...

"I know a good place to build castles if you are interested." A familiar voice could be heard over the roar of the cars.

"Ran? Is that you? How in this world are you?" Josh could hardly hold his excitement. He had so much to tell Ran. He wanted to tell him about the storms, the worlds, the visions, the...

"If you are going to just stand there I will have to leave you here," Ran said as he opened the door of his car.

Josh's Garden

Josh had never been in a car. He always rode the horse. He felt safer that way. He grabbed the door and sat on the seat next to Ran. Ran pulled the door shut and they were off.

"I cannot wait for you to meet my father. He is at home now. He does not travel much anymore, not since..." His voice trailed off.

Josh could see the pain the storm had caused.

"My father is not the same man. He is very quiet now. He teaches me every day. I like having him with me. How did you know how to find me?"

"My father told me when I was on Jemini," Josh replied but did not go into detail. He would show his friend his abilities when the time was right, and not before.

"Is your father with you? Will he be staying on Shurfate? Will you open the business here? How are your sisters and brothers? Are they here with you also?" The questions did not stop. Ran wanted to know everything.

"No, my father, mother, sisters, and brothers are not here. I left them on the homeland. I am afraid for them. The..." He stopped. He did not need to tell his friend of the wars. If Ran knew of them he would wait until he brought them up. Josh was not to tell anyone of the wars. "I have come here on my search for the 'land of Naru'. You remember the stories, don't you?" Ran nodded. "My father is still doing the business on the home world."

"Really?" Ran sounded as if he were surprised to hear this. "I was sure by now that they had all become soldiers for the wars. My father says that I will have to go soldier soon. All of the boys will." Ran seemed happy, in a weird sort of way.

"You have heard of the wars then? My father is making hides for the soldiers now. The whole family is." At least as far as Josh knew.

Ran pulled up to a very large building. "This is where my father and I stay. Our house is at the very top. It covers the whole top floor of the building." Ran jumped out and went inside the building. Josh followed behind him, cautiously. He had never seen a house so big, and did not know that you could own just one floor of one. He glanced around at the expensive lighting hung from the very high ceiling. The rugs on the floor were hand woven and looked hand cleaned. They almost sparkled.

They walked through a door into a small room. Ran pushed a button on the wall, and the floor began to move, no, the whole room moved. Now it was Ran's turn to laugh. "It is a portable room. It runs up and down on large cables." Ran loved that he could show his friend the wonders of a city.

Josh did not let go of the rail that ran around the room until the small door opened. He almost ran out of the room, not sure if it would fall or what it would do. He turned around and glared at it, amazed at its simple but complex mechanisms. He was astounded by the mere idea of it moving them from one place to another. The door had not changed, but the room had been transpired into a vast open area with the ceiling not quite as high as the first room they had been in before entering the transportable room. The windows were full length from the floor to the ceiling. There were no coverings on them, so it was easy to see the tops of the other tall buildings and the horizon behind them.

Ran's father sat in a chair in front of the large window which formed the wall. Josh had never seen anything like this before, but he liked it very much. He could see the horizon very well from here. He would very much like to stay here on Shurfate, but on the edge of the horizon he saw the white storms. They circled in many directions like a pot on a cook fire ready to boil.

He could see many transports in the sky, most of them carrying soldiers or supplies for the soldiers.

"Father, this is my friend Josh. You remember me telling you about him, don't you?" His father looked up from the window.

"Yes, Josh, how do you do this fine day?" He sounded just like Marhya. Josh missed her, and he assumed that Ran did too.

"I am fine, sir. This is certainly a very nice home you have." Josh was polite as usual.

"Thank you for rescuing my son. I am glad that I still have him. I should not have been away for so long. Marhya was all that I ever had. She had given me two wonderful boys, and now she is gone and with her she took one of my sons." He hung his head down, turned back to the window and said no more.

"My father has been like this for many weeks now. He stares out the window as if he were waiting for mother to come and pick him up. He just sits there and waits." The concern in Ran's voice was apparent. He worried for his father. It was not good to just sit. He would surely die, if he did not move once in a while.

"I am sorry, my friend." Josh could think of nothing else to say. The hurt in his friend's heart could be seen easily. He wanted to bring his mother back, just to see the skip in his father's step again; to see the joy in his eyes as they embraced after a long trip. That would never happen.

"Hello, Josh?" a woman's voice could be heard.

Josh turned around to see Ran's girl woman behind him. She was more beautiful than the last time he had seen her on the homeland. "Hello, Shraze, how have you been?" Josh could not take his eyes off of her.

"I am fine, but if you continue to stare like that, you will end up with Ran's hand in your eye," she teased. Ran would never do anything to harm his friend. He owed him his life, and someday, he planned to repay him. They sat in front of the window together and talked of the happenings of the last few weeks.

Josh told Ran of his abilities and the vision of his father. "I can see a lot of things. I can even see inside of a flying transport. Sometimes I can feel your presence, also. My father did not teach me much, but I assume that I will learn as I go. He probably figured since he could contact me anytime, he would teach me as I travel."

Josh spoke with great excitement. He was glad to be able to spend time with his friend. It made it easier to know that he had a place to come back to while he searched for the land of Naru.

"Have you figured out why the white has stopped falling on most of the worlds?" Shraze asked him, hoping that he knew something that would make them come back.

"I know why the white has stopped falling, but I have not figured out how to stop it from not falling. The enemy has special transports that carry a fine powder laced with the disease. The Law wants to stop them, because they need the people to help fight the enemy, best as I can tell anyway."

65

Josh stopped. He had become very tired and wished to rest. "Ran, may I stay here with you and your father? I still have many places to look and I have already covered the worlds that are close to the homeland."

"You may stay as long as you like. I will put a wash basin in the spare room and you can sleep there." Ran got up from where he had been sitting on the floor and went into another room. He soon returned with the wash basin and a set of materials to put on the bed.

Josh had never seen such a house. Each room was separated by doors, and the beds were made of feathers and sat on top of metal frames above the floor. There were no hides to cover up with, only thin materials. All the cooking was done in a separate room, and the warming fires seemed to come from somewhere else in the building. Josh could feel the heat of them in the small metal plates on the floor.

Josh followed Ran into the spare room and politely excused himself so that he could rest. It had been a long journey so far, and he just wanted to close his eyes and rest.

"Hot plates will be ready when you are rested. I will have Shraze keep one for you. Do you want to be awakened later, or should we leave you to rest until you have rested enough?" Ran waited for his friend to reply.

"Please, wake me when the hot plates are ready. I have been eating cold jerky and rolls for so long; I'm beginning to wonder if there is such a thing as a hot plate anymore." Josh rolled to his side and stared out the window. After a while his eyes closed and he rested peacefully, though, not without visions.

Josh was startled awake from a vision that he had not seen or heard before, "Son of Naihu, you are closer than you think to the land that you look for."

Josh sat straight up and wondered where the vision had come from. He was sure, until today, that his father was the only one that would send him visions.

"Josh, are you okay?" Ran had entered the room.

"Fine, I think. I have had a vision that I am not sure of. It was not from my father, but it called me 'son of Naihu." Josh was dazed. He sat for a moment trying to clear his head of the vision that had startled him awake.

"Hot plates are ready if you want one still." Ran wanted to make sure that his friend was all right. He stood in the doorway of the small room and waited for his friend to either dismiss him, or invite him in. He preferred the latter.

"Yes, I still want one, but I need time to clear my head. Come sit down." Josh hesitated as he waited for Ran to cross the room to the bed. "There is a lot you don't know about me anymore, my friend. I want to spend time here so that I can share these things that are as new to me as they will be to you when I tell you about them." Josh did not feel as lonely as he had in the last few weeks. He was glad to have the company of his friend.

"Well, I have plenty of time to listen. Just don't feel like you have to tell me these things just because we are best friends and we have always shared everything with each other. There has to be a time in a person's life that they have to hold some things to themselves," Ran finished. He waited to see if there was anything else that Josh might have to say.

"I speak with my father every day, mostly quick visions that he sends with word that everything is fine. Give me a few minutes to get dressed and I will join you all for hot plates. Then we will have time to talk again."

Josh went to the window and gazed out at the openness around him. He stood there until Ran had closed the door. Would there be a vision from his father today? He hoped so.

When he had finished dressing, he opened the door to the room to find Shraze, Ran, and Mr. Tis sitting at a large table waiting for him.

"This is the traditional way that I learned to have a meal. Not like the hot plates that we had when we lived on the other world. My mother always had a hard time sitting on a bench in front of a fire when it was time to serve the plates." Ran finished his sentence with a small hint of the sadness that he still had for losing his mother and brother to the disease.

The table was shaped like an oval. It had cloth on the top of it that fell over the edges and ended with lacy, scalloped edges. There were three bowls of food, a plate and eating utensils at four different places on it. A glass was filled with liquid for each plate.

"I am sorry, I did not mean to keep you waiting," Josh apologized as he sat in the empty space at the table. It sure was a different way of having hot plates, he thought.

Mr. Tis handed a bowl of food to Josh and the meal was officially started.

Ran and Shraze both reached for the other two bowls. Ran handed his to his father, and waited for Josh to hand him the one that had been passed to him.

They ate in silence, afterwards the three young people sat together and talked of all the new experiences that Josh had had in the last few weeks.

It felt good to tell the important people in his life what was happening, and to know that they understood it all made Josh more at ease.

There were so many worlds that Josh would have to search. He wondered if he would be able to before he was too old to care anymore. Ran helped Josh locate as many worlds as he could think of, but he didn't ever remember seeing any that did not have the large storms, which seemed to be causing such devastation to the entire dimension.

Josh spent over a season on Shurfate. The wars had not required the boys to go be soldiers yet, and Josh was not going far until he could go with his friend. Besides, he liked the different pace of the big city and he enjoyed the company of his lifelong friend. They had not been able to spend much time together in the last few seasons, since Josh had started working with his father.

The two boys spent most of every day together. Sometimes they would go to the other buildings and look at the fine materials. Sometimes they went to Ran's favorite place to build castles.

Josh continued to look for the 'land of Naru'. He would only travel for a few days, and he always returned to Shurfate. He stayed with Ran, Shraze, and his father. There was plenty of room for all of them.

Ran and Josh spent many days' together, building castles with soil from the ground and reminiscing about the homeland. Josh missed his family, but he knew that he would have to find the 'land of Naru' before he could return.

Sometimes Ran traveled with him, but his father did not like to let him go. He feared that he would lose Ran, and he would not be able to bear that kind of devastation again.

Ran's father soon came away from the window as if the vision he was looking for had come and told him to go on. He traveled a little, but never more than a week would go by before he returned. He did not like the idea of leaving Ran. He was all that he had left.

The time had come for the boys to become soldiers. Mr. Tis was not especially happy about Ran having to go, but at least Josh would be with him. He liked Josh. There was something about him that made him feel less uneasy when Ran was away.

The two boys traveled to many worlds together. Most of them were nothing but rock. They did simple patrols to the different buildings, checking each one for anything that didn't look right. The only thing the boys felt didn't look right, was the fact that there were no families in them.

"Josh, I wish I understood this mess that the Law has become involved in. The enemy has captured and destroyed so many worlds, and the people on them. There just has to be a way to stop it." Ran was disgusted with the whole idea of the war.

They had turned ten seasons and within a week the Law sent them papers telling them where to meet and at what time.

"There is a way to stop the enemy, but I haven't quite figured out what causes the disease that they spread all over. I can see them in their transports, but it is as if they know someone might be watching what they are doing and they hide it well," Josh said to Ran.

Josh did not understand why the Law had not picked up on the fact that he had great abilities and he could be a great asset to them. Instead he walked around all day and looked into old buildings. Most of the time, he enjoyed it because he and Ran made an adventure out of every day. It was like they didn't even belong to the Law. Ran always had fun with Josh, too.

"What will you do if the Law wants you to work somewhere other than the patrols?" Ran knew that he had no special talents to do anything but the patrols. At least it was only for three seasons. Maybe someday he would get to do Workhouse Patrols, but he wouldn't count on it.

"I guess I will ask if you can go with me. I need you to help me think sometimes, and besides we are partners." Josh knew that they would never allow anything like that unless Ran had abilities that neither of them knew anything about. So, they assumed he didn't.

The time came when they were separated. Josh and his abilities were needed at the base world. The Law had found out about his abilities when they checked into why he had signed in on Shurfate and not his homeland.

Josh's father did not tell them exactly why he had gone to Shurfate; just that his friend had lost everything and he was there to comfort him and his father.

Josh was transferred to the base world without Ran.

Ran did patrols and after a while he was transferred to do Workhouse patrols. Sometimes he wished that he had not wanted to do them. They were awful places. There were times when the women and children would get so exhausted from the heavy work that they would collapse right where they stood.

The Law had learned that Josh could see the transports that dropped dust out of them on top of the storms, from great distances. They really did not know the extent of his abilities, but this would prove to be to Josh's advantage. His mission would be to locate the enemy flyers and radio their exact location to the patrol flyers for the Law. These were the enemy soldiers that Zac had told him about. Zac had also told him when he could figure out how to stop them permanently he should do what he could to get that part of his mission accomplished.

Josh didn't see Ran again for a long, long time. He was not allowed to go to Shurfate any longer. The enemies had taken the city, and would love to have Josh or someone like him on their side, even if they had to steal that someone from his own troop.

Josh visited many worlds after he was stationed at the base camp. He would travel to each of them and watch for the enemy craft. When he did not see any after a few days, he would return to the base and find out where he should go next. He also tried to envision the 'land of Naru' and every so often he would get the vision and message from the lost elder who called him, "son of Naihu". These visions had become scarce since his last visit to Shurfate but the Law would not allow him to go there for fear of his capture. He looked, with his mind and abilities, for the special world that his father had sent him in search of, but he did not find it. He was beginning to wonder if it existed at all.

He made trips to the homeland with the head man of the troops every once in a while. The head man would go to see how things were going in the Workhouses and if there were any other problems that needed his attention at the time. Most of the time there was nothing but the same old thing going on, but he allowed Josh to see his father and brothers.

Josh loved seeing them. His brothers had become big boys now, and they helped Father with the hides. They had become very good at stripping them, and that left Josh's father to do the easy work of tanning and stringing. It made Josh happy to see that his father had gotten to a time in his work that he was able to take it slower.

Josh's mother and sisters had been taken away shortly after he left on his journeys. There was not much left of the homeland. The trees were all gone. The ground was rock hard. The land had been turned into nothing but a place for the Law to mine the rock and hold the enemy prisoners. There was no escape from this harsh place. There was no hunting, nothing left to hunt. All of the food and clothing was brought by transport. The hides were from animals that were kept in cages and bred simply for their hides. The meat was left to rot or burned in most cases.

Josh wondered if Zac was still in his house or had he taken his children and left, before the land died?

One time when Josh was visiting his father he had asked, "Father, is Zac still here?" hoping that the answer was yes.

"Yes, he is somewhere, but...shhhhh." His father could tell that there were ears around that should not hear this conversation.

Naihu and Zac had formed an alliance of people to fight the enemy and the Law for what they had done to all the worlds. The Law considered them rebels, or at least they had considered Zac one. They did not know that Naihu was as big a part of the alliance as Zac was, and many others at well.

Zac had taken all of his belongings and stored them below his house. He made the top floor look like it had been ransacked, so the Law and the enemy would believe that he had moved on.

The only other person around them was General Har. Was he a bad person? Was he disguised as one of our soldiers? Did his father think that his ears were the ones that should not be there?

Josh understood very well what his father was telling him. Josh could feel the presence of the ears as well. He had only practiced this talent a few times, because he never felt it necessary to use it very often. The Law did not allow Josh to go very far by himself. His special talents were what the soldiers of the Law needed to protect the people of the lands so that they could have them around to mine the rock. The enemy wanted to kill off as many as they could with the disease, so that they would not be without their mineral. The Law needed the people to keep the enemy from getting to the rock, because they wanted it all for themselves.

Josh always felt that it was futile to understand either side's true mission for the warring. He wanted to know why they didn't think to pool their resources together and work on the same side. However, he never expressed this to anyone. There would surely be trouble if he did.

"I am going to the ridge, Father. Can you join me?" Josh asked, knowing the answer.

"No, I must finish loading these hides, so they can take them on the next transport. I am sure that the lawman over there will not let you go alone, though," his father whispered, knowing what Josh wanted. Naihu would do all that he could to help him.

"Mr. Har, sir, there is a place not far from here that I remember from my childhood. Would you mind if I go there and have a look around?" Josh asked very carefully, so he did not tip the lawman off to his adventure.

"Sure Josh. Is it far from here?" he asked as if he would go with him, especially if it were a long way off.

"No, it is only a few minutes by horse. Would you like to come?" Josh knew that he would not, but to keep him from being suspicious he asked anyway.

"No, Josh, you go. It will do you some good to have a little time to yourself." Mr. Har busied himself with helping the boys.

Josh tried not to run to the horse. He had not been on one for a long time and he really needed this time alone. He readied the horse and he was off, slowly at first. Then as he rounded the first corner and was out of Har's sight he kicked the horse hard and made it run. It was easy to get around on the rock ground. There were no trees to go around.

Josh got to Zac's in record time. He tied the horse inside of the main floor, and raced to the communicator room. As he threw the door open, a man with a powerful weapon jumped up from a chair and pointed it at Josh.

"Who is it?" the man demanded.

"Zac, is that you?" Josh asked carefully.

The lights had cast a shadow in front of the man and he could not tell. But he had used his abilities to check for bad presence and found none. He did not know who else would be there. Maybe it was another rebel.

"No, there is no Zac here. Who are you and what do you want?" the voice demanded again.

"My name is Josh Naihu, and I am looking for..." the other man interrupted him.

"Naihu, you say. Josh, is that you?" The man came from behind a curtain. It was Zac. He was very careful. "Sharhi, come here, love. There is someone here." He called over his shoulder, as he grabbed the now larger Josh and hugged him like a long lost son.

"Sharhi!" he hollered, "Hurry."

Sharhi had come from behind the curtain. When she saw who the visitor was, she rushed to Josh and hugged him, not like a lover, more like a sister.

"Josh, you...you have grown so tall, and you are much more handsome now. How have you been? I assume that you are here to pick up your family."

She was eager to hear about his travels though she had seen the Law materials that he wore. The disgust showed in her deep brown eyes.

"No, I am just visiting. I am a soldier now, as you can see." Josh pulled on the shirt of the soldier uniform. "I work at the main base now. I have not found the 'land of Naru'. I don't think that it even exists. I think that my great grandfather made it all up, so that my father would not continue with the hide business. It did not work, however. He is still doing hides, and now he is not only short one son's help, but also the help of mother and my sisters." He sounded angry.

He hated his great grandfather, for putting such an idea into his father's head. But, he hated the Law even more for allowing his father to continue with the business, even if he was shorthanded.

"Did you come alone?" Zac looked concerned though he knew that Naihu would not let him come with anyone else. "I have been hiding the communicator from the enemy. Your father's was destroyed. They found it under a pile of hides. The Law has not figured out that he sides with the rebels. He told them that he had used the communicator for the business to ship the hides. The Law told him he would not need it any longer. They would pick up the hides and take them to the shuttle pads for shipment," Zac finished.

"Yes, I came alone. I am concerned about the man that I came with on the transport, though. My father thinks that he is an enemy, disguised in one of our uniforms. If he is, then I will surely finish my mission with him and be done with soldiering." Josh could not keep the distaste out of his mouth as he spoke about the general.

"I must be going. They will think that I have run off if I don't return soon. I would like to contact my father with my mind before I go, though. He has things to tell me and I cannot talk to him face to face with this enemy around."

Josh was very mature now. He must be around ten seasons now, thought Sharhi. His disgust with this new development showed in the tone in his voice.

"Go ahead Josh; you will have good reception here."

Zac took Sharhi by the hand and disappeared behind the curtain.

Josh stood very still in the darkness. He listened. His eyes were closed. He just listened.

"Josh, my son, you must return." The signal was very strong, he opened his eyes. Fear had crept deep inside of him. He wondered if the Law man had started to cause trouble.

"Zac, I must go!" Josh yelled loudly at the curtain door, but did not wait for his friend to reply.

He turned and ran the length of the stairs in three steps, grabbed the horse, checked outside, and in a flash was gone. "Home, girl!" he bellowed at the horse.

They ran all the way to the running water, taking all the short cuts they could. Josh let the horse drink while he listened for his father. He was but a short distance away now and he would know if there was trouble. It had not taken Josh long to get there. He knew of many shortcuts, especially now that the trees were gone.

"Josh, I can feel you. Good. You are close. We are finishing up the load now. Things are good."

There was concern in his father's voice, as he listened carefully. "Har started to snoop in the workroom. He had heard about my communicator. Little did he know that my communicator is in my own head."

Josh could hear the teasing tone in his father's voice. He had not heard this tone for many seasons. It was as if the Law had turned him into a cold man with no feeling. Josh did not like his 'new' father. The old one was much nicer, and gentle.

Josh knew that it would be okay to return now. His father's humorous business tone was one that Josh knew well. He trotted the horse in and yelled to Har how different everything was. His voice had a sinister tone. Har did not pick it up. "When you are ready, sir?" Josh had put the horse back in the gate and waited for a reply from the senior man.

"Say your good-byes, and we will be off then." He sounded pleased. All had gone well, and he was looking forward to some rest of his own.

He had brought Josh with him this time, because he knew that Josh would not be able to come back for a long time. The storms were destroying more and more worlds and they needed Josh to concentrate on fixing the problem. The Law knew that he would need to keep his mind clear of worries so that he would be able to come up with a plan to destroy the enemy, once and for all.

The two men jumped aboard the truck with the hides on it and headed for the shuttle that would take them back to the base camp.

Josh sat silently next to the general. He pretended to be working on a plan in his head. Little did the man sitting next to him know that the plan he worked on would include making an example of the Law and all that it supposedly stood for.

Josh knew that he would have to sharpen his ability of knowing good people from bad. It would be difficult with the soldiers around him all the time.

The truck had pulled up to the shuttle landing site where several soldiers started unloading the hides from it. They would load them on the transport and take them to the nearest recruiting site.

Josh and the general stood close by and made sure that the soldiers did a good job and handled the hides with care. Once the hides had been transferred to the craft, all but two of the soldiers boarded it along with Josh and the General.

"Thank you, sir. It was good to see my father again. He looks good. The boys are a big help to him. He has taught them well." Josh was making small talk with the man that sat next to him while the transport prepared to take off. He wanted to escape this man who sat beside him on the transport, this enemy. He would not be able to trust anyone, not anyone but his father and Zac.

CHAPTER FIVE

Josh soldiered for a little while longer. He still traveled some, and wherever he went he scanned the worlds. He still longed to find the one they called 'land of Naru'. He continued to work on the plan that would stop the enemy transports from dumping the dust into the storms, the dust that caused disease and destruction of the lands.

When he slept he dreamt of the horrible things that had happened on his home world. There were few people there anymore. Most of them were rebels like Zac, or in business, if it was needed to supply the soldiers or work houses. Josh had never seen the work houses on any of the worlds. He heard talk of them from other soldiers, but they never gave any description. It would give the positions away and the enemy would destroy them. The Law could not afford this. They needed those houses for their precious rock!

The thought disgusted Josh. He just wanted to escape. He had to figure out how, without tipping off anyone. His thoughts of making a plan had caught him off guard.

"Hey, soldier, are you off daydreaming about that faraway place, again," came a familiar voice. "I know guys that have been put to work on the front for daydreaming," the voice teased.

Ran? Could it be? Josh did not say anything. He could not be sure of anyone any more. "I'm sorry. I was trying a formula in my head, Sir?" Josh came up with something quick.

"Well, if it were me I would be building white castles in the sand." The voice was almost laughing.

"Ran, is it really you?" Josh was very careful.

"I swear on the land where disease took my family, the land I will return to."

Josh turned around to see his old friend holding one hand on his heart and one in the air. "How in this world are you?" Josh grabbed his friend like a lost relative and hugged him. He did not let go for a long time. The men silently cried together there in the light of the far off moon.

"How have you been, Josh?" Ran held his friend away from him to look at him. They had not seen each other for many seasons. Ran had gone back to Shurfate after he traveled with another troop for some time. He had continued on with soldiering for the Law for an additional three seasons.

His father's health had failed but not from disease. Ran guessed his many seasons, probably. He had married Shraze and he was at the main base to get his release signed. He had sent Shraze to the 'harshland' that they had always considered home. As soon as he received his release papers he would join her there. He could not bear to live on his home land for fear of the enemy. Ran figured it would take a few days, and he was excited about seeing Josh.

"I have done many things, my friend," Josh came back with a delighted tone in his voice. He could not believe his eyes or ears. "I have so many things to tell you. How long will it be for your release? I assume that is why you are here, correct?" His mind could tell this was his old friend. They kept no secrets, even as men. This was one other person that Josh could trust. There would never be more than those three and his brothers. When they were older, they would understand, he knew.

"Yes, that is why I am here. My time has been served to the Law and I am free to go." Ran had become quite the theatrical clown. He again placed his hand on his heart and the other in the air.

"Where did you learn such a crazy gesture?" Josh laughed at his life time friend. Then, as if he could hear other sounds, Josh placed a finger to his mouth and pushed the air between his teeth, "shhhhhh."

He put his hand to his friend's mouth and listened. "I don't think it is safe here together. We must be very careful. Go and find your room. I will find you later." He turned and walked away.

Josh had disappeared as fast as Ran had appeared. He knew what Josh had been feeling. He felt it, too, but not with any ability. It was a feeling that he had been getting from time to time, even though he was never close to the enemy. He wondered if Josh thought that there might be enemy spies disguised as Lawmen.

That is why he was returning to the harshland. At least he would have Josh's father as a trust-worthy friend until Josh came to take them to the 'land of Naru'. Ran had seen paper with those letters on it, but no one knew of the place. Most of the lands he had seen were harsh, like Josh's homeland, and he had seen plenty.

Ran stood and chewed on a stick for a minute before he walked the corridor to his room. It was a small room with a place to sleep and a place for materials. Ran undressed to his waist and waited for his friend. He knew that he would come as long as there was no trouble.

Ran drifted in and out of sleep. He kept thinking of the times that Josh and he had spent as small boys. He thought of a place that had trees and animals, a place Ran knew did not exist anymore. It nearly destroyed him to think that there was nothing left, nothing but a bunch of underground houses and tons of women and children working in the mineral mines. Ran had seen them. He had done watch in them. It was a horrible site, the women loaded the rocks into sleds and two children hauled each sled off. They worked until the cool hours began and then returned before the sun became high.

Ran awoke from his dream. He had heard something. Could it be Josh? He waited, with his eyes closed. He pretended to sleep, but he was alert, as if the enemy had been listening to his dream.

"Ran?" He heard the faint whisper of Josh's voice.

"Yes."

The door opened and closed so fast you could hardly see it move. Ran lay very still. He could not be sure it was Josh until the silhouetted figure moved into the light. Before he knew it, Josh had sat down beside him and was holding his mouth shut.

"Hey, what's the big idea?" He whispered, barely.

"There are bad ears here. Just be quiet for a few more minutes."

The two men sat in silence for a long time. Ran could not hear a thing, but he knew his friend could.

"I cannot stay here. Take this message to my father. I will have to catch you up later." Josh sat for a while longer. He could not sense the enemy any longer, so he gave Ran a few more things to tell his father. "I am due to leave soldiering as well, but I will find the land that I promised I would when I left so many seasons ago. If you cannot wait for me, go. Get as far away from the enemy as is truly possible. I will return to the homeland when I have found the 'land of Naru' and I will take him there. I must go now, my friend. I have found that you will be on the soldier transport tomorrow just before the cool hours begin. Your papers are all signed. General Har cannot risk the two of us together for very long. He is afraid I will tell you things that only a few select people know. He's right, I would! Good Luck!" He hugged his friend again, as if to make sure it was not a dream, and then he was gone.

Ran was shocked. He sat in the silence for many hours. He did not think of anything except the message his friend had given him. He did not worry for Naihu. He knew that he was a very powerful man, and he knew he had never given the Law any part of the business. He would just as soon pack the place up and leave the Law to figure it out for themselves, than to ever be pushed by any of them. Ran had also visited Josh's family from time to time.

Ran woke after fitful sleep. He had not rested at all. The words of his friend rang in his ears as if they were reminding him not to forget. He packed his things and left to get his release papers. Shraze would be delighted to see him so soon. After almost half the day was gone, he received the papers and headed to the nearest shuttle site. One thing Josh was wrong about was the time he would leave.

Ran did not know or question why he had not been on the first shuttle. He did not see Josh during his entire morning running. As he boarded the transport, he thought of Josh. He wished that he would come back to the homeland. They could make their own 'land of Naru' there. Ran just wanted the few people he could trust all in one place. Then there would be no chance for distrust.

Josh had prepared things all during the cool hours. He was tired, but he must continue. He worked feverishly on his new plan. The Law would not release him until he came up with a way to stop the enemy. He had finally devised a plan that would at least get him released. He hoped.

After his last visit with his father, he had worked non-stop on the new plan. The new twist of involving the Law with his plan made it a little harder to accomplish, but with the help of his father and their abilities, he would complete it in no time.

"Sir, I have been up all of the cool hours. I think I have a plan for the enemy! There is only one problem. I am due for my release papers so I am afraid I will not be here for the outcome. I am sure that it will work." Josh stood rigid in front of the general. He came across with great confidence. He was very good at being a businessman. His father had taught him well.

"Well, Josh. This is not a surprise to me. I knew that you were close. I could feel it. You have been working all hours on this. I am sorry to hear that you will be receiving your release papers and will not be able to enjoy the outcome." Har had become very sarcastic. He did not need Josh anymore. He had what he needed and would be happy to sign his release. Then the enemy could do as they wished with him. "When would you like to be released, Josh?" Har asked coldly.

"I will set the plan up and see that it gets a good start. That should not take more than maybe a week or two, if all goes well, Sir," Josh replied as planned.

"Well, then, I will sign your papers tomorrow and date them for two weeks from now. Thank you, Josh. You have been a great asset to the Law." Har reached his hand out to shake Josh's. The two men shook hands, and Josh began his work.

He knew that if he could complete the plan in a week Har would change his release date. He worked furiously, high sun and low. He would catch sleep when he could and be right back at it. He spent the last few hours of the week making the final preparations.

On the last day, he received a letter from his father. Ran had delivered his message and this would be his reply, he thought. He opened it and read 'Josh, my son, I hear it is time for you to visit again. If you can get a transport here, please come.' That was it. Nothing about any part of the message Ran was to deliver. Josh could not return to the homeland, not just yet. He had to find the 'land of Naru.' He knew that he was close. He could feel it. He dreamed of it most of the time. He could see the image clear in his mind, but he could still not see the path that led him there.

Josh had completed the initial startup of his plan. General Har had done as he suspected and changed the date on his papers. He sat at the shuttle site and waited for the first transport to wherever. He boarded and prepared to watch everything that he could see. The engines on the craft had come to the usual high roar as the pilot radioed for takeoff. Gently, he lifted the craft into the air and in a tight circle headed the transport to its destination.

Josh watched everything. The beginning of the flight was the best part. Before the sky turned black Josh could see all the storms of white, but they were so small. The only time he had seen larger ones were on worlds that had not been destroyed. It only took a short while to go from the light part of the atmosphere to the darkness beyond.

The darkness allowed Josh to see several worlds all at once. He knew that it would be difficult to travel after the first transport, but he would figure that out when he arrived at his final destination.

Josh spent more than two seasons searching the worlds and the paths of the shuttle crafts. He had seen many, many worlds. Most of them had rock surfaces though he did come across a few that had still not been hit with the fine powder of the enemy. Maybe they were the only ones that were considered the 'land of Naru' and there were no lands, but the Harshlands, that did not get white.

He had become tired of travel. He wanted to see his family. The wars had moved further from the homeland. Josh had begun to think that he should return to the homeland and gather his family. They would have enough money to travel together now, especially since his father had not given up the knowledge of the business.

Josh found the nearest shuttle on the world that he was on and waited until a transport came that would connect him to a flight to his homeland. He could feel the excitement of seeing his family again. He had enough power with the Law that he could get release papers for his mother and sisters and they would all travel together.

Josh arrived on the homeland several seasons after he left soldiering only to find nothing. He had not seen the homeland since the last time he saw his father. There was talk that the Law was hunting him, so he stayed away from his family and his usual stopping places. There would be no way he would allow the Law to punish him for a plan when he had not been around for the outcome.

Josh sat and cried for hours. His father was gone. No one even knew of Ran Tis. It was as if he never existed on this land. He followed the road to Zac's house. The windows had been broken, and there was nothing inside not even on the lower floors where he had talked to Zac. His heart sank.

He climbed down the rickety steps to the communicator. It was there, but it had not been turned on in what looked like a long time. He wondered if he could get it hooked up. He tried the switch on the microphone. Nothing. Not even a crackle. He tried for a while longer, but no luck. The communicator had been damaged somehow, and Josh had never worked on any because of his ability to communicate without them.

Even though Josh was devastated, he would not give up the search, ever. He knew that his father was fine. He could feel his presence at the business. It was a faint presence, but there nonetheless. He would continue his search until he found his family. He traveled the whole homeland world. He asked many children if they had heard of Naihu. Some had, some had not. Those that had did not even know where he was from. He continued.

He found a young lady and asked if she had a horse for sale. He would pay her handsomely. She agreed and Josh did the rest of his search on horseback. It made it a lot easier, and he was able to cover more ground though he found that some would not speak with him. He could not figure out if it was because he had a horse or because of the materials on his back. He did not have any nice clothes. The Law would not allow it.

He had left most of his supplies with his father shortly after he started soldiering. Now that his father and all of their supplies were gone, he had nothing. There were no storekeepers left in any of the towns so far. He would try to find something. He must know where his family had gone to.

Where was Ran? Did he ever get to his father? Why had he not come when his father had asked him to! He continued to search the land.

Occasionally he came across soldiers of the Law. Ducking behind whatever was available, he avoided them at all costs. He was determined to find all that he had lost, and the Law was not going to stand in his way.

He discovered a few of the old work houses. Most of the people inside would not give him the time of day. They did not have to. They had spent most of their lives living under the enemy. They had no reason to trust anyone, not even the Law, and for good reason.

Josh had covered most of the land, and was about to search for a transport site when he came to another work house. He would try one final time to see if any one inside would speak to him. He went in. there was a woman sitting on the floor tanning a hide. She glanced at Josh and continued her work.

"Excuse me. I do not intend to interrupt your work, but have you heard of a man they call Naihu?" Josh questioned the woman. He did not get a response, so he turned to go, hanging his head in desperation. He had failed all his life missions except for one, and he did not care to remember the plan that he left with the Law.

"Did you say Naihu?" the woman replied.

"Yes. Have you heard of him?" Josh could hardly hold his excitement. He turned around quickly to face the woman again.

"I have." She stopped. "What's it to you, Law man?" She was cold.

Josh still wore the material that his father had made for him many, many seasons ago. It seemed like a lifetime to Josh. His heart was heavy with pain and sadness.

"I am Josh, eldest son of Naihu. I am in search of him and the rest of my family. I have not seen any of them for many seasons." He stopped, so that the tears would not cloud his speaking.

"I am Ruba. I have worked here since the enemy came. I knew your mother. She is the one who taught me this." Ruba held up the hide. "I have not seen your family for many seasons now either, three or four possibly." It sounded as if she was guessing. She continued with the hide. "Your father came for them and headed for the nearest transport site. He had said something bad about the Law upon his arrival here with his sons, and they were gone; left in the cool hours." She looked up to see if Josh had been hearing her. "Would you like some better clothes? You might get better reception from folks." She held the hide out to Josh.

He took the hide from Ruba and admired its quality. Mother had taught the woman well. She had told him that she no longer had family to give it to so he might as well take it. He took the hide and thanked the woman.

Mounting his horse he headed in the same direction. He had to find a transport. It would be hard to find his family. There were many worlds to search, and Josh had not been able to see his father in visions since he had left the base camp. He could still feel the presence and he would only go until the feeling became weak.

He kept his search on the closer worlds. It took him a long time to find open transport sites. After nearly half a season of searching other worlds, he returned to the harshland and searched there one more time. The feeling of his father was strongest on the homeland, but it wasn't strong enough to see him or communicate. This made Josh wonder where his Naihu could be.

He found another shuttle site, only to learn that the next transport for the other side of his world was not due for some time. He decided he would wait. He searched his mind for his father's image. It was not there. He could still feel his presence. Where was he?

When the shuttle craft arrived, Josh purchased a pass to ride and gathered his few belongings. It did not take long to receive permission for takeoff, and they were headed to the other side of the home world.

Josh drifted off to sleep, weary from his travels and the letdown of not being able to find his family, nor was he able to find the land that he was still fairly sure did not exist. If it did, then there was no way to get there.

CHAPTER SIX

Josh opened his eyes. The sun had been high for some time. The heat was unbearable. Not remembering the landing, he rolled over to see where he was; his last memory was of boarding the transport. He had been exhausted physically, but mostly, mentally. His heart ached, his head was full.

"What the..." he pulled his hand up and shook the warm wet water from it. He sat up. This was not your usual transport site. Where was he, he thought to himself.

There was water everywhere. All he could see was water. He sat very still. He thought if he tried he could see the far horizons. The water would not hold still though. He was too exhausted and hungry to try any harder.

He had nothing but a satchel full of money and the two hides. He wore the one that the woman had made. He put the Law one up for a shelter in this floating room. His father's presence could still be felt as he drifted in and out of sleep. He finally awoke.

The water had stopped moving. Maybe he could scan the horizons now. He sat up to look for something familiar, but the only thing he found was trees and fruit and nuts and solitude. The water washed to the sand and then ran out away from it again.

Josh had never seen anything like it. This must be the land of Naru, the place that Josh had searched for his whole life. He climbed out of the floating room and headed for the trees with fruit on them. His insides felt like he had not had anything to eat for days. For all he knew, he hadn't.

He had no idea how long he had been on the little floating room, but he felt like it had been quite a while. His skin had turned an almost reddish brown from the heat of the sun.

After he had eaten all that he could, he stood still and scanned the horizons beyond the water. He was looking for the storms. He could see a very faint one. It was almost white, and very small. Josh still remembered the talents his father had taught him so well, his father and Zac.

He continued to wonder if the family had found the place. Josh did not even know if there was a transport site. His last conscious thoughts were of boarding the transport and taking off. He had dozed in his seat almost immediately. Something must have happened during the flight.

Whatever it was, he wished that he had been awake to find out, though he was almost sure that he would not have made it out alive. Nor would he have made it to this place.

At the moment he did not care. His father's presence had grown weak, almost as if he was just feeling the memories. Josh thought that he could feel another presence, but he brushed it aside.

The first thing to do was figure out what world he had landed on, he thought, even though he did not remember landing. The whole place felt familiar, somehow.

Josh's mind raced with so many thoughts. For the first few days he tried to concentrate on the landing. He was sure that his exhaustion had caused him to forget all about it. Not understanding why his memory of the flight eluded him, he soon tired of concentrating on it.

He tried to concentrate instead on his father. He still felt his father's presence from time to time. Though, as his father's presence seemed to slip away from him, another presence seemed to grow. Josh wondered what this meant. It was certainly not in any of the learning that he got from Zac or his father.

There had been so much to think about. Things like, where had his family gone? Why couldn't he find Ran on the homeland? Why was he here? Where was here? Why did his father leave? What had happened to Zac? Had he and his father gone together? His mind wandered. The questions that rushed through his head reminded him of his childhood when he would question his father incessantly while he learned.

Josh built himself a shelter from the long leaves and branches of the trees. He made a store room that would keep the fruits and nuts. He had grown tired of having to go out every day to pick what he wanted to eat, though there was plenty close by, and it never took him very long to eat what he wanted. Still, the store room gave him time to search the new world that he had landed on. It was a peaceful place, the animals and the birds were a nice change from the other worlds that he had visited.

Josh had decided that he did not want to leave this place, not because he couldn't find a transport site, but because of the splendor and beauty. Since he had failed all his life missions, and still did not have his family nor did he know where the land of Naru was, he spent most of his time clearing the bad and useless thoughts from his mind.

After a few weeks on the land surrounded by water, he decided that he wanted a new start. His life had passed over him, and as far as he was concerned there was nothing left from his past that he cared to remember.

There seemed to be only one memory that he could not get rid of. Something kept bringing him back to his homeland. What would it take to erase this memory from his head? He had become angry with himself. He should have returned when his father asked for him. All he wanted to do was forget all the beginning seasons of his life.

The days were full of sunshine and warmth. He soon learned to enjoy the solitude that he had found: no transports in the sky; no war ships or soldiers clamoring around. But soon enough he became tired of the silence and not having anyone to talk to. Every so often he would awake after the strange vision he had encountered on Shurfate would startle him. It was a very clear vision, but there was still no face to the silhouetted figure. The message was the same, "Son of Naihu," but it would end there. The message seemed to be the same one but it was always cut short when the vision started to become clear. It was as if Josh was not to see the figure clearly. He would push the thought away and ready himself for another day of sunshine and solitude.

The trees and the animals were no match for the human companionship that he found he desired. One day he decided to go and explore the rest of the land. He climbed a rock face and could see, with his ability, the whole piece of land. It was rather large. He discovered that there were a lot of people here. He could see groups of them in the water. They would laugh and speak, but it was a tongue that Josh did not recognize. There was a great piece of the land that had nothing but trees and animals.

It seemed like the people stayed on the flat part of the land. The rest had very steep rocks and more fruit trees than he could have ever imagined one place to have.

Josh spent a long time on the other side of the land away from the people. Though he desired the companionship of talking to someone other than himself, he was tired of people in his life. Only bad things had happened to the ones he cared to know, and the rest were evil. They were lawmen and enemies.

It had become a place that Josh wanted to stay. It made him wonder if this was the land of Naru that his father had told him to find. Maybe it was, but it would never be a land of Naru to him, because he had not found his family.

As far as he knew, there was no way off the small piece of land that he had found. Sometimes he saw transports way off on the horizon, but he had no idea how he would ever reach them. The floating room that had brought him there would surely never allow him to reach the place where he saw the crafts flying.

After some weeks on the land surrounded by water, he learned that there were animals in the water that he could catch like he and his friend had done as children.

Only he did not let these go. He made a cook fire and cooked what he caught. He remembered the lessons from his father. He understood many of them, now.

So much time had passed. Josh had lost track how long he had been there. The storms came and went. As he watched them he noticed that they did not fall white. They fell water. He could see white from the top of the land, but it was only very small patches of it. This land was way too warm to allow white to last very long.

He came to the conclusion that he had found the land of Naru. Though he wished that his family could be here with him, he decided that he wanted nothing better than to stay here for the rest of his days. He would walk for hours on the sand next to the water, enjoying the sounds of the animals and the water crashing against the land.

One day he was spotted by one of the people of the land. The person waved to him. It was a man, not much older than Josh, he guessed. Josh waved back, hoping the gesture meant the same greeting here as it had on all the other worlds that he had traveled.

The man came closer. Josh became defensive, though he did not run or try to hide. He used his sensory ability to feel if there was evil in this person. He could feel nothing, though he was not sure if it was nothing or if he had lost the ability because of the lack of practicing it.

"Guo vi ma." The man held out his hand.

"Hello, my name is Josh." He spoke very slowly and used his hands.

The man gave him a questioning look. He had not understood a word Josh had spoken, nor Josh him.

The man tried again, "Guo vi ma, me hoy sa Malrui Blanca." The man reached his hand out again.

Josh reached his hand out and shook the man's. It was a mutual greeting. The man took Josh to his village and introduced him to his people. All he would say was, "se Josh" and the people would reach for his hand.

Josh spent many hours watching the villagers. His new friend taught him the words that he spoke, and Josh did the same. Josh did not get any bad feelings or images from these people. They had no cares. Life was easy for them.

He learned to make the things that the villagers used in everyday life. He taught them how to smooth the hides of the animals for materials. He did not need money here. There was nothing to buy. Everything that was needed was made from the land. He learned how to weave the long branches of the trees to keep the water out. He learned to make the sand solid to drink from. After Josh had spent a great deal of time with the villagers his friend suggested that he buy the hut at the top of the path, it would be much easier to see him if he didn't have to walk the sand. Josh agreed.

He had put his first hut as far away from everyone as he could get it. It was a time when he did not have any trust.

Josh had learned of another village. Though he had seen the people before, when he sat on the top of the land, he assumed that all of them were from the same village. Much to his surprise, they were not. He did not venture into the other village. He just watched the people in it.

Josh had always loved watching people, ever since the day he had left his family for the first time. This group of people had different ways, different from his new friend's village. The children there had beautiful materials.

They did not sit and make things from the land. All that they had was expensive, things that Josh had never seen. He wondered where they would purchase such wonderful pieces of material and the beautifully crafted daily supplies that they used. They wore beautiful rings around their necks, arms, legs, and feet; everywhere.

Josh liked to watch the inhabitants of the two villages. The differences were like light and dark. He sat on the hill above the strangers' village almost every day. At times he would feel his father's presence and that would make him go to the top of the land.

There were no cool hours. The sun went away, like the places that Ran had told him of. The heat stayed. He would watch until it was too dark to see clearly, then return to his hut for sleep.

The presence of his father would fade in and out, almost like he was trying to reach Josh, but didn't know exactly where he was. It was the only part of Josh's past life that he had been unable to dismiss from his mind. After time, he barely remembered any of his past. He had become a new person and had learned a new language also.

One day, as he watched the people of the strange village, a woman came from one of the larger huts. She was different. Beautiful! Her hair was light, not like the other villagers. Her skin was olive, and darkly tanned from the sun. She walked very softly, her whole body swung from side to side as she headed to the water.

Josh could not take his eyes off her. He did not want to return to his hut. He wanted her. He had not felt these desires since the time he spent at Zac's, a time he chose to forget.

The next morning he asked his friend about the woman. Who was she? Did she belong to anyone? Why hadn't he seen her before? His curiosity nearly killed him.

His friend would find the answers to his questions, but it would take a while. He did not dare go to that village. They were not of his kind. He probably did not even speak the same tongue.

Malrui sent Josh to his hut. He would see him in the morning. Josh tried to sleep. The visions in his head were of her. He had to know her, or at least find out about her.

The sun rose above the horizon as it had done each day since his arrival here. Josh stretched and put on his materials. He had decided that he wanted to go to the other side of the land again and have time to just be alone. It had been a rough night without sleep and he needed time to relax. As he walked out the cloth door of his small shelter, his friend Malrui met him at the door.

"Vi ma. I have your answers. She is the daughter of the King Shahi-Nehra. You have not seen her because she has been away. She does not belong to anyone but her father." Malrui was out of breath as he gave his deliberate answers to Josh, as if he had practiced them.

"What is her name?" Josh had to know who she was, besides the daughter of a king.

His friend did not know, he had forgotten to ask. That was okay, Josh thought. He would find out for himself. He found the only thought on his mind was the woman, every day and night.

Josh spent many more days watching the woman. She bathed in the green water, then lay on the sand to dry.

Her body was sensuous. Her skin was a golden brown, which made her hair almost white in the sun.

Josh could not believe that not only had he found the land of Naru he had found the woman that his heart desired. He had to know this woman. She was very mysterious. His desires for her were stronger than he had ever learned of. No one had taught this feeling to him. It came from deep within him. His body shivered with the thought of lying next to her. To hold her and caress her darkened skin.

He saw visions of her in his mind like they had seen each other in another time. They were clear, similar to the ones that he would have of his father from time to time. Only his father's would fade quickly, hers stayed with him.

He watched the children gather around her and listen to stories of their king. She did not spend much time out of her large hut, and when she was out she was never alone. This made it even more difficult to meet the woman. The feelings he held inside of him were making it difficult enough.

There were not as many people in this village; mostly children, and elders. Some of the elders would spend their time with her in the hut. Then they would all come out except for one, and the woman; the mystery woman who held many secrets.

What did they do in the large hut? Why didn't the woman spend more time alone? Was she special, did she have talents, like Josh? His mind raced with questions, questions he knew he could not share with her. Would there ever be a time that she was completely alone?

Josh would have to find the answer to that one, if it took him the rest of his lifetime.

Josh remembered some of the skills he had learned as a soldier. He had to make a plan, and then entice her to a place where she would be alone. He spent an entire day and night observing her every move. He would record all of her actions in his mind.

He waited to see if she would come out by herself in the time of no sun. He had never watched all night. He got as close to the hut as he dare, and he waited. He would have to be cautious to move away before the sun came back so that he was not caught. She did not come out the first night. Josh continued his observation of her. After three nights he saw the door move in the hut.

He crouched down, just in case it was the elder woman who stayed with her. He watched as the blonde hair waved in the breeze around the small opening of the door. She moved slowly and secretly, as if she were trying not to be found out, alone.

Josh followed her to the water. She stood very still. She looked to the sea as if she waited for it to speak to her. After some time she hung her head and sat hastily in the sand.

Josh could feel the pain. Did she wait for her father? Did she wait for a lover? Whatever it was that she waited for had saddened her. Josh sat close enough to her now that he could hear the sobs coming from under her folded arms.

Josh walked out to the sand and came to her. He did not say anything at first. He stood behind her and listened. He cleared his throat and walked around to the front of her. She looked up at him. The tears fell, like rivers that would not stop running, from her eyes.

Josh reached his gentle hand to her cheek and wiped away the water. Her eyes were as green as Josh had ever seen, though he never thought of them as special, only in his own eyes.

"I am Josh. I have been here for many seasons. My hut is on the other side of the land where there are no villages." He stopped, wiping the tears from her cheek. "Why do you cry so hard? A beautiful woman should not have such pain in her heart." He again caressed the smooth skin on her face.

"I am Zerasha Shahi-Nehra. I cry because I wait for my father. He should have returned many, many suns ago. I do not understand why the wars have kept him so long this time." She had become very businesslike. Though, the fear inside her could be felt easily by Josh.

"I have watched you for many suns. Your golden hair and darkened skin is all that I have been able to think of since I saw you the first time with the children on the sand." Josh was not sure if the woman liked him being there or not. "You must have been but a small child when I left here for the wars. Or surely I would have known you then, with all of your beauty."

She blushed. "Who are you? Where did you spend your time in the wars?" she questioned, almost interrogated.

"I said, my name is Josh. I am son of Naihu. I spent my time, mostly on the base world." He did not give any details, as he bowed to the woman on the sand.

"Why have you come to this side of the island? You say your hut is on the other side, with the rocks?" She was still interrogating, as if she did not believe his story. Why should she? Very few strangers ever came to her village. It was secluded from the rest of the villages on the land surrounded by water. She had become very untrustworthy of most people, as others had, since the wars had started.

"I came because I had seen your beauty on an adventure walk I took many, many suns ago. I had just returned from soldiering and wished to see if the land had changed any, like most of the worlds that I have seen. Your beauty beheld my heart and I could no longer wait to speak to you and see if the beauty you held on the outside was on the inside as well. I can see that it is, but it is clouded with a thought that has saddened your heart." He could hardly believe his own ears. He had never had the desire to speak this way. The words flowed from his lips like he had rehearsed them.

"I have never heard of Naihu. Where is he now? And why do you not go to him?" She questioned, eager to hear where the strange dark-haired man had come from.

"Naihu is no longer. He was taken from here before I came. I do not remember much, except the stories that I heard while I was soldiering. He was a hide maker for the Law, and I was never allowed to visit him." He told the story with such confidence that he almost believed it himself.

"I must go. My mother will not be pleased I am out alone." Zerasha rose from the sand, and turned to go.

"Tell her you were not alone. I would like to see you again," Josh almost begged the woman.

"Fine. Then you may tell my mother yourself. Come to the hut after the sun comes up." She darted through the trees like a goddess with her hair blowing in the wind.

Josh could hardly hold his excitement. He sat for the rest of the darkness, preparing the best that he had. He cleaned his face and put on his best materials. He hoped that her mother would not throw him off the island.

He desired, deep in his heart, to spend the rest of his life next to Zerasha. He was sure, however, that her mother would know he did not speak the truth.

All he wanted to know was what Zerasha would tell him of herself. All the things that made her happy, the places she had been to, the things that made her happiest in her life. He hoped that someday one of those things would be him.

He had completely erased most of his past from his head. There were certain things he wished to keep fresh in his mind, but most he preferred to leave hidden. This would surely be a new beginning for him.

He walked nervously to the beautiful woman's hut. He could feel the water from his body all over him. He had never felt like this. It was similar to the feeling he had as a child venturing away from home for the first time, but somehow different. He called her name as he reached the cloth doorway to her hut. There was no reply, so he called again. He would not leave until he saw her beauty again.

After a few moments, her head came from behind the cloth. "Hello, again, my mother is waiting for you on the back veranda. She is very pleased to hear that a man has come calling on me." Zerasha blushed, as though she had never had a man call on her. "Come this way, Josh of Naihu," she called him by his ancestry.

"Mother, this is Josh of Naihu. He has come to tell you something." The elder lady's eyes had deepened with concern when she heard the name of Josh's ancestry.

Josh bowed to the elder woman and kissed the back of her leathery hand. "I am pleased to meet you, ma'am. I would like the pleasure of your daughter's company as often as you will allow." Josh tried not to be nervous.

"Slow down, young man. I would like to get to know you first." The elder woman was kind. She seemed pleased to have Josh come. "You say you are of Naihu. I knew a man named Naihu, but it was from another time." She broke her conversation off. She did not want to tip Josh off to anything that she might know of him already. "Zerasha, please go get us something cool to drink, will you?" The elder woman wanted some time alone with this handsome prince who called on her daughter.

After Zerasha left the room, the answers came from the elder woman. "I am the Queen of Shahi-Nehra. My husband of many seasons left this Island for a land that needed his expertise, more so than his own island, many seasons ago. Zerasha was but a tiny girl, only a few days old. I know of all activities on this island paradise, and I know that your hut was only built a few seasons ago. I do not know why you want to hide your true ancestry, but I am most positive that you have a very good explanation." She finished very politely, but the business woman in her showed very well.

She had been taught by the finest people. Josh could see this when she spoke. "The true King was an elder from many generations before even my time," the woman continued. "He made this land all that it is today. His stories are still told today to the children of the island. It is to keep the history of the legends continuous. When he left the island, he would tell only the people that needed to know of it. The rest would not be welcome. He told of a time when there would be peace in all the lands and the island would be the start of it all. Shahi-Nehra left this island and only returned as he saw that he needed to and only when he was able to.

"My husband, the eldest son of Shahi-Nehra, left this island in search of a young man for his daughter. This is the way the legends have called for, all the seasons of the Shahi-Nehra. So, what are you hiding from? The Law, possibly?" She waited.

"No, I only hide from the bad memories that I have of a land and family that no longer exist the way they did when I was but a young child myself. My father sent me away to find the 'land of Naru' that his father's father had told him of. I was to be the child of Naihu that would find this place which I am now sure does not exist. I have traveled to many worlds, only to find the same devastation everywhere I went. When I returned to my family, so we could continue to search together, they were gone. No trace of them was left. I am sure if the place exists that is where my family is, and I am doomed to live without them.

"So, I found myself afloat on your sea, two or three seasons ago. I have dismissed the thoughts of my youth and travels. I am ready to start fresh with my life with little or no ties attached," he finished.

He did not go into any details. It was a part of his life that he had not thought of in many seasons, and he did not want to start now.

"My, what a story. I was truly not ready for that." The elderly woman was quiet for a long time. When she spoke again she was sincere in her tone.

"I told you that I had heard of Naihu. My husband was a great friend of his. The two families have known each other for many generations. My husband left here shortly before the wars started to find the man that his new daughter would marry and to find the lost tribal members. When he found Naihu, he prepared him to know the Law and the enemy. My husband should have returned many, many seasons ago. He was to return with the man for Zerasha. She thinks that she is doomed to live alone, until her father returns.

"Our culture decides a woman's betrothed when she is born. If there is no one for the woman on her day of birth, then the hunt is formed to find her a suitable companion with the right teachings. I am afraid that something terrible has happened and that is why he has not returned." She hesitated as Zerasha came into the room with mango cider to drink.

"I am sorry, mother. Were you not finished?" She waited at the doorway for an answer, as if she were a child that had just been scolded for interrupting.

"No, that is all right, Zerasha, Come in." The elderly woman would catch up later on this new addition to the island. "Josh is of a fine culture. I will allow the two of you to see each other, on one condition. Zerasha, when your father returns, you may remain friends with Josh, as long as your betrothed does not mind." She drank her cider and stood to go.

"You will take very good care of her, won't you Josh!" It was not a question. She nodded her head at him and left the two of them in the room alone.

"Did you have a nice conversation with Mother? She can be overbearing sometimes. Please come and sit for the elder men's stories of the Legends of Shahi-Nehra. These are my ancestors, and some of the stories are almost believable." Zerasha put her glass down and turned to lead him out of the hut and down to the sandy story place.

109

He had watched her listen and tell stories for a long time, but he never thought that he would be listening to them right beside her. He could not take his eyes from her. He sat across the group from her so that he could listen to the stories and still behold her ravishing beauty. He did not touch her when they walked. He did not want to go against her mother's wishes. The stories seemed familiar somehow but he could not place his mind on why.

They learned what they needed to of each other. Josh tried hard not to keep any secrets from her, but there was a part of his life that he did not want to let her enter. Not now. There would be a time, and when that time was right he would tell her. Until then he answered her questions of where he was from and what his childhood was like with great caution.

Josh was able to spend many hours with Zerasha's mother. She told him that her husband was Zachariah Shahi-Nehra. Josh remembered his friend Zac, and wondered from time to time if they might be the same person. It could not be, though. Josh's father had told him that Zac was a friend of his for many seasons. Zac had also said that he was from the land that he lived on.

Josh dismissed the thought. He was sure there were many Zachariahs in the many worlds. However, Josh was certain that the woman knew of his father. She spoke of Naihu, as if he were a king himself. He had many talents, and he could smooth the hide of an animal like no one she had ever met. The words rang in Josh's head. Josh wanted to know more of what she knew of his father, but the conversation usually surrounded the subject of her beautiful young daughter.

"Josh, what are your intentions for my daughter? She is not getting younger, you know." The elder woman sounded concerned. Her husband had been gone now for more than six seasons. She doubted his return.

"I would never go against the wishes of the legends. However, ma'am, I do desire your daughter to be my companion. She is not only the most beautiful creature that I have ever met in all the worlds, but she is intelligent, thoughtful, and warm of heart."

"Her father left so many seasons ago," she started. "He left to help Naihu, and also..." the elder woman hesitated, not sure if she should tell Josh who that man was or where he was from, "to bring back the man to whom she is betrothed. He was not picked at her birth. There were no eligible men at the time. There are secrets in her life that you do not need to ever question her of. She thinks that you are from the far side of the island. This must remain that way, until... her father returns, or is returned to the island."

"Ma'am, you speak of my father's name, but..." Josh was not sure that he wanted to bring his past into this new life that he had found and had truly enjoyed for many seasons. He still had the feeling of his father's presence, but he could not find the vision.

"Josh, there are things that you and I will need to spend the next few weeks or so discussing. I speak of your father because he is a very important part of the legends. If you stay here for a while you will learn of him during the story hour for the young. However, when you start hearing about him, you must promise to not tell Zerasha, until the time is right. These are things from her life story that she is not going to be ready to hear until she has heard from her father again. Do you understand, Josh?" The elder woman was gentle, but very businesslike, and proud of the legends.

"I understand very well. I must ask the same of myself about my past. There are things that Zerasha must not find out about me, at least until I feel the time is right." Josh hated the secrecy, but there were many parts of his life that the woman of his dreams would not understand until she has her betrothed beside her.

"I understand, young Josh. You have learned a great deal of lessons on your own. You are a traveled man, but at a very young age. The legends have been heard for many seasons, and they go even beyond your time. But, like your father, you are a part of these legends. Your father is a very powerful man. He has been a great asset to the true legend, much like his ancestors. When my husband, Zac, left here for the first time, he searched for the prince that his daughter would be betrothed to.

"In the legend, as you know, the tribes were separated many thousands of seasons ago. The wars, the disease and the near collapse of the tribal vows sent our ancestors out to stop the evil from spreading. The wars created chaos to the portals, and the Enemy nearly discovered the entrance to our land of Naru. There is a part of each of the tribes on some of the worlds. Zac landed on one that he had not been to before. This was truly an accident. When he settled to have a look at the people of this world, he came across a burial ground with a few of the names that he recognized from the legends. Naihu was among those names. This is from a time when you were but a wish in your father's eyes."

"This is not the same Zac," Josh interrupted, "the one that sent me on my journeys? The same man that taught me some of my abilities?" Josh became more confident as he watched the woman nodding her head.

"Zac told me that he was an abandoned child..." his sentenced drifted off in awe of what he was learning.

"Yes, that is the way that he keeps the legend true. He could not tell you who he was, because the legends forbid it unless the tribes are all in one place. This is why you are now a great asset to the legends as well. The legends were never able to pick up neither the news of war nor the outcomes of such. There are but a few elders left now who are able to foretell future legend. Your father is one of those elders like his father, and his father's father, et cetera. I think that you get the idea.

"Zac learned of your grandfather and spent many seasons learning from him. He traveled back and forth and learned something new with each trip. He spent many days with your father playing and learning together. After the small wars of your grandfather's time there was difficulty getting to the world of your ancestry. Because of the sickness, there were few left to find the way to most of the worlds. Your father was not very old when Zac found him for the first time. It took many attempts for Zac to try and find the world that he so desired to learn more from the elders. I have not seen him since his last attempt. Something has caused him not to be able to return this time.

"Now that you are here to tell me that you actually had the opportunity to meet him, the legends will remain. This only means that he has found the tribe and..." she did not know where to finish.

There really was no ending. She did not know if her husband had found the man betrothed to her daughter.

She needed Josh to stay among the tribespeople to know and learn the legends, and know them well.

"Josh, I need you to stay here on the island and learn of the legends. You are now a part of the group of elders that will continue the legends. However, remember that you must not let Zerasha find out until the time is right! The elders will change the stories enough for you to catch on, but not let the others know what is happening," she seemed to finish.

She sat for a long time, like she had gone into a trance. It appeared like she was meditating, or...

"Ma'am," Josh waited. "I will do all I can to learn the legends of the elders, but I must know if I may have Zerasha for my companion in all other things that I do. I do not know of her pledged, but I will listen to the elders and then I will go to a new world in search of the tribe that is part of my ancestry."

"Josh, you may have Zerasha as your companion, for I do not think that there is a way to the world where Zac has found her betrothed. That is why I wish you to think about remaining on the island for as long as there is life." She was thoughtful, almost rehearsed.

"Josh, I know of the presence of your father. He is the only presence that you have been unable to dismiss from your mind. His presence will lead you on many journeys in search of him. Zerasha will not be old enough to go with you, if you desire, for several seasons, maybe more. You will have to listen to your mind. When you know the time is right I will tell you if Zerasha is ready or not." She had turned her tone to the teaching side of her.

She did not want to tell Josh when the time would be right. He would find out for himself soon enough.

"Mother, it is just about story hour. Did you have a nice conversation with Josh?" She waited for her mother's reply. She respected her mother. She had learned most of her lessons from her mother and also knew how protective she could be.

"Yes, we had a very nice conversation, dear. Josh has explained to me his desires. Though I hate to admit this to you, child, I fear that your father may never return. I have allowed Josh your companionship for as long as he desires, or until..." She did not finish. Zerasha understood very well.

Josh and Zerasha left the hut and headed for the story teller. Josh was truly excited this time. He had permission to take the woman of his desires and be able to learn of his and her ancestry all at one time.

Josh waited each day for the story teller, though he knew that he would not be a story teller until he could find the tribe that his ancestors had come from. The elders taught Josh many things though they did it in a way that the other villagers did not know of. They still considered Josh a stranger, certainly not a part of the legendary tribes. He learned all of the knowledge of his great grandfather, his grandfather, his father, himself, Zac, and many others whom Josh had never met and would not meet until a later time in his life.

He learned that Zac had come to his homeland when his father was but a boy. He was not much older than that himself. When Zac arrived, he had no way of finding the way back. He learned that Zerasha was not much older than he was, but the abilities made him seem so much more knowledgeable of things. This is the way of all the elders.

The stories made Josh return to the part of his mind that he tried to erase. The presence of his father was very strong during the story hour, as if he sat and listened. Josh had better control of his mind. He could recall pleasant things and leave the bad out.

The only thing that he could not control was the presence of his father, and Zac. He still did not desire to return to the homeland. It was a place that he remembered as devastating, a great loss to his heart.

Josh and Zerasha spent a few seasons together on the island. They were happy seasons, the ones you find in fairy tales, and stories that the elders told from time to time. She was the happiest she had been since her father had left.

In the seasons that followed, they never talked of their pasts. They knew that each had secrets and they were best kept as secrets. The days were always beautiful. There were no storms of white, the sun was always warm. The trees were heavy with fruit and nuts, and the flowers bloomed all the time. He wished from time to time that his father could see the 'land of Naru' that he had finally found.

He quickly dismissed the thoughts, as if he had also deserted them and wanted to keep the 'land of Naru' all to himself. To himself and the beautiful woman that he kept by his side.

Josh and Zerasha spent their time together doing many different things. Learning and telling each other the things that they had done in their young lives. Zerasha loved to hear the stories of the soldiering that Josh had done. Josh enjoyed hearing about the market place that her village used to buy supplies.

Josh remembers the first time he touched her in front of the others. They laughed and teased, which made Zerasha blush and pull away. She knew of her betrothed. Though her mother did not think that he would ever see her, she was not comfortable in front of the others, because they knew that she was betrothed as well.

Josh took her to the other side of the island. They slipped out together from his small hut outside the village. That way they would not be followed and they could have their time together. He was passionate with her. He loved the smell of her rich blonde hair. They danced and laughed on the sand and then fell to the ground. Josh had many things to tell Zerasha, and teach her.

He knew that she was strong and knowledgeable. He told her there were parts of his past that he could not tell her until the time was right. Zerasha had secrets of her own, but most of them were of the desires she had for Josh. She could not tell him the deepest of her desires, because she is to save those for another man.

There were many happy times for the two young lovers. They made love anywhere their hearts desired at the moment. Sometimes it was on the sand, sometimes in the middle of the day in Josh's hut. It did not matter to them where. It was just one of their many desires for each other.

Josh would sit on the furs of his bed and watch her. She had a very beautiful body that he could not keep his eyes nor mind off of. He could not be away from her.

They were companions for many seasons, until Josh woke from a dream that excited him so much that Zerasha questioned him insistently about. He could see his father's vision. It was the first time since before he landed in the water not far from his new island paradise. He did not speak to or hear the vision. It had only lasted a few moments before it was gone. It wasn't even clear, and the longer Josh remained awake, unable to sleep, the more unclear it became. He had to go to Zerasha's mother, uncertain of what this might mean.

"Are you sure you are okay, my lover?" Zerasha questioned for the fourth time that day.

"I am fine, but I would like to see your mother today, if that is okay with you, my beautiful lover." He reached to kiss her.

"That is fine, but if you don't mind, I would like to go to the water and bathe while you two talk about me. That is why you want to speak to her, isn't it?" She teased him.

"Yes, my love. You are so very brilliant, in so many ways." Josh spoke to her this way most of the time. His voice was soft and deep, and it carried a happy tone when he spoke with her. He knew that he could not explain to her, not now.

He wrapped his arms around her and laid her on the furs of the bed and caressed her bare skin, until he would reach the ties on her foot hides, then the ties to her shirt. He would untie each of them very slowly and smoothly, like he had practiced it all his life. Little did she know that he had. He would pull the hides from her feet and kiss the insides of her legs. Then he removed her shirt to release the full rounded breasts from under it. He caressed her so that all her desires would race through her body. He made her skin tingle at every soft touch he made on her soft, warm body. He made love to her for a long time that day. He could not put his desires aside until he had his entire fill. Then he made sure that she did.

She awoke. There was something different about their lovemaking from a few hours before. She could not put her finger on it, though. She dismissed the thought and dressed herself to go to the water and bathe. She loved the feel of the warm water after her desires had been fulfilled. She reached across the furs of the bed to kiss Josh and tell him he should get going if he were to talk to mother before she slept for the afternoon hot hours.

She gracefully walked out the door of the hut feeling sexier than she had ever felt before. Josh headed to the large hut to speak with Zerasha's mother about his vision.

"I have had a vision." He spoke to the elder woman with caution. "I have had it twice now since yesterday. It is clear for only a moment, then it fades. There are no words with it. My father either does not wish to speak, or is unable to for some reason." Josh was almost businesslike with the elder woman.

"I know." She said, not so cautiously. "It was felt by the elders as well. It is now a time that you must make a decision. The elders wish for you to find the vision. It is integral with the legends. However, since you are not of this tribe and your king is not here to guide you, it must be your own decision."

"I know of the legend, and in order to complete the cycle of legendary tribes, I must go and find my father." Josh knew something was not right. He could feel his father's presence more and more. "My only desire is to take Zerasha with me." He waited for a reply.

"Zerasha is plenty old enough now to accompany you." The elder woman was pleased to hear that Josh still had the desires for her daughter, even though his father's vision had returned.

Josh spent many hours alone every day. He asked Zerasha for this time without questions. He must have it, and she must understand. He would go to the other side of the island, where he could see the whole land. He had to see what his father's vision was all about, and there was no one that could tell him except his father.

He waited on the top of the island, every day. Some days he would see the vision, the one that woke him from sleep a few days ago. Some days he saw the vision very clearly. It would almost speak to him, and then disappear. It seemed to happen at the same time every day. This made it easy for Josh to be away from Zerasha. He knew that she understood.

As Josh climbed to the top of the island for one of his quiet moments alone, he barely reached the top, when...

"Josh, you must return to the homeland." He could hear the voice of his father as he turned to see the vision very clear now. "I cannot give you the correct path, but if you look hard from the front of a transport you will see the path. Must go..." The vision disappeared as quickly as it had appeared.

That was it. Josh ran down the side of the island and raced as fast as he could to Zerasha's side. "Come, my love, I must speak with your mother." He grabbed her around the waist in the knee deep water and swung her to him. Her wet naked body excited him, but he could not waste any time just now. He waited for her to dress and they were both off and running to see her mother.

When they reached the hut, Zerasha was not allowed to go in with Josh at first. He told her not to worry, all would be fine.

"Ma'am, the vision has spoken to me to return to the homeland. I wish to take Zerasha with me to a new world. This is the way that I will explain it to her. I want to be able to have a beginning with her and I desire her to accompany me on this journey to a new world." Josh could hardly contain his excitement. His only true desires were to see his father again, and to have Zerasha.

"Have her come in," the elder woman motioned to one of the villagers who stood by the door. "Zerasha, Josh has something that he would like to share with all of us, together." She was almost cold. As if she did not want to lose her daughter, especially to a place that she may never be able to see or one that her child would return from.

"Zerasha, ma'am, I would like to take your daughter to a new world, where we can have the time to really get to know each other and keep our souls and desires within reach of our dreams." He said it as if he had rehearsed every word for many days. He waited for the replies that were needed. All of the elders had joined them in the small hut.

"Mother?" Zerasha looked to the only ancestor she had among her for guidance.

"Zerasha, you and Josh have become very close to each other in the past seasons. There is nothing more for you to learn here. Your father has not returned and there is no reason for you not to go and learn of new worlds. You will then be able to come and tell the stories to the children." The elder woman did not continue, for she knew that there was little chance of her daughter returning.

"I would very much like to accompany Josh. I desire his companionship as much as he desires mine," she started. "I shall go and get supplies ready for our journey. I love you, Mother, for all that you have ever taught me. Please tell father when he returns, that I have gone with Josh and I will return to my betrothed when I hear that he has returned with him."

She turned and left the room so that her mother could have the chance to speak with Josh and the elders. She would meet Josh at the boat landing where they are to go across the sea to the nearest transport site.

"I know that you know what your final mission is, Josh. We will not go over it with you. It will only cloud the vision that you have. Find your father, and have a safe and happy journey." The elders each bade him farewell. They knew that someday, he would be able to return to the 'land of Naru' paradise that the ancestors have spoken of for many generations. Only a few people from the old tribes are the ones that truly know of the paradise, and soon all the tribes would be in the same paradise together again.

Josh bowed to the elders and thanked them for all they had taught him. He knew now that he should find his father, and that he would return to the paradise, and to Zerasha's betrothed. He turned to go from the hut and gather his supplies for his journeys to the "new" world, a place that Josh and Zerasha would have even more time to get to know each other. At least he thought that they would.

CHAPTER SEVEN

Josh met Zerasha at the boat landing, where his friend from the other village was loading her supplies on board. Josh put his supplies down, kissed his most beautiful desire, and shook Malrui Blanca's hand.

"I have many thanks for you my friend." Josh would never forget the friend that found the information of the princess of Shahi-Nehra, the woman of his deepest desires. Even if that meant he would never have a betrothed, then so be it. He would never be able to share the things that he and Zerasha shared with anyone else. And this did not bother him in the least.

He bowed to Malrui and bade him farewell, as he boarded a much larger 'floating room', to a place that he would refer to, in Zerasha's presence, as the 'harshland world'. They would buy a transport for Josh to fly. He would follow the vision of his father.

When they reached the land again, there were many boats and people. They dressed in groups, much like the villagers of the island. He could see many groups. It was like a market place. Josh had not seen one of these in many worlds. He did not know there was so much diversity on this world. It was truly a different place.

He remembered a place like it when he was a soldier, before he spent time on the base world. He could not remember much of that time, though. He had done a very good job of erasing it from his mind. It had been so many seasons ago. Josh had never desired to leave the island, until he saw the vision of his father. Now he would search for the man that he called Father, because he knew deep down that he was still waiting for him. There was still much to learn from his father.

The time had come for him to use his abilities again, and to find at least the part of his family he desired most to see.

Zerasha had found a transport market not far from where she found Josh. "I think we can get a transport for a good price. You must look at it though. I cannot read anything about it. It is written in a tongue I am unfamiliar with."

She knew that Josh was a man of many talents, though she did not know all of it, by far. She thought of Josh as a very highly educated, intellectual, not to mention sexual man though she knew it as learning, not by instinct. She knew nothing of his instinctive abilities, and that is the way Josh would keep it, until the time was right. Not even Josh knew when that time would be. He just knew when it was, he would know it.

Josh thanked Zerasha and took her by the hand, as he always did, and headed for the transport market. He had learned to fly many transports in his seasons of soldiering. He hoped that this one was similar to ones that he had flown. When they arrived at the market, Josh could see the transport, but he knew if he headed right for it, he would not get a fair price.

He had dealt in the markets when his father was a hide maker. Did he remain a hide maker, or... The thought crept into Josh's mind like it was yesterday when he saw his father at the hide business. He turned his attention to the transport market keeper.

"Do you have a transport for sale? A small one would be better, if that is possible," Josh began the business transaction.

"I have several. Do you have a transport license?" The man was straightforward.

"I need a small oriun type. It really doesn't matter what world it is from. The language of flight is all the same." Josh paid no attention to the man's question. He did not like to be questioned for something he knew he had; otherwise he would not want a transport. Although he did know of the thieves that would buy transports, and not have a license one, he was insulted just the same. "May I look at a few of the ones that you possess?" He was polite, but very business mannered.

The man shrugged his shoulders and led the way to the small flying crafts. "I require the sight of your license, Sir, before I can let you test drive any." The man was meek. He had not learned much about doing business, or he was in trouble with the law for allowing so many transports out without license. Either way, Josh knew that he would definitely get a good price, especially now, because he did have his license and this man would not sell anything otherwise. He probably had not had a good sale since the law busted him. This is what Josh guessed his nervousness was attributed to.

"I do not wish to test drive any. I would, however, like to look at half a dozen or so, if you don't mind." Josh was almost soldier-like. He remembered some of the manipulating ways they had taught him.

The man led them to a lot where he stored the small transports.

"Thank you. I will call you if I should desire to purchase one." Josh dismissed the man, like he had done it time and time again. He looked at each transport carefully. He had to have the right one. It would be the only kind that would be able to take him down the path that would lead him to the 'harshland' world. He finally came to a small one just big enough for him, Zerasha, and the supplies they would need to survive.

"Zerasha, this is the one, but I will try to talk him into a better price. With what we have, love, it will not really matter." He kissed her and made her blush. "Sir, I cannot decide. There are three or four that fit my needs, but..." He stopped. He knew if the man was a true salesman he would know where Josh was leading the conversation.

"Well, sir, maybe I can help you decide." He explained all the features of the transports and gave a price for each to Josh.

"I would really like this one, but the price, its... well, you know, a bit out of my satchel," Josh replied with a wink of his eye, hoping the man would at least go down to the next lower price. He did.

Josh was relieved that his businessman skills had returned to him, without a flaw. He paid the man for the small transport, showed him the license, and prepared to have it readied for travel. While it was being readied, he and Zerasha would go to a quiet place, so she could bathe, and Josh could find the vision of his father.

"Josh, you are the most wonderful man that I have ever met. I have traveled, but I always paid someone else to fly the transport. I am so ready for travels with you. I want to see this new world that we are heading to, wherever it may be." She turned to go bathe, as he watched her from behind.

"Josh, I only have a short minute. Are you alone? Good." The vision of his father appeared before him, and since his time was short he did not wait for an obvious reply from his son. Josh could only see the vision of his father. There was nothing else, only blackness behind him and all around him. "I am waiting for you."

He was gone! Josh hated that their 'communicators' were failing as if his father had learned to turn his on and off. Maybe that was the case. He may be in trouble, or hiding from the Law. He vaguely recalled the woman from the workhouse who had told him about his father coming and leaving in the cool hours. He had said something bad about the Law, and that was about all Josh could remember of the conversation. He hated that he had tried to erase those things from his mind, sometimes. Not always, though, as he turned his attention to Zerasha.

She had undressed and gone to bathe, all he could see were her materials, and the silhouette of her sensuous body under the water. He yearned for her. However, it was hard to keep her in his thoughts and to keep the thoughts of finding his father in his head at the same time.

He wondered why this could happen. He did not see her as a vision like his father's. He saw her more as a dream, one that he could wake from and feel her presence beside him. His father's vision was different. He could talk to his father's, not to Zerasha's. He could only behold her beauty.

"Have you finished? Did you have a nice swim?" He had grabbed her around the waist and started to tickle the inside of her slender, long legs.

"Yes. Thank you my love," she answered as she brushed his hand away so that she could get dressed and they could be off on their travels. She loved the way he touched her. It made her tingle all over. She wanted him, but she knew the time would not allow, not now. Their transport would be ready to go soon. She would have to put her desires on hold, hopefully for just a little while.

Josh had begun to prepare some new supplies that he had purchased for the new transport. He would need these to keep him on the patterns with the other transports. He would be able to see them long before they would see him. He had to have the proper supplies for transport. He would not travel against what the Law said, no matter how he hated them. He could not risk detection before he completed the mission, once and for all.

When he was done, he sat Zerasha beside him and told her a few things that she would need to know. He explained little details of the harshland, what it would look like, in case she had never seen one. He kept secret only the things that he needed to. He told Zerasha everything else.

She was ready to know, and understood very well. She did not think that Josh would have secrets, but she knew he knew things that he did not explain to her. She accepted this, because her desires were for him as he was. She did not care to know much more than she already knew of him. Her true desires were held for a man she did not even know, and may never know.

Zerasha never told Josh of these desires. She did not want him to feel like she did not want him. She did. She just could not tell him what her true desires were. Sometimes, she was not sure of them herself. She kept most of her thoughts of Josh. He was truly a kind man, and he had learned to love very well.

She shivered at the thought of him touching her skin. It delighted her so. She wanted him badly. She desired him at every thought of him that crossed her head. He was certainly the man of her dreams. She only hoped that her betrothed would be as kind and gentle as the lover that came to her that long ago day.

The transport was ready for takeoff as the two lovers arrived at the market to inspect it and put the rest of the supplies aboard. Josh climbed into the pilot's seat and started to flip several levers. The turbines whined and sputtered and then finally started with a roar. Josh made a few more checks of the craft, then made sure that Zerasha was ready for flight. She had joined him in the cockpit of the small craft.

Seeing that she was more than ready, Josh flipped one more lever and then moved the handles in front of him towards himself. The craft lifted lightly off the pad that it had been sitting on. Zerasha watched the ground move farther and farther away from them as Josh climbed to a suitable altitude to clear the buildings and high points on the land. Flipping one final lever, they moved forward in a tight turn to head in the direction of their flight path.

They traveled to many worlds, but they stayed only long enough to refuel and take off again. He flew in many different directions. He had to find the path that would lead him to the land that he came from. He was more determined this time than he had ever been before.

He tried to keep his mind clear for the vision of his father. He looked down every path, marked or not. He knew that when he found the path that would lead him to his father, he would see the vision clearly.

As they took off from their last fuel stop, not far from the island paradise world, Josh could see the vision of his father very clearly. Only the path that he was seen in was not a path at all. It headed right for the moon of the world that they had stopped on. How could that be? If he flew down that path, they would surely crash into the moon.

Josh's thoughts were almost audible as he mumbled the question. He turned to go around the planet. Maybe there was a different approach, one that Josh could not see at the angle he was looking from. When he came around the world in a pattern that was not a true flight path, sure enough, the vision of his father could be seen and sent him to the other side of the moon. He warned Zerasha to hold on, they would be veering from the normal path, and it looked like it might be rough going.

As they cleared the other side of the moon, the sky had turned dark at first, then bright white like they had flown into the path of a storm. The small craft rattled and shook, then seemed to take on speed, even though Josh had not touched any of the power levers. Zerasha sat next to him with the most astonished look in her eyes.

Josh was not sure where his father's vision had led them, but he was sure that if it didn't end soon, there would not be any of the small craft left. When everything turned back to normal, after a few minutes, the worlds had changed. They had flown into another dimension. Josh had heard of this while he soldiered, but to the best of his knowledge he had never flown into one. Except, of course, the time when the transport that took him to the island, somehow veered off the path.

He could see many familiar worlds, now. He had traveled all of them either while he searched for the land of Naru, or on his travels to find his family. They even stopped on Shurfate. Josh thought that maybe he could get directions at the transport site.

They landed on Shurfate only to find the transport site abandoned. The city was nothing but ruins. This is what Ran had escaped from. Josh would have to find the homeland on his own. He traveled on, only this time he concentrated on visualizing all the worlds that he passed. This was the only way that he would be able to tell which world his father was on, if indeed his father was on one of them.

The presence of his father was very clear. He felt like he could hold a conversation with him. Though the vision had not returned, Josh knew he was on the right path. When he flew passed Jemini he knew that he was getting close.

He concentrated very hard now to see the vision of his father. It had been almost two days since they traveled through the dimension. He could only feel the presence of his father, but it was a presence like Josh had not felt for a long time. It kept growing stronger, so he knew that he was still on the right path.

Nearing the homeland he radioed to land his transport. No answer. He radioed again, still no answer.

Josh's mind turned to his father, "Father, if you can hear me and it is safe to reply, please, I need to know where the transport site is. There is no radio contact." He waited. The least his father could do would be to flash a vision of the transport site. He still waited.

It must not be safe for his father to answer. As he neared the world, the presence of his father had become very strong. He could also feel the presence of someone else. He dismissed both of them as best he could and concentrated on finding a place to set the transport down safely.

Zerasha had become so excited she joined him in the flight area of the transport. She knew what the land would look like, but she wanted to see the view from the transport. She acted like a spoiled child who had been given one of the finest toys to play with.

Josh set the transport down on a smooth hill. It looked like it had a transport site on it at one time. Nothing on the land was familiar to Josh, though he had been there many times before. This was probably a good thing. It would be much easier to keep the memories of the place he had actually grown up in from Zerasha.

He looked over at her and gazed into her beautiful green eyes. He did not speak to her. He just wanted to look at her. She held a special talent with Josh. He could hold his attention to her for many hours, sometimes days.

He enjoyed having her beside him in a strange place where they could start a life of getting closer to each other, close in ways that only true friends could be. He wanted so much someday to have Zerasha as close to him as his lifelong friend, Ran, was. He needed that companionship from her, though his body still desired her from deep within him. He wanted a companion to keep his secrets with, like he had with Ran.

Josh could feel the memories of his childhood start to grow more familiar as he sat there next to Zerasha. He took her by the hand and prepared to find out where they were. He had to know if he was on the right transport site. Otherwise it could be days before he found the right place for them.

They walked to a nearby building. It did not look like anyone was inside, but one never knew. Josh pushed on the door. As he felt it open, he pushed harder, to get in. There was no one in sight. He could feel the presence of his father again. This time it was if he were going to see a vision. He stopped at the counter, took a look over the other side of it, and propped himself on top of it.

"Well, what do you think of the new transport site for these parts, ma'am?" he teased Zerasha, the way she liked.

He made things always seem fun, no matter how dreary. He had made her mother laugh delightfully, the day she boarded the boat with her man companion.

"It is... Well, I... I am having a bit of trouble finding the correct words, my love," she teased back.

He knew that it was going to be rough for her at first. There were no trees left on the land. He could see storms on the horizons, though they were very far off and not moving, just sitting. It was a good sign for now.

Zerasha had only seen white on the top of the island, and that was a great distance from her village. She would have to get used to having it for many days at a time if white ever fell on this land again. Josh could tell that it had been since before the wars that white fell on this world.

"I think that we should shelter here for the ni... coo..." Josh was not sure what he should call it. He could not remember calling it cool hours on her homeland. "cool hours." He finished waiting eagerly for one of her brilliant replies.

"Cool hours, it does not feel like it would get very cool here," she mused.

"That is the type of world that it is known for. There are many worlds like this one. You can tell by the way the sun looks. In your world, the sun goes away. In this world, the sun will shrink, but it never goes away. I will let you watch it tonight." He tried not to show his excitement.

"I don't know if that is a good idea or not. I am not sure that I want to see a sun that only shrinks. Why doesn't it go away?" She was afraid. The fear had crept into her voice.

"I don't know. Why does the sun on the island go away? Why doesn't it just shrink, like this one?" He was teasing her. She started to blush then she pouted, like a child who had been scolded.

Josh had to be careful how he explained things to her. He must remember to refer to it from the travels of soldiering. He brought enough supplies from the transport to eat and sleep in the building for the cool hours. He would have to get used to the ways of the homeland. There would be times that he would need it.

He prepared the cook fire in the stove next to the counter. It was really a warming stove, but for obvious reasons, it had not been used in many seasons. While he did that, Zerasha unfolded the furs of the bed. She tucked them behind the counter. That way they would not be in sight of the doorway. Josh had taught her that, seasons ago, when he first met her. It was something, she assumed, he learned from soldiering.

She was ready for a hot plate and a good sleep. The journeys had truly exhausted her. She ate silently next to Josh. He was content with this new world. She could feel how peaceful he was. She stood to take and clean the plates. She was ready to lie down beside her companion and rest with him. She knew that the next days would be busy for them both.

They would have to find a hut to stay in and then all the supplies would have to be put in proper places. It would be fun. Zerasha had never had a place to call her own. She could hardly sleep because of the excitement of the new world.

She rolled over to Josh to see if he had taken to sleep. He had not. He was staring at the roof of the building. She wanted to hold him and make wishes with him. Her desires for him became stronger and stronger the more she stared at him.

Josh could feel her presence. He turned to look at her, only to find the desire in her eyes. He could always tell that she desired him when she stared at him. He would tease her sometimes, and pretend not to notice her gazing eyes. If he waited long enough she would come very close to him and lay her head on his chest. He could feel her sigh, every time. He loved to play this kind of game with her. She always took them with a good heart.

As he gazed into her green eyes, he could feel the presence of his father getting stronger. He wanted so much to find the place that the vision came from. He had not seen the vision since he rounded Jemini.

It was well into the cool hours, and neither of them had taken to sleep. It was an exciting time for both of them. He took her by the hand and they went out the door. He was eager to show her the sun that shrank, instead of going away. She tugged with resistance on his grip. She was truly afraid.

He stopped and wrapped his arms around her. He did not move again until he had calmed her with the smooth caress of his hand on her head. She finally had calmed down enough to look at him. She could see the peace and calm in his eyes and knew there would be nothing to be afraid of. Josh would never let harm come to her.

She looked over her shoulder to see only part of a sun. It was still round like the one from the island homeland, but it was small. She seemed delighted to see that it would not hurt her. She relaxed in his arms for a long time as they watched the sun as it got a little smaller, then it started to grow again.

Josh knew that they would not go anywhere the next day. They would be exhausted from not taking to sleep. Besides, Josh needed to find supplies before they could go to find a house. He saw a car on the far side of the hill from where they landed the transport. He would sleep for a while and then he would go get it.

She could see if there were any other buildings, close by. He did not want her to go far without him by her. This was a strange land to her, and she may not get good reception if she were to come across any other beings.

He took her by the hand again, and laid her under him on the furs of the bed. He would surely exhaust them both with the desires that he was feeling. He caressed the inside of her legs and then up her belly and her breast. He kissed her with so much passion that she could feel her own desires awaken. He made love to her until her whole body was limp. He rolled over, and they lay in each other's arms until the sun was high in the air and the heat became very unbearable in the building.

Josh could remember this heat. It was when he had dug his family out of the first storm, the one that destroyed the land, the people, everything. That was a time that Josh tried to keep as far from the front of his mind as possible. He could feel the shivers run up his back. It was not a pleasant feeling, and he wished it away. He could not dismiss it. He had tried when they first landed and the memories came flooding back to him. He tried then to dismiss them and they returned, several times already.

He opened his eyes to Zerasha holding a hot plate above him. She was threatening to dump it on him if he did not sit up and eat. He would need the nourishment to get the supplies that they would need to travel on the roads of the land.

He sat up quickly, so he would not have to wear his food all day. He had not found a place to bathe, yet. That would come when they found a house to stay in permanently. When he was through with his plate, he handed it to her, then left the building.

He had to have time for his father's vision before he could get the car. He walked to the top of the hill. He waited. Would he still be able to see his father's vision, or would it be just his presence? Josh could feel the presence growing stronger.

"Josh, there is little time. You should find a house. Try to get close to the town of your boyhood. This will help you," his father's voice came and went very fast.

Josh wanted to talk to his father, like he had done on the ridge the first time he used his communicator ability. He could still only see darkness surrounding his father. Maybe it was because there was nothing on this land but dark rock. He had so many questions to ask him. He supposed that he would have to learn the answers on his own, like his father had told him to do when he was a small boy.

Josh went to the car. It started easily like it had been left there just for him and Zerasha. He turned it around and headed for the building. They would put their supplies in the car and go looking for a home. It would be near here.

He could feel the memories from his childhood. They were very strong here. He saw a vision down one of the roads. It showed the business of his father, though the building in the vision was still boarded up, like he had seen it last. He would take Zerasha there and they would stay in that house, if it was possible. He would never let on that he knew of the place.

He reached the building where Zerasha waited for him. She knew that he desired the time to be alone, so she did not go to find him. She knew that he would return. It was a feeling that she had felt since he asked her mother for her companionship. She would never let that thought change.

"Zerasha, I have found the road that we should travel first. This car will get us where we need to go to find a house. Then, we can set the supplies up, and learn all that we can of this new world, and, of each other." He wrapped his arms around her and pressed his lips to hers, as if he wanted this to be the beginning of another new life together.

They put all the supplies that would fit into the car and headed down the road of Josh's vision. He could see the children of another time, playing and enjoying the trees and the animals. The small houses had all disappeared. He could see the remnants of some of the taller chimneys, but most of them had all been torn down, or had fallen from the wars. He searched his mind for any familiar visions. So far, none could be seen.

They rode down the road for a very long time. Josh could remember that the transport site that first took him away from his homeland had been four or five days, walking. He did not remember how long it should take in a car. He had never traveled that way on this world and he could not let Zerasha know that he had ever traveled on this world.

This would be the place where, sooner or later, he and Zerasha would know all of each other's secrets. Josh felt that sometimes he had too many, and if the time did not come soon, he would be shaming her for holding so much inside of him and not sharing his whole life story with her.

CHAPTER EIGHT

They traveled nearly two days straight. Josh had a yearning to find the place of his childhood, and he would no matter what it took. He came to the top of a ridge where he could see the vision of his father on the far edge. He wanted to stop and run to the vision, but Josh knew that the house would be close by now. He would have plenty of time to explore the ridge of his boyhood.

As he pulled over the top of the ridge, a storekeeper's shop came into view. This looks like a great place to start, he thought. His memories of the old storekeeper's house in Josh's mind were as clear as the first day he went there with his father. Josh wondered if there was anyone from that long ago time still here in the small town where he grew up.

"Well, my love, what do you think about this one?" He gazed into her green eyes. He wanted to hold her close to him.

"It looks pretty much like all the rest of the towns we have been through. Though, it does feel a whole lot friendlier." For some reason, Zerasha could feel a peace inside her that she had never felt, not even on the island homeland.

"I thought the same way, my love. I will go in and see if there is a house that we may be able to purchase. Do you want to come in and take a look around or stay here?" He had opened the door of the car and started to step out, as he waited for her answer.

"I would like to come in and take a look around. I feel a wonderful peace about this place. I hope that there is a house available." She could hardly hold the excitement inside.

The couple walked to the door of the storekeeper and went inside. Josh's heart raced as his excitement of seeing the old store grew. The place had many more supplies than it did the last time Josh had been inside. The same storekeeper was there from all those seasons ago. Josh would have to be careful that the man did not recognize him in front of Zerasha.

Josh started to feel a little uneasy about having to live so close to so many of the memories of his childhood, without letting on to Zerasha that he had been here before. She would eventually find out, but the time had to be right, or all that the legends taught would be lost.

"Hello, sir, I am looking for a place that would be suitable for my love and me to stay in. Is there such a place nearby?" Josh had winked at the storekeeper, to keep him silent about who he was.

"Is there a particular place that you might have in mind?" he questioned Josh very carefully. He knew that he did not want the ravishing woman to know something, but he was not sure what it was.

"No, but it should be a large place. I must have space for myself, and I would like to have a place that has a cook room separate from the sleep room." Zerasha had interrupted the conversation between Josh and the storekeeper. She had reached her arm through Josh's and waited for him to get an answer from the very kind man.

"There is a place. It is not far from here by car." The storekeeper had seen their big fancy car. Not many people on this world had one, and the ones that did left them in their storage until they needed them for something important. This fancy car was familiar to the storekeeper but he knew that it had been left for Josh and he was happy to see his return, even if there was a strange silence about him. "If you follow the road down to the next ridge, there is a turnoff. Follow that for a short distance. As you come over the hill, you will be able to see the chimney. It is a rather old house. They have had boards on it since before the wars ended."

The storekeeper had become very sad. He remembered the storm that had taken Josh from the land and the disease that followed for so long. Many strangers had come to the land since then, but most could not handle the harshness: no trees, no animals, all supplies had to be purchased from the major storekeepers. Most of them were at least a day's drive from here in a car. Most strangers to the land would leave within a matter of months, but he knew that these strangers would be here for some time. Or, at least, he hoped that they would.

Josh had changed his appearance many times since the storekeeper had seen him last. It was when he and Ran had come for supplies for Josh's father. Then the big storm came, and all was lost. At least all that ever mattered to this land was gone.

"I would like to look at the house before I decide to buy it. Would that be all right?" Josh knew that it would. He could see the joy in the storekeeper's eyes again. To see someone from the time before the wars made him very happy. Most people who left did not return. They could not bear the memories of their pasts or the loss of the ones they loved.

"That would be fine. Help yourself. Let me know tomorrow what you decide." The storekeeper handed Josh a set of keys "There is a large lock on the main door. You will need this to get in."

"Thank you so much, sir. If we are not back tonight before the cool hours begin, then I will bring you the money for the house in the morning." Josh tipped his velvet cap to the man, winked his secrecy, and took Zerasha by the hand to show her the house of their new beginning.

They got in the car and in a matter of a few hours, they arrived at the large house. There were boards on all of the windows of all the floors. Josh could not wait to see the inside of the building. Neither could Zerasha. She was astonished at the size of the house.

"Someone important must have lived here." Her eyes had become very bright. This was exactly what she had in mind when she told the storekeeper what she wanted. "This would be a magnificent place to live. I only wish that there were more trees and animals. I have never seen so much desolation in all of my seasons." She had almost become sad. She was remembering the homeland

and picturing the large house on it instead of the hut that she had lived in there.

"I would have to agree with you there, my love. This is a very large house. I am not sure that we will be able to afford the price of it, however. I will leave you and the supplies here. Since it only takes a short time to get back to the storekeeper, I will go and find out if the price is a good one or not. Do not put anything away, yet. But, you can start a cook fire and make some hot plates. I will want to stay somewhere at least until the cool hours have passed. I will return in no time at all, my love." He bent over to kiss her, and got in the car and drove back down the road to the storekeeper's from his childhood.

"Hello, my friend Josh. It has truly been a great time since you have been seen in these parts." The storekeeper was overjoyed at Josh's presence in the small town again.

"Hello. How is the business going for you?" Josh waited for a reply from the storekeeper. He had hung his head down, as if he had shamed him by asking such a question.

"It is not doing well, Josh. I have very few customers, but the Law insists that I stay open. They say they have enough soldiers in the area to keep me in business for many more seasons. I do not see many soldiers. However, the Law does come and pick up supplies for many people about once a month." He had become very sad. He had lost a great deal from the wars, and the most important thing was his freedom. He had lived under the Law since they took over all the businesses needed for the supply of the soldiers and the work houses.

"I am sorry to hear that. However, I hope that we can discuss the cost of the old house. I do not know if it is still in my father's name. Did the Law buy him out?" Josh was concerned about the storekeeper. He would need the supplies from the store to keep him and his love here for as long as it took to find at least his father. "I must ask that you not let on that you know me from the seasons of my childhood. Zerasha does not know of my past life on this land, and it is something that she should not find out about until I know the time to be right." Josh knew that he could trust this man, but he would not tell him the true reason why he had returned to the land of his childhood. "I have brought my love here to start a new beginning with her." Josh hoped that this would keep the man from his past satisfied as to why he had returned.

"I understand, Josh. You can count on me, you know that." He confirmed that the same man Josh knew long ago was still here and would help out in any way that he could. "I saw Ran about three months ago. He stopped in for supplies and I have not seen him since," he finished the conversation.

"What about the house, sir?" Josh was curious to find out if his father had turned the business over to the Law.

"Your father boarded it up after a big scandal with the Law. He took all that was inside and headed for the work house where he would find his wife and daughters. I have not seen him since that time. He told me that someday he would return to the house where he raised his family. It is yours for no cost, Josh. I know that is what your father would want."

The storekeeper took Josh to the outside of the building and led him around to the place where he kept the horses. "Your father left your horse here. He would not need it in his travels, so he asked that I keep it for him. I figure you could use it to get a good start here. Good luck. I will see you again, I am sure." He shook Josh's hand and turned to go back inside of the building.

Josh was pleased that the old mare was still here and very strong. She would make a great start here for him and Zerasha. He took the reins and led the horse to the door of the car. He would have to drive slowly, but it still would not take him long to get back to the house of his childhood. When he returned to the house he would take the boards from the windows, and Zerasha would be able to put supplies away. He was very excited, but he would have to come up with some kind of sale price to tell Zerasha. He would not be able to tell her about the house belonging to his father.

***

"Hello, love? Are you still here? Or have I frightened you away?" Josh's teasing voice came through the doorway. He could not see Zerasha anywhere.

"I am down here," she called to him from the work floor. "This is a marvelous old house. Look at these hides. They look like they have been here for many seasons. We will be able to tan them and make them our bed." She had so much excitement in her voice that she had almost forgotten to ask if they could stay permanently in the house. "What did you find out from the storekeeper?" she finally questioned.

"The price was very cheap. We can stay here permanently!" He was overjoyed when he saw the excitement in the dark green eyes of his lover and confidant. She jumped up and threw her arms around him. She could not hold her excitement any longer.

"This is the best news that you have ever given me. I can't wait to set things up my own way. I never had a say in the homeland. My mother did all the decorating. I guess I should not complain. It was her place, and she, like I, wanted things to be perfect." Zerasha did not understand why or how she could be so excited about a place with no trees or animals. She had proceeded to finish the hot plates, and then she would put away the rest of the supplies.

Josh had gone down to the work floor of his childhood. At first he could remember the conversation from his father that terrible time when he was sent away to find the homeland that Zerasha had come from.

Now his concerns turned to finding out where his and Zerasha's fathers had gone to. What was the secret? Why would they leave and why together? What was the Law trying to push over on his father all those seasons ago? As the questions ran through his mind, he lifted the hides that Zerasha had found only to find the destroyed communicator that the Law had found.

Josh wondered if the floors in this old house continued below the work floor. He would certainly attempt to find out in the days that followed. He picked up the pile of hides and took them to Zerasha. They were the old bed furs from long ago, but with a little outside air they would be as good as new.

Josh could feel his father's presence most of the time now, but he could not see the vision. He would take the horse to the ridge after he finished his hot plate and see if the vision would come to him.

"Josh, are you ready for your hot plate?" Zerasha called down the stairs to him. She waited for an answer, though it did not come right away. He had been very preoccupied in the last few days, like he was in search of something. She only wished that she knew what it was.

"Yes, my love, and then I will go out on the horse to give her a stretch." He had met Zerasha at the top of the stairs, only to see the childlike excitement in her eyes when he had mentioned the horse.

"A horse?! Where did you get a horse? I have never seen one, much less been on one. The elders have always spoken of them as great animals of transportation. Wow, we have one of our own?" She could see the teasing look in his eyes now. He loved to tease her with things that he knew excited her.

"The storekeeper sold me one. She is very gentle. I will let you ride her after I teach you how, but not tonight. She has not been ridden for some seasons now, so she might not take kindly to having both of us on her for her first stretch." he mused.

He knew that he could not take her with him because of the chance that he might find his father's vision. He finished his hot plate and reached his arm around his beautiful woman. He wanted to make love to her right there near the cook fire. His desires for her had become very strong since the day they landed the transport. Some day he would be able to tell her the truth of the legends, but until then he would satisfy her in ways that all women wanted to be satisfied.

He rose from his seat on the floor, placed his plate in the pan of water, heating on the cook stove, and gave her a kiss to satisfy her desires for the moment.

Josh had readied the horse and was about to board her when the vision came. "Josh, it is good to see you in the old house. You must take care of it. It is all that this family will ever have that does not belong to the Law." Josh could hear the distaste in his father's voice. "I cannot give you my location for I do not know it.

"I do know that I am on the homeland. It is very dark all the time. Your mother is fine, and the children also. Zac was taken some days ago. I do not know where though I assume it is on the homeland, because I can feel his presence. You must not let the Law find out that you have come back for me. Keep the secret, just as you do with Zerasha." His father seemed to have lots of time now. He did not try to cut the vision short.

"Father, it is very good to see you. I worried for a while that you were no longer here. How do I find you, and where do I start?" Josh was ready for the adventure.

"We are at least four levels below the top surface, but I can't remember exactly. I do not know what work house we are in, and there are many. I found your mother and sisters in one after I had looked at almost 100 of them. The Law does not allow us to go anywhere. We are fed, though not well. Right now they have gone for supplies, somewhere. You must not let them find you, Josh. Do you understand? The legends are very important and they must be continued. Does the white fall on the land again?" He sounded old and frail, though Josh knew that his father would be strong if he needed to be.

"No, Father, the white does not fall here yet. There are still no trees or animals." Josh had gotten on the horse and started to ride, so that Zerasha would not wonder what he was up to. He continued the conversation with his father for quite a while. "Father, how do you know of Zerasha? Have you seen Ran?" Josh wanted to know all the answers to all of his questions right then and there, but he knew that would not be possible.

"I have not seen Ran since he delivered supplies some three months ago. I know of Zerasha because she is the daughter of my old friend Zac, and he talked of her often. I sure wish I knew if he was still okay. It worries me to think that the Law has punished him for siding with the rebel cause. I suppose that is why I am here also. Because I fought the law, and it seems that they have won. Son, you must pull the boards from the floor of Zac's house, get to the communicator and fix it. If he is not with the Law, then he will be near a communicator. We cannot speak to him with our communicators because he does not have the ability. I must go!" The vision and voice disappeared without a trace.

Josh hated that the Law was holding his family for some reason unknown to him. He had learned to hate the Law more and more since the day that he last saw his father in person.

He took the path to Zac's house. He would spend a few hours working on the floor before he would return to his Zerasha. As he approached the house, he had the feeling that there was someone there, someone that Josh did not care to be found by. He ducked behind an old out building not far from the house.

As he watched, he saw the Lawmen coming from the inside of the house. He was instantly angry! Why were they inside the house of one of the rebels? What were they looking for? Josh could see that the soldiers were young, and he would have a fair chance of learning something from them. He boarded his horse, and galloped around the hill and came at the soldiers from the opposite direction of his own house.

"Hello. Can you tell me if the owner of this house is here?" Josh used his business tone.

"No, sir, why do ask?" One of the soldiers was quick witted, though not as quick as Josh.

"I had heard of there being a few houses for sale in this area. I just need a small one, only me here and I'll be coming and going most of the time. I seemed to stumble on this one when I saw you come from within." Josh waited for one of the lawmen to reply.

"No, we are just on patrol here," the younger one started. "There is a storekeeper not far from here. He would be the one to ask about places for sale." He looked at his partner to see if he had said something he shouldn't have.

"You do know that this land is mostly owned by the Law, don't you, sir?" The other one questioned Josh, almost like he was doing an interrogation.

"Yes, I had heard that before I came here. I also heard that there were places, small ones that I could buy and keep some of my things in. I do a lot of traveling, so I don't always like to carry a ton of supplies with me. It's easier that way, you know." Josh was starting to feel

151

uneasy, a feeling he got often when he had to deal with the Law for very long. He could remember the day Har had come with him!

"What is it that you travel for, sir?" The higher ranking of the two men was trying to get under Josh's skin and it made him angry, though he did not show it.

"I travel to see the condition of the lands that were destroyed during the war. I take readings of the air quality and look to see if the soil has received any nutrients." Josh was good. He knew he could convince the soldier. "It really is quite a simple job, but I like doing it."

"I do not believe this one is for sale, but the storekeeper will be able to tell you which ones are. Good day, sir, and good luck!" The soldier had lost the battle. But Josh knew that it would be difficult for him to win the war at this point.

"The storekeeper, is that way?" Josh gestured with his hand in the direction of the storekeeper's, not far from the house he stayed in.

"Yes, sir," The younger soldier had not said much else since his first statement.

Josh galloped the horse to the ridge where he knew he could watch the house. The soldiers wandered off, but he was sure that they would return. He quietly rode the horse back to his house and beautiful lover even though she was the last thing on his mind at this time.

The events of the last few hours were swirling around in his head. Now he was more determined than ever to accomplish this mission. All he had to do was figure a plan on how to get into Zac's house without being caught.

He arrived at the house to find Zerasha outside. "It is such a beautiful sunset, that I thought I would watch it for a while. It is very warm in there." She pointed to the house.

Josh took her by the hand and led her to the work floor. He pulled a wooden bench from under the shelf and set it in front of the doorway. He knew this would cool her, and she could still watch the sun.

Zerasha was amazed at Josh's knowledge. He knew so many things. She had seen very little of the rest of the worlds. She had traveled some away from her homeland, but mostly by boat to the other land. She sat for a long time watching the sun, almost forgetting that it does not go away on this world.

Her thoughts were drawn to Josh. She had never met anyone so kind. She could hardly believe he had been on her homeland all those seasons, though she could barely remember the wars. She was but a baby in her mother's arms then. He always treated her gently and kind. His words were sweet with passion every time he spoke to her. She truly loved the way they spent their time learning what the other liked about everything.

She appreciated that he gave her time alone during the day, and she knew that he needed the time also. His dark hair and green eyes intrigued the passion inside of her slender, sexy, young body; his strong frame above her as they lay on the bed, his gentle touch massaging her whole body, his soft lips pressing against hers, his gentle words in her ears. She longed to have him by her side every minute of every day although she knew he had things he needed to do, especially now, to fix this wonderful, beautiful, old house. She would be satisfied to have him in the evenings and early mornings.

"Zerasha, love, are you ready to come in now?" She could hear Josh's voice coming from the top floor of the large house.

"I am coming, love. Are you ready for a hot plate?" she called up the stairs to the top floor.

"No, come here first. I want to show you something that I found up here. I think that you might really like it." Josh couldn't wait to see the look on her face when he showed her the chest that his father had left behind, probably because it was too big and bulky to take. There was nothing in it, just the smell of the wood when the lid was opened. It was a sweet, pungent smell.

"What is it that could be more exciting than eating?" Zerasha could hardly finish the sentence before her mouth gaped open. "It is simply beautiful. It must be hundreds of seasons old. The handle is beautifully carved. Why do you suppose it was left?" She could not contain her excitement. The child inside her had come alive.

"I suppose it was left for lack of room. There was nothing left inside, so I would say that it was just too bulky." Josh just wanted to lie on the bed furs and watch her as she fondled the box. He loved to show her things that he knew she enjoyed. "Are you fixing hot plates tonight, or do I have to fix them for us, so you can play with your new present?" Josh teased her, only to see her turn in his direction and pout the way she always did when she wanted to do the fun thing that he gave her a choice on.

"Okay. I get the picture. I will call you when it is ready." Josh got up and headed to the cook room. He liked to cook. It was something that his mother, and Ran's mother, had taught him. His mother always said it would be something he would need to know later in his life. She was right. He had needed those skills many times while he was searching for the 'land of Naru', the paradise where he had found Zerasha, and would take her and his family back to someday.

After he finished the hot plates, Josh had plans to go and watch Zac's house. He needed to know when the soldiers were there and when they were gone and for how long. That was the only way that he would be able to get into the house without getting caught.

He remembered the first day they had arrived on the harshland of his home world. Why didn't he see the soldiers then? He wondered if they did patrols to different houses in the area. If that were the case, he needed to know when they left and for how long they would be gone. He cleaned his plate and told Zerasha that he would return soon.

He wanted to go to the ridge. It was a beautiful night for thinking, and this is what he had told her for his excuse to look at Zac's house.

He sat on the edge of the hill where he could see the house well. So far there were no soldiers in sight. Though he did not dare go any closer, he would just sit and watch. He could almost feel a presence with him, though he was not sure whose it was. He hoped it would be his father, but he was sure that it was not. It did not feel like his father.

He had to be very careful while he was out. He did not know the routes of the soldiers yet. For all he knew he could be sitting right in the middle of one. He watched for several more hours and then decided he should go back to his own house, before Zerasha became suspicious.

He would have to come back the next night at the exact same hour so that he could see if that was a time when there were no soldiers. He boarded his horse and headed in the direction of the storekeeper's. He wanted to know if there was any information that Keiler could tell him.

"Hello, Mr. Josh, mighty late for a visit to the storekeeper. How can I help you? Did you forget something the other day?" He winked his eye as he spoke to Josh, indicating that there might be someone else there with him.

"Yes, as a matter of fact, there was. I won't be but a minute." Josh could feel the intensity of the storekeeper's fear. He wanted to stay and find out if there was going to be trouble. "Sir, I need some feed for the horse. Do you have any?" Josh was careful not to let on that he knew the storekeeper.

"Mr. Josh, you said it was Josh correct?" He hesitated, but not long enough for an answer, "there is feed in the back. I can meet you out there in a few minutes." The storekeeper motioned the directions to Josh as if he did not know them.

Josh left the building and headed to the back of the storekeeper's house. He located the feed that he was sure Keiler was telling him about. It was not in bags, like it used to be. He grabbed an empty bag and proceeded to fill it, very slowly and deliberately. It was almost like he had never filled a feedbag before. He kept one eye on the feedbag, while he watched the front of the store. At this angle he could almost see the doorway for entering the building. Josh had filled one bag already and started another when Keiler came up from behind him.

"Do not speak now, sir," he whispered. Then in a normal tone, "Did you find what you needed, Mr. Josh, sir?" He grabbed the other end of the bag and helped Josh fill that one and another yet. "Those are the soldiers that come for supplies once a month. They asked if you had found a place to stay. I told them yes, but it wasn't really what you wanted. They seemed pleased with the answer. When did you run across them?"

Josh seemed a bit confused. How did the storekeeper fit into this? Was he one of the rebels, or was he there for another reason? "I saw them up on the ridge yesterday while I was enjoying what landscape is left in these parts." Josh was careful. He knew the storekeeper from another time, but he did not know how much the Law had influenced him. He had always seemed to be a weak man. Most of the storekeepers were. It was hard to make much when everyone is able to cut your price on goods, with very little bargaining.

"Don't pull my leg, young Josh. I am still a mite wiser than you are and the legends have not changed that much. I would like to see you after the soldiers' last trip. I have some things that you will be interested in. I hope that you understand. They will be in this area for about two days. It would be a good time to see about the communicator at Mr. Zac's." Keiler knew the legends and was not afraid to tell Josh about them. He had to be a part of the rebel tribes.

"I am very sorry, Keiler. I have had a hard time trusting anyone since my last visit. I can trust my father, and Zac, and Ran, I think, and now you. This will make things much easier for me." Josh was very relieved. He could hardly believe the rebels that kept popping out of everywhere. He would never recognize them if they did not tell him. "I must go now, but I really don't need any feed. Will you be able to sell it?"

Keiler nodded and patted Josh on the back. "I will see you in a few days, sir."

Josh could still not believe all the things that were going on, but he must get back to Zac's house tomorrow to see if he could fix the communicator and possibly find some more help. He would have to be very careful.

Zerasha had waited as long as she could for Josh before sleep overcame her. Josh found her on the furs of the bed lying naked so that the air would cool her skin. She did this a lot, something that her mother had taught her very young. Josh could hardly hold his desires. He wanted to touch her soft skin, but he dare not wake her.

He wanted to see if he could contact his father. He could feel his presence for most of that day. He walked to the work room and waited. He had not yet learned how he saw a vision, although he did know that it had something to do with concentrating on the presence. He had tried this many times, but all he ever felt was the presence.

His father would know before contacting him where he was, and who was with him. Josh just wanted to know how. He sat for a long time in the silence and the darkness of the work floor. At one time he thought he caught a glimpse of something, but it was a last puff of smoke from the cook fire. Josh rose in disappointment and went to the side of his wonderful love.

He had become very lonely the last few days, a loneliness that he had not felt since he left his homeland for the first time. He had rid his mind of it when he met Zerasha and decided then that he would never return here. He wanted the fun days of the paradise to be back, but the presence of his father haunted him. He could not think of much else. Finding his family once again was an obsession now.

"Are you all right my love?" Josh had bolted straight up out of bed, screaming. Zerasha knew of visions like that during sleep. Her mother talked of her father having them.

"I am fine, love." He tried to be convincing. It did not work.

"Do you want to talk about it? My mother used to tell me of my father. They would talk and it would make him feel better, at least for the time being." Zerasha was truly sympathetic to her love.

"No, my love, it really was not that bad. I do that when I am very exhausted, and I have had a busy time since we arrived at this, our final destination." He started to tease and act out his glory for the Harshlands, such that they were.

He became very sarcastic, "This will be a place that all people will want to come to." He held his hand to his chest and saluted with the other.

Zerasha began to laugh. Josh could always turn a bad thing into something good and funny, in no time at all. She liked this quality in him. He lay down beside her and wrapped his strong arms around her. He knew exactly how to distract his mind until morning.

Zerasha could feel the heat of his breath on her neck. She could feel his desires as he kissed the back of her neck, then down her back. She rolled over to meet his lips with hers for a long passionate kiss. They made love and lay in each other's arms until the sun began to come high.

She woke before he did, feeling very fresh. She started the cook fire and made large hot plates for breakfast. Josh still did not come down from the sleep room by the time she had finished, so she took the plate to him. She found him staring out the window, almost in a trance.

"Love, here is a hot plate for you. I thought maybe you were still in bed and you would enjoy eating it up here today." She was very apprehensive as she spoke. Josh had not even acknowledged her presence yet.

"Josh, love, are you okay?" She walked over to him and placed her hand on his bare shoulder.

"Huh? Oh, I'm sorry, love. I was just enjoying the morning. I miss the animals talking in the morning like they did on the homeland." Josh was speaking of his own homeland, but he made it sound to Zerasha as if he had only one homeland on the island paradise. "You brought hot plates! Wow, after last night, I am famished!" He grabbed her around the waist and kissed her lightly so that she could remember the passion from the night.

"I miss the animals, too." Zerasha handed Josh his plate, and they both sat down next to the window and ate.

"I will be very busy today. I want to clean out the work room. Maybe we will be able to use it someday for something." Josh finished his plate and started toward the work room floor.

He spent the next two days alone in the work room, as he had requested that Zerasha spend her time learning to care for the horse. She needed to know how.

Josh found many old things that his father had left behind. The white tunnel machine, the pan that was used to scoop, lots of hides were all there. He cleared the pile of hides and hung each one on a rope that crossed the top of the room.

As he reached the bottom of the pile, he saw the hinge that would allow him to see the rest of the floors below the house, the real work floors. Was this something that his father intended to hide from the soldiers?

Josh finished hanging the hides on the rope and pulled up the part of the floor that would lead him to a place he was unsure of. As he reached the end of the stairs he could smell the musty ground. He could not see much. The only light was that of the open door above him. He would have to go get a lamp so that he could see what other surprises might be awaiting him.

He climbed back up the stairs to the work room and quietly closed the door on the floor. He did not want Zerasha to find out about this, yet. He had to make sure that it was a safe place to venture into first. He had neatly arranged the hides in front of the door, so that she would not be able to see behind them to the secret doorway that led to, who knew where. Josh intended to find out.

He checked to see if Zerasha was okay with the horse, as he knew that she would be, but he wanted to protect her from everything he possibly could. He grabbed the lamp and headed down the stairs to the work room, then the floors below. His curiosity was deep. His heart raced as he felt the excitement of secrecy build inside him.

He lit the lamp when he reached the bottom of the stairs. He could see several hallways leading from the room that he was in. There was a curtain wall, much like the one at Zac's house. He pulled the curtain aside. There was a door with a large lock on it. Josh did not know where the key would be. Did his father have it? He had so many questions. Where did all the hallways lead to, and what was behind the locked door? When did his father discover the real work floors? Was it when he left the place? Did the Law want his home for a work house?

Josh's thoughts were rampant. His father had hated all that the Law had become. Josh knew this from his conversations with his father shortly before his last visit, so many seasons ago.

Josh felt the presence of his father in this place. It was very strong. Would he be able to speak with his father today, or would it just be his presence to warn him of any dangers? Josh could feel the secrecy that the rooms held within them. He decided to follow one of the hallways to see where it led him.

"Josh, do not leave the floor door open. It will cause you trouble, no matter how fast you try to talk your way out of it." Josh heard the voice of his father, but he could not see the vision. Was this another ability that Josh had yet to learn? The voice was gone, but it rang clear in Josh's head. He headed up the stairs to the floor door. As he neared the top he could feel a bad presence. He took the last few steps in a bound and closed the door.

He peeked through the hide curtain that he had thrown up to see if his feeling was legitimate. As he peered through the curtain he could see nothing, just the stuff in the work room. He had not uncovered the windows on this floor, as they would not use it and it would be easier to explain to anyone that might come around.

Josh threw a pile of hides on the floor and headed up to the cook floor. He wanted to check on Zerasha. The bad presence was still there. As he looked out the window he could see a soldier talking to Zerasha. He listened with his mind to see if he could hear what they were talking about. It sounded like just a regular conversation, so Josh went out to meet the stranger.

"Hello, I am Josh. I see you have met Zerasha." He approached the soldier with his hand held out.

"Hello. I did not realize someone had bought this old house. We have not patrolled it in a long time." The soldier was friendly. "I came over the hill and could see the last of the smoke from the cook fire. I thought maybe there might be someone in there that shouldn't be."

"Are there many vagrants around these parts?" Josh quizzed the soldiers.

"No, only the POW's that somehow escape undetected. Most of them are caught. That is why we patrol." The soldier had given Josh plenty of information so far, but he wanted to see if he could get more.

"We are not from this world. We don't know much about it." Josh offered the information like he meant every word. "Would you like to sit for a spell and have something to drink?"

"I would like to, but I must finish my patrol. I took a shortcut today, 'cause, well..." The soldier started to explain himself like he had just been caught doing the wrong thing. "There's a house over the hill that we are supposed to patrol, but there isn't much of it left, and it certainly doesn't make a good place for shelter. You won't tell anyone, will you?" The soldier had become scared, like he had seen the punishment of a soldier who does not patrol his entire perimeter.

"I will not tell anyone. Besides, who would I tell?" Josh had sent Zerasha for something to drink. "Don't worry son, you have nothing to fear. Sit and have a drink. Where does your patrol route go from here?"

"Back to the storekeeper's, then around one more time before my relief gets here. I will ride back to the camp on the supply wagon. My relief then patrols the same path once and then he moves on to the next path and storekeeper. His patrol will last all of the night hours." The boy was friendly. He was not afraid to tell Josh things. He could feel that Josh was trustworthy.

"Here you are, some juice for you. Josh, would you like some also?" Zerasha had returned with the pitcher of juice and some glasses. She sat down next to Josh and listened to the rest of the conversation.

"What do you patrol for, just vagrants?" Josh tried to sound curious.

"Yes, sir, and rebels!" The soldier had a great deal of excitement in his voice, like it was all a game to him and soon he would be able to return to his own homeland.

"Rebels!?" Josh seemed astounded.

"Yes, sir. They are the people that are against what the Law says and does. They are very sneaky, and it is hard to catch them. But, when we do, it is really exciting. We go into their house and destroy their communicators then haul them off. There is one in particular that we are looking for, but no one has seen him for many seasons. Seems this man made up a plan to stop the Enemy, but he did not finish it and it caused the Law a great deal of..." he hesitated.

"I really must be going. It will take a few hours to get to the storekeeper's and I must get there before the supply wagon." The soldier finished his drink and bade the two new comer's good luck and good bye.

Josh had finished his break and started to head towards the house when Zerasha interrupted him. "Do you believe what he says about the rebels?" She sounded afraid.

"Yes, love. I know of the rebels myself from my time of soldiering. But I do not wish you to tell them that I was a soldier. They need not know that. Okay?" He glanced at her to make sure that she understood. He was thinking about the young soldier's last statement.

"Why, my love?" she questioned him like a small child.

"That is a part of my past that I do not want to tell you about, my love. When the time is right I will tell you of all the places that I have been and all the things that I did. Until then, you must continue to trust me." Josh was very understanding. He knew that she would understand also.

"I understand, Josh. There are parts of my past that I do not wish to tell you now, either. So, I guess that makes us even, right?" She was teasing him, but she knew he would take it that way. She knew that he could read her well. He could always tell when she was frightened, or extra happy, or extra sad. That was okay for her. It kept her from having to explain the way she felt at certain times.

"I still have some work to do down in the work room. Do not call me for hot plates. I will try to be done before that, or at the very latest shortly after you have finished them." He bent down to kiss her on the forehead and headed for the house again.

He reached the first hallway and lighting his lamp, headed down to see where it would lead him. As he walked he could see an opening at the end. It did not have a door on it. He quickened his pace to catch up to his racing heart. The excitement in him was overwhelming. He reached the end of the hallway to find a very large room with tons of equipment in it.

On the far wall there was a microphone, and when he reached it he could see a whole other room, or dungeon, or something. It looked more like a mine pit, but the only ones that Josh had ever seen were the ones above the ground. He looked at the wiring for the microphone to see where it led.

There had to be a communicator somewhere, or at least he thought there would be one. He followed the wire to a speaker, much like the ones that are on transports. Josh was very confused. He was not sure what he had stumbled upon here, and he wasn't sure that he liked it.

Was his father part of the work house horrors that Josh had never seen during the wars? Why didn't he tell him? What really went on here? The questions raced through Josh's head faster than he could keep up with them.

He decided to go down another hallway, so he headed back up the first one. On his way, he saw a door. It did not appear to be locked. Josh was almost afraid to open it for fear of what he might find inside. He grabbed the handle of the door with great apprehension and turned the knob. He pushed the door open slowly and put his lamp inside. There was another door on the other side of the room. Josh was ready to explore all that he could.

He tried the door, unlocked. He pushed it open very slowly. His curiosity was a little stronger than his fear. Inside the tiny room were a bench, almost wide enough to sleep on, and a cabinet. The cabinet had a set of soldier's materials inside of it. This must have been a sleep room for the soldiers during the wars, maybe not this last one though. Josh looked at the materials. They were of hide, but they did not look like any of the materials he had ever seen on a soldier.

"Josh, this is all from the wars of your great, great grandfather's time. This is why I had to go. The Law wanted to use the house as a work house instead of a business. I would continue to run the hide business, but the soldiers would come and go as they pleased. I would have nothing to do with it, so I packed all that I had and left. I did not put the house for sale, though Keiler listed it occasionally for strangers such as you. He would not put the family house in danger of being overrun by the Law." Josh's father's vision had appeared before him in the small room.

"The key to the communicator room is on the outside of the chimney, twelve rocks above the ground. Make sure that you do not let anyone see you get it. It will surely be a tragedy to the legends that still exist today. The supplies will come today, so I will not be able to appear to you for quite some time, not until the next supply run.

"Please, my son, I need you to find out all that you can. They have taken Zac from here. I do not know where. They became very suspicious of him. He would not tell them where the rebel base is. They do not know that I have this knowledge also. But if they break Zac, they will come to me next. I will die before I give them any information.

"It sounds as if they are going to open a few of the work houses to pull more rock out. Josh, you must do what you can to stop them. There is information behind the locked door that will help you. Find Keiler. He is one of our biggest assets." Josh could feel his father's tension.

167

"Father, I am so confused. Where is your communicator? I did not know that Zac was with you. Where is mother? How are the children? What..." Josh was acting like his true self from long ago. It almost felt good. "What should I tell Zerasha? She will surely question me."

"You must tell her as little as possible. But, son, only tell parts of the truth. Do not ever lie to her. She plays a very big role in the legends of the united tribes." His father could not stay much longer. "Keep your abilities sharp, my son. Try seeing through the presence that you feel. You must first have a strong presence, then you must be in a place that is neutral to the presence surroundings. If you practice this during sleep, you will be good at it in no time while you are awake. Good luck, my son."

Josh could feel the presence of his father's hand on his shoulder. "Ran is out there somewhere posing as a Lawman. He is waiting for word of your arrival. The patrol soldiers will..." The voice was gone. The presence was barely there at all.

"Father?" Josh spoke aloud. "Where did..." he stopped. The presence was getting stronger. Josh concentrated hard. He could see his father. Though he was sure that his father could feel him, he knew that he could not be seen. Josh did not see much more than just his father. There was very little open space around him. Josh could hear footsteps.

He lost his concentration for fear he was hearing them in the hallway. He turned quickly and left the two rooms. He knew that Zerasha would have hot plates ready. He glanced quickly down the hallway before he left the outer room. As he entered the empty hallway, he realized that the footsteps he heard were from his vision of his father.

He hoped that all was well, as it was every other time that Josh had seen his father's vision. He knew that he would not be able to contact Father for some time. He would practice his ability on Zerasha. These were some of the things that Josh had showed her when they first met.

He entered the room with the locked door and stopped before he went up the stairs. He concentrated on her beauty and gracefulness. In just a few minutes he could see her by the cook fire finishing the hot plates. She had set his on the top to stay hot and finished dishing hers. He opened his eyes and started up the stairs.

He liked being able to see what others were doing. It would help him to know if there was trouble inside a house. He would be able to picture the inside of Zac's house before he went in. He had seen most of the floors, just none of the hallways. Now that he knew what they were like he would be able to envision them in his mind.

He pushed the door open and peaked to see if there was anyone around. He covered the door and headed to the cook floor. Whatever was on that hot plate sure smelled delicious, Josh thought. He came up behind Zerasha and kissed the top of her head. He was very glad to see her. She handed him his hot plate and sat down beside him on the bench.

They both sat quietly and ate as though each had a story to tell of the day, but neither wanted to be the first to start. They were acting like two children that had just met for the first time.

"I found some really neat things down there. There is a whole pile of hide. The person that lived here before must have been in the hide business." Josh started the conversation, finally. "Most of it is just a bunch of junk. I could see why they left the stuff."

"I learned to ride the horse, but I am not very good at running." She stood and lifted the material from her legs. She had fallen off the horse when it stopped too fast after a run. She laughed about it now. So did Josh, but he was a bit concerned for her frail and tender body.

He bent over and kissed the mark on her leg, then took his hand and lightly rubbed across it. He could tell that it had some pain with it still. She would heal though. Josh did every time he fell from a horse as a child.

"I will go to the ridge again tonight. Do not wait for me. I will probably be late. I found an old house on the other side of the ridge last night, and I would much rather have a smaller house for now if I can find one. You don't mind, do you?" He always checked this kind of thing with her. He wanted her to be happy.

"Well, I am kind of use to this one already, but if smaller would be better, then okay." She was compromising and Josh knew it. He would go and look anyway.

He cleaned off his plate, kissed Zerasha passionately, almost as if he would never return, and told her as always, "I will return, my love."

Josh reached the ridge just in time to see the soldier from earlier finishing his final patrol. Only this time he did not cut across the ridge. He followed the path to finish the patrol properly. He would have to report all of his stops. Though, Josh was sure he would make something up for the abandoned house that he missed earlier.

This would give Josh plenty of time before the new patrol arrived at Zac's house. He walked around the ridge, so that the soldier would not see him. Entering Zac's house from a window in the back, he walked to the hole in the floor where the door used to be for the lower floors. He went down the stairs and looked behind the curtain.

There was nothing there but the old communicator. Josh would see if he could get it working this time. He checked wires and panels, hit buttons and turned keys. All of a sudden the lights came on in a few of the panels and the microphone crackled.

"Z?...Come in, Z." The voice was familiar, but Josh could not place a name to it. "Z?...Come in, Z." The message crackled again. Josh concentrated on the microphone. He would practice the ability his father taught him. He could see the microphone. He concentrated harder. "Z?...Come in Z."

Josh listened and concentrated. All he could see was the back of a man's head. But this man did not wear the material of the lawmen. He concentrated. Who could this person be? What would happen if he answered the communicator? "Z?...Come in Z. This is R. Come in." Josh thought, who is R? Would he know of Josh, or would Josh be endangering ever coming to this communicator again?

Josh had lost his concentration. All the questions in his head were distracting him. He sat down in front of the microphone and pushed the button.

"This is J." He let go of the button, just as Zac had taught him many seasons ago. "Z is not..." he waited. Should he continue?

"J? How is castle building?" the voice spoke the words quickly.

171

R was Ran! Josh stopped and envisioned Ran and the microphone. He could see him clearly. "Ran, how in this world are you?" Josh spoke to him, but not with the microphone. That was how his father had kept from being detected for so long. "You know where I am now. When do you do patrols?" Josh waited for the stunned Ran to reply.

"Patrols?" He turned to see the vision of his friend Josh, the look of shock still on his face. There were still many abilities that Ran did not know Josh possessed. Josh barely knew them all himself.

"I will go out on the next run to your area. How in all the worlds do you do that?" Ran was completely amazed.

"It is something that my father taught me not long ago. What happened to you when I saw you last? Is it safe to talk?" Josh was curious to see what his friend had to say.

"I bought the abandoned house on your patrol route. When they found out that I had soldiered they asked me to help on the patrols. I had spoken to your father about it and he nearly pushed me into the materials. He said that I would be a great asset. When I am not patrolling I can do as I wish. I am kind of part time soldiering. The rest of the time I spend helping the rebel cause. I knew of it when I returned here, but I did not know I would be able to view it from the enemy side. It is a fun thing to do, though really not as fun as castles." Ran could still not believe that he was communicating without the use of the communicator.

"I will meet you on your patrol route. My father says that there is information in a room in his house, and Keiler has information for me, as I am sure that you do, also. It will be good to see you face to face, my friend." Josh finished the conversation and pulled his vision back.

Ran stood in amazement for a long time. He was glad that his friend had made it back to help the cause. He turned off his communicator and locked the door to the room as he left. He had been trying to reach Zac for some time. Naihu had told him on the last supply run that he had been taken, but not by whom or where. Ran was concerned.

The Law was playing dirty with the rebels, and he feared if Josh did not find some way to help, then Naihu would be next. Zac and Naihu were considered the Leaders of the Rebels, and the Law felt if they could be destroyed then they would not have to continue with this warring game that they played for a few bits of minerals. There was not much of the mineral left.

Most of the worlds that still mined it from under the surface only found enough to keep the Law happy. There was virtually none left on this harsh land. They had mined it all during Josh and his soldiering days.

However, the Law did not know of all of the work houses in this world. That is why they were holding Naihu and Zac. They wanted information from them about the other houses that had mines under them. Only the elders knew of these houses, and most of the elders were gone now. Naihu and Zac seemed to be the only ones left.

Ran did not know if he could wait for his next patrol to see Josh. He had not seen his friend for a very long time. Ran had come to the top of the stairs when he got a feeling. He stopped, listened, and waited. He wasn't sure, but he thought he had heard a horse. There were not many soldiers that rode horses. General Har and some of the top ranking ones were the only one that Ran could recall at this point.

Ran could feel the fear building inside of him. Had they detected his communicator? He double checked the door and covered it. He stood very quiet and waited. If it was a soldier, then he would call out before he entered, Ran hoped. He could hear footsteps above him. Who was out on his roof, and why were they here?

Ran's fear turned to anger. He went out the door. He could not believe that there was actually someone on his rooftop. As he cleared the door and turned around he could see the back of a man turning around and going toward the other side of the house. He called to the man, but he did not turn around. He grabbed his knife out of his boot and headed around the house. The Law would surely be happy if he brought in a vagrant even though it was not time for him to soldier yet. By the time Ran reached the far side of the house, no one was there.

He looked up in time to see a man jump from the roof right at him.

"How about we do some castle building my old friend?" Josh had just missed Ran when he jumped, though that was his plan.

"How did you know where I was? You will have to be careful. I still work for the Law, you know!" Ran teased his friend, though he was serious about being careful.

"I did not. I told Zerasha that I wanted to look at this house because it looked abandoned, and a smaller house would be much nicer."

Josh did not realize that it was Ran's house until he had come upon it and could feel his friend's presence. It was something that Josh had become very good at. He practiced it a lot, and his father kept him in practice by making him feel his presence. "I guess that I will have to tell her that someone else has already bought the place. Nice to know the neighbors are friendly." He slugged Ran lightly in the arm.

"Wow! Do we have a lot to catch up on! Shraze went to the storekeeper. She will be happy that you have come back. However we must not meet here again. It is too dangerous. I am too close to the Law, and they will take you prisoner. They have been looking for you since you finished soldiering. It seems you left a very important part of your plan out." Ran spoke as fast as the words would come out. He could see the smirk forming on Josh's face. He kept looking around to make sure there was no one nearby.

"Would you relax. I can find my way out as secretly as I found my way in." Ran did not know that Josh had improved his ability to pick out a bad presence. "I have checked the horizons. There is no one near here. Besides, don't you think that I have enough sense not to put your life or mine in jeopardy?" Josh sounded angry, but he was just letting Ran know that they were on the same side.

"I made the plan that way on purpose. The Law double crossed my father and then tried to do the same to me. I had to come up with something that would fool them long enough to get away, and far enough that they would think I no longer existed. I must keep it that way."

"Josh I had no idea that you knew of the double crossing fools when I last saw you. I would have insisted on staying on there and waiting for your release. We could have been working on this a long time ago. I did not see your father when I arrived here. Though, later I found out that he had sent you a letter. I, we, assumed that you would come soon. Soon became long and your father had all but given up on you. He continued to push his presence to you, but he had a hard time concentrating with all of the lawmen at his place all the time." Ran wanted to continue, but Josh had held his finger up to his lips for him to be quiet.

"I think that I hear someone coming, though it does not sound like a soldier's walk." Josh listened more carefully, tuning out everything around him. "I believe it to be Shraze. She will be happy to see me." He grinned mischievously.

"You are correct, my friend. She is coming over the top of the hill now. You are getting very good with your abilities."

Ran stepped outside of the house to meet his wife. "Hello, my love. There is someone here." He tried to sound concerned.

"Who?" She questioned him in a whisper being careful not to show the fear in her eyes. She liked that Ran was working for the rebel cause but she hated and feared him working for the distrustful Law.

"Come inside. I will help you put the supplies away." He still held the concern in his voice.

Shraze had become accustomed to the tones in his voice when there was trouble with the Law. Ran had become accustomed to changing his voice to suit the conversation. He had to, so he could keep the Law from suspecting him. She stepped inside the door and turned to Ran to make sure that everything was alright.

He put his arms around her and kissed her lightly. He knew that would reassure her a little, but not enough to feel completely out of danger.

"Hello, Shraze, it is nice to see you." Josh spoke as plain as he could. He was in a darkened part of the room and Shraze could barely make out the features of his face.

"Hello. Nice to see you, also." She did not know who she was talking to, so she answered quaintly and headed to the cook room where she would put the supplies away.

"Ran," she started with a whisper, "what does that man want? Have I met him before, or does he know me by watching us?" Ran could see the fear and anger in her beautiful dark eyes.

"Shhhhh, my love. Why don't you go back out there and get a better look? I know that you will feel a whole lot better after you do." He placed his strong hands on her shoulders and turned her around to the doorway, then gave her a slight nudge. She hesitated at first, then she went into the warming room.

"Have we met before?" She reached out her hand to the stranger sitting in the corner.

"I believe that we have, though you were not as beautiful then as you are now." Josh always had a way with words when they were meant for a beautiful woman. He reached for her hand and pulled it to his lips and lightly kissed the back of it.

By this time Shraze could see that it was their dear old friend from their childhood. "How did you get here? Where in all the worlds have you been?" She wrapped her arms around his neck and hugged him tightly. She felt like she should never let him go. She had tears of joy in her eyes when Josh reached up for her hands to get a better look at her. He took his hand and lightly wiped the water from her blushing cheeks.

"I do not believe that I have enough time to tell you of all the places I have been. And, furthermore, if I told you how I got here then you would know my secrets, and there are few people who know me that well. Not even Zerasha knows that much about me." He had become very sarcastic with his tone.

"Who is Zerasha?" This was a name that neither her nor Ran had heard and now Ran had heard it twice. His curiosity was peaked, and Shraze's also.

"Zerasha is my lover and companion," he paused and lowered his head in shame. It was fairly common practice for a man and a woman not to marry, but usually because one had lost their true love. "I met her many seasons ago, on the island of paradise in another dimension. She is betrothed to someone, and her father never returned with him, so she is accompanying me until she has word from her father." Josh felt that his two best friends, in all the worlds, deserved to know that much of the love of his life, which he would never have because of a legend that his name and his father's name stood for.

"When do we get to meet her?" Shraze was curious, almost jealous. She had always told Ran, if there were ever a time that she would have to find another love, it would be Josh. Ran agreed to that with her, and approved of her taste. He knew that if there were ever to be someone else, then Josh would be the one that would take care of her best.

"I must complete all of my tasks that I came here for before I can do any social visiting, love. It shouldn't be long now that I have caught up with my good friends here."

Josh seemed pleased to be able to put a piece of his forgotten memory back in place.

He had not thought of the two of them since he landed in the water near Zerasha's homeland island. "If you should ever meet Zerasha, she is not to know that we know of each other from this land. It is very important to me. She will find out when the time is right and I will tell her." Josh sounded concerned that he had brought her name up.

"Do not worry, my friend. Remember, we are all on the same side." Ran's words were comforting. "Meet me on the ridge tomorrow. I will show you a short cut to the storekeeper's, and we will be able to meet there in the next day or so. We must wait for the supply wagons to finish buying supplies. Keiler's is the only store for miles around that has any decent supplies left. Most of the rest of them have closed up and left, probably for good."

Ran shook his friend's hand and waved as he disappeared very quickly.

Josh could not wait to get to his house. He would surely wake the love of his life tonight. She would be delighted to hear that they would be staying in the large house that she so liked.

He knew that she was sleeping before he got to the door. He could feel her presence at rest. He slipped inside the door quietly and headed for the sleep room. He stood at the top of the ladder leading to the top floor of the large house. He could see her beauty lying peacefully on top of the furs.

He slowly unbuttoned his shirt and removed the rest of the material from his dark body. He lay down beside her gently and massaged the back side of her body. He could feel his desires inside of him. He wanted to hold her and kiss her until the sun came high in the sky, then he wanted to keep her inside all day and love her more.

She started to stir as Josh's desires peaked. He rolled her over and gently made love to her as he had never done before. He feared that he was very close to finding her father, and then she would return to the island homeland with her betrothed one. Josh would always remain her friend, but he had started to fall in love with her. He had to learn to occupy his time with other things or his heart would surely shatter.

"Wow," Zerasha breathed the word out of her mouth. "You were out late tonight. Did you get lost in meditation?" She teased him. Her whole body was exhilarated. She had not had that kind of love from Josh since the first time they met, though she was sure that the first time was pure lust.

She could feel the desire inside her deepen for him. She had the same fears of falling in love and having her heart shattered when her father returned, though by now she was sure that he was never to return to her. The thought almost made her happy. Then, at least she would not have to worry about her betrothed, though she would never be able to marry. She was content with that thought, but the thought of never seeing her father again, saddened her deeply.

Josh rolled over, "I have some news for you, but you seem to be in a world of your own, so I suppose it will wait until the sun is high in the sky." He teased her as he rolled away from her, pretending to take to sleep.

"Josh, what news? I,..." She reached out and hit him in the back. "Hey, you must not keep things from me.

It is not healthy for our type of relationship," she teased, and hit him again.

"Well, since you keep beating me, I guess I can tell you now, so that I may get some rest." He rolled over to find her patiently waiting for whatever news it was that he wanted to tell her. Her arms crossed in front of her and a look of great disgust was on her face.

"The little house is occupied. A young couple lives there. So you are in luck. We will keep the big house." He rolled over the other way, and closed his eyes, pretending to sleep again.

Zerasha giggled, kissed her love on the back and snuggled up against him. She was glad that they would not have to find a place for the supplies in a smaller house.

Josh's mind raced back to the events of the day. He tried very hard to find Zac's presence. He knew that if he could feel the presence he might be able to find Zac. He concentrated for a long time. He could feel a presence, but he was not sure whose it was.

It was a good presence. There were no bad feelings at all. He had been feeling this same presence for a few days now. He wondered if it was Zac. It had been so many seasons that he had seen him. He was not sure what he was looking for.

He tried to concentrate on Zerasha, but he could still feel the presence. It started to grow stronger the more he tried to ignore it. Josh tried to put his vision ability that his father had taught him that day to work.

He could see Zerasha, but she was on the island. She waved to a boat that was leaving. Zac could be seen on the boat. He was much younger then. Josh gave up and lay down beside his love. He could not get rid of the presence though. He had periods of brief sleep. He continued to concentrate on the presence.

Maybe he would be able to see something in his sleep though he had never been able to remember the things that he saw in his sleep. Of course he had not concentrated on them as hard as he did this night.

He woke abruptly again, but he did not scream. He could see Zac, at least 6 or 8 levels below the ground. He tried to reach him while he was awake. He could see the small room that he was in. It looked much like the room in the hallway of the floor that he found under his own house.

He tried to speak to Zac, "Zac, if you can hear me nod your head." Josh waited. He could feel the presence stronger than ever now.

"Josh, is that you?" He sounded weak and cold. Not at all like the Zac Josh had met so many seasons ago, it seemed.

"Zac, are you alone?" Josh waited to see if he could feel any other presence before he continued.

He could still feel the presence that he had been feeling since he arrived on the land of his childhood, though it was not Zac's. "I see that you are. I also see that you are not well. Your daughter will not be pleased to see you in that condition." Josh mused with the elder.

"Josh, I am in a work house not far from the one I was in with your father. I do not know where though. I must be some eight or ten levels down. You must find Ran and have him tell you where the work house of your father is. He has been there, only it is unsafe for him to speak, as he comes disguised as a lawman.

You must figure a way to stop the Law from mining the rock. It is what the elders used to make good white fall from the sky and nourish the plants and animals. I do not know what they use it for now, but it certainly is not for making white. The Law does not like the white for it covers the land and makes the plants grow so dense that they are unable to find the mines. Do not come for me yet. When you have figured the plan to stop them, then come for me, and bring my Zerasha with you.

"I hope that you are caring for her properly. I know where to find her betrothed now, and then the whole tribe will go back to paradise and live in peace from the Law. I hope that all the lands will be able to return to what they used to be before the wars started. We have beaten the Enemy. We will not have to worry about sickness and disease with white anymore, thanks to your plan. Now all we need is a plan to stop the Law, if that is possible." He stopped. It was as if he could hear something coming.

Josh could hear it too, but he was not sure of what it was. He pulled the vision back and fell into a deep restful sleep. He knew that he must make his plan fast. Zac was in no condition to have to wait very long. He awoke to find the sun half high in the sky already. Zerasha was still sleeping beside him. They both must have been exhausted. He leaned over her and kissed her on the cheek. She stirred. She looked ravishing, like she had rested well all night.

"Good morning, love. I had the most wonderful dream. My father had found my betrothed and I had returned to the homeland. There were a lot of new people there, but you were there also." She was well rested, and Josh knew that her father had put the vision in her head.

"I must get going. It is really late. I too had good sleep, but I did not have any visions that I remember."

Josh was already up and dressed before he had awakened his love. "I will take some jerky and rolls for something to eat. I will return, my love." He kissed her and headed to the cook floor and then out the door.

He met Ran on the ridge as planned, though Josh was not happy with Ran for not telling him immediately where he would find his father. "Why didn't you tell me where my father was yesterday? I could be halfway there and have him out of that awful pit that they keep him in." Josh's tone was angry. He wanted to hit Ran with all his strength.

"I am sorry, my friend. I have been ordered by your father not to give that information to you until you have figured out a plan for the Law. Did you get the key to your father's communicator room? We will need it before we go to the storekeeper. Besides, it is too early to go there yet. The soldiers will still be loading supplies until later today."

Ran was apologetic about the information, but very businesslike also. He had never gone against an order from Josh's father. He respected the man for who he was and all that he put up with from the Law.

"I spoke with Zac last night in my dream. He is not well, my friend. It seems that he is somewhere near my father, though he is not sure where. He is about ten levels below the ground. I was truly surprised that I could locate him. He put a vision in Zerasha's sleep, so that she would not worry for him or her betrothed." Josh was anxious to get started. The two men headed for the large house.

Josh sent Ran to the work room door that connected to the outside. Ran remembered it well from his childhood. Josh concentrated for any bad presence, or any presence for that matter. He took the key from behind the rock that his father had told him about and slipped through the doorway to the work room.

Zerasha would not suspect that they were even here. She never went to the work room. She had no desire to see the empty cold floor made of rock. Ran had the doorway in the floor open and the two men ducked inside of it and closed it. They took the steps two at a time. The excitement was building in them both.

Ran knew no more about the contents of the locked room than Josh did. Josh unlocked the door and glanced at his friend to see if he was ready. He opened the door to find a huge room with tons of equipment and supplies in it. All of the old sleds were there and many of Josh's old clothes. There was an entire wall filled with bottles of something. Josh and Ran could not figure out what the labels said. They were in some sort of code. Ran sat down and started to copy all the labels down. He would need to remember them all to tell the storekeeper, though he was not sure of their importance yet.

Josh had found a small communicator. He turned the switch to see if it worked. The small microphone crackled a message, "...I do not care what you do with him. He is useless to me, unless he can locate the mines that I wish to know about!" The man's voice was very familiar. Josh turned the volume up a little. This was not an ordinary communicator. It was only used to listen. Josh would not be able to send any messages this way. He listened for a while longer. "I need that mineral to keep the white from falling. It is the only thing that the elders have ever used to make that awful nourishing thing that the plants and animals must have to survive. I want it all!"

Josh did not dare listen any longer. Ran had been listening also.

"Wow! That was an informative conversation, wouldn't you say, Josh?" Ran was pleased that they had heard the plan of the Law. This would make it easier to make a plan of their own to keep the Law from what they desired the most; to keep the lands barren.

"I would! Suppose we finish up here and head to the storekeeper? I am getting a plan in my head. I will work through the details on the way there." Josh would need the help of as many rebels as they could find. Keiler would know if there were any others to be found, otherwise it would be the three of them.

Josh had run the plan through his mind, but he was unable to come up with how to get the rock into the air to meet with the storms so they would move and produce white. He hoped that there was a rebel that had knowledge in this field of expertise.

He departed from Ran so that they would not be seen together. Josh showed up at the storekeeper's first. He went in to find the soldiers finishing their supply list. He waved to the storekeeper and went to look for some supplies to keep himself busy. He did not know if the lawmen carried a picture of him or not. He wondered though, since his plan from seasons ago had worked out perfectly, for him anyway. Of course he knew that the Law would be disappointed, but that was the plan in the first place.

CHAPTER NINE

By the time the soldiers finished loading their supplies; several more had come in and out. Josh made himself busy behind the building. He could not afford to be noticed at this point and time. He hoped that Keiler would be finished soon. Ran had been there for some time, but he chose to stay in the building and talk to the soldiers and lawmen. It made it easier if he did not try to avoid them. He was always very businesslike with them, though.

Josh started to get anxious about the time it was taking. He concentrated on the inside of the building. He could see Har, his old superior from his soldiering days. It seemed he was questioning who moved into the Naihu place. He was unaware that it was for sale.

Keiler made his way around the story fast, though he was very convincing. He told Har the story that Josh had told the soldiers by Zac's house. He was a stranger from another land and he took some kind of samples from the air. It was the only thing that Keiler had to offer the man and his companion.

187

Har was appeased for now, but he seemed dissatisfied, somehow.

Josh pulled the vision back, as Har and his crew of soldiers headed out. They had many stops, according to Har. Josh was glad that he had chosen to go outside. Har would surely have recognized him otherwise.

Josh was relieved that they had gone. He was beginning to wonder if he would be able to look busy for much longer.

"Josh, my friend, please come in. The lawmen will not return to this area for 15 or 20 days. It has been their pattern for seasons now." Keiler held the back door open for Josh, as he shook hands with his friend Ran. "Come; let's go to a more secluded spot, shall we?"

Keiler led the way to the floor below the main one. It also had a door in the floor, but when they reached the bottom of the steps, there were shelves and shelves of supplies. Josh had never seen so many supplies in one place before.

"Wow, Keiler, do you use all this for the soldiers?" Josh could not believe his eyes.

"No, this is all reserve, non-perishable items for large white storms, like the last one that was seen on this land. You were here for that one, Josh. You too, Ran. That was the last time there was white in this world, and many others, which is why we are gathered here today.

"We must come up with a plan to get the rock from the land to the air and get this white a fallin'." Keiler had become theatrical by the time he finished his small speech.

"Josh and I have found some formulas in Naihu's lock room. I have written down symbol for symbol what is in each jar. We overheard a conversation between two of the higher ranking soldiers, maybe the highest, talking on the one way communicator. The one said, 'I don't care what you do with him. He is useless to me unless he tells me where the other work houses are,' and he also said, 'I must have it [the rock] all.'"

Ran only relayed the important parts of the message to Keiler. He did not want to get him started. He was easily made angry, especially where the Law was concerned.

"Well, we must get this plan in action. Josh, do you have anything to add to this plan, maybe something that will get us a good start?" Keiler knew of the plan to stop the enemy. He had mastered it well.

"With the symbols from the jars, I assume they are chemicals that my father stored from the storms. If I could figure out how to get the rock crushed and loaded into a transport with a drop bottom, I could locate the storm on the horizon and dump into it. I already have a transport license. Can you tell what these symbols are, Keiler?" Josh had the plan all set. He was anxious to get started. He was the only one that had seen the true condition of Zac. They would have to get him out of there and soon.

"Well, most of them are just chemical combinations, though I am not sure if they are what we need. Did you see a mineral crusher among the equipment in your father's lock room?" Keiler knew how to get the rock crushed. Now all they needed was to find the crusher.

"I saw it. It was on the bottom of the shelf right at the base of the steps. I have seen them in the work houses. Do you think that we should crush our own? It will take a long time to get enough to add to any storm clouds." Ran was just as ready to end all this nonsense with the Law. He wanted to get on with his life with his wife.

They all worked tediously into the cool hours. It was getting late, and they should return to their families until morning. Keiler opened the door to let them out and wished them a good sleep. They would start and complete the plan immediately, as soon as they all got some rest.

Keiler had plans to check out Josh's transport. He would go during the cool hours so that it would be less likely that the Law would see him. He grabbed what supplies he needed and left through the back entrance so that he would not be seen. He walked to the transport. It only took him a short time to get there. Josh had moved it to a closer transport site when he had found the little town of his boyhood.

As he approached the transport he could see that Josh had picked a good one. It would fly fast and be mostly undetectable in the skies. It also had a secret drop door. Keiler figured it was one of the transports from the wars. He made sure that everything was still operational and then gathered his supplies. They would be all set for the beginning phase of their plan.

Josh reached his house nearly exhausted. He did not wake Zerasha. He undressed and quietly lay down beside her. He did not even concentrate on any visions or presence. He knew that the next few days would be long and tiring, so he just wanted to sleep. He hoped that he would be able to sleep with all the excitement from the day swimming around in his head.

Ran arrived at his house just as the sun was starting to come high. He told Shraze to wake him in a few hours. They needed to get things in motion if they were to beat the

Law. He undressed and went straight to the sleep room where he collapsed on the bed from exhaustion.

He thought how good it was to work with and see Josh again. It had been many, many seasons since they had worked together, and it seemed even longer since they had seen each other. Josh had decided to go find the 'land of Naru' instead of following Ran back to the homeland. Though Ran was happy that he had found it, it just seemed that if he would have come back first, then all of this would be long since over, and there would be happiness for everyone, in all the worlds. Ran drifted off to sleep finally.

Keiler had not slept. He stayed up through the cool hours to prepare supplies and direction sheets for each of them. Josh would need to look for Zac, and then his father, so Ran would fly the transport. Keiler had found enough of the rock to crush and mix with the solutions in Naihu's lock room.

He was starting to get a little anxious for the boys to show up. It had been a long time coming with all of the elders in one place. There was only one that Zac had not found in all of his worldly travels. Naihu had always wondered, after his presence disappeared, if he might have transported into another dimension, unlike the one that Josh had flown through. None of the elders had heard, seen, or felt a presence from him since before the boys were born.

Where are those boys, anyway? Keiler came back to the present, and still no sign of them. He went to the back room to rest until they arrived.

"Zerasha, my love?" Josh knew it was time to tell Zerasha part of the plan that would take place in the next few days. "Zerasha, are you awake?" He waited to hear her reply. Nothing. He got up, dressed and headed to the cook room for some morning hot plates, and then to the work floor. He had to get the supplies ready, and the solutions for the rock.

He would wake Zerasha when he was ready to depart. They would talk then. He knew that she understood the wars. He would not have to go into details about that part. However, she did not know of Josh's abilities. How was he going to explain to her that he had seen a vision of his father, and that was the main reason to come to this land?

He would not have to tell her of her father, yet. He had a vision in his sleep from an elder who gave him specifics to tell her, nothing more, and nothing less. Josh could still not figure out who the man was. He did not recognize him from the island paradise. The elders had not mentioned anyone like him in the stories that were told while he was on the island paradise. Josh wanted to talk to his father. Maybe he knew.

It was almost like a dream, only it was very clear to Josh, and remained clear, even though he was awake now.

Josh had finished gathering all the things that he needed for his travels. He now took the time to contact his father. He concentrated on the small dark area where he had seen his father's presence many times. He could see the shadow of his father. It looked as though he were sleeping. He was lying on the small bench, with his face to the wall. Josh waited to see if there was any bad presence around the area where his father was imprisoned. He did not feel anything except the peace of his father sleeping.

"Father, I see that you are alone. Are you awake?" Josh waited to speak again, until he saw his father's face.

"Father, I have seen a vision in my sleep. It is of a man who knows the legends and of the elders. He gave me some specifics to tell Zerasha, and then he was gone. I remember him vividly. I had the same feeling from his presence that I have had many times since I came back here. It was always a presence that I could feel, but I had never seen."

Josh stopped. He could see the astonishment and excitement in his father's eyes.

"Josh, my son, can you try to reach him again? That is the lost elder. His presence has not been felt since just before you were born." The joy in Naihu's eyes told Josh how important this was.

"Father, he finished his instructions to me with 'Son of Naihu, I will see you in paradise.' That was all that he said. I did not get to see where he was. I can concentrate on his presence, but I am not sure that he wants to be found, at least not yet. I must go now, Father. I have some things that must be told to Zerasha, and Keiler is waiting for Ran and me. We will start the plan today!" Josh finished and pulled his vision back. He could feel it getting dangerous to be there any longer.

"Josh, where are you?" Zerasha's sleepy voice could be heard faintly at the top of the sleep floor stairs.

"I am in the work room, love. Grab those hot plates and come on down. I have some things that I must tell you." He closed the door to the lower floors and covered it with the hides. This was a place that Zerasha did not need to know about. If the Law were to come around while he was gone, she would be better off knowing as little as possible.

"What is this all about?" she questioned as she came into the light of the work room. She had noticed the sled of supplies as she approached Josh. She could feel something different about him, but it was not bad. "Have you heard from the elders? Do you have news of my father?" Her eyes danced with excitement as she took a seat, facing Josh on the floor.

He could never lie to her, he thought. "Yes, my love, I have heard from the elders. I must go and make the white fall again, so that the lands will have nourishment. I have found my father, which is one of the reasons we came to this world. I must rescue him. Maybe he has heard of your father. I will be gone for many days. You will be fine here. Do not let the Law know where I have gone. You must try to forget what I tell you.

"If they suspect that you know, they will not hesitate to do whatever they want to get the information from you. So far, they do not even know that I am still alive. I would like it to remain that way for as long as possible. As you know, I have green eyes like yours, only I am able to talk to the elders without a communicator. I have had visions of my father since before we left the homeland." Josh stopped to eat and wait for her to reply. He could see the astonishment in her eyes. She had heard about the special men of the tribes, but she had never met any of them.

"My love, then you would be able to reach my father!" She was so excited that she found herself staring deep within the darkness of his green eyes. "Have you seen or felt my father's presence?" She waited for Josh to empty his mouth.

"I cannot lie to you, Zerasha. I have felt your father's presence, but I did not know that it was your father until my vision last night." He had to stretch the truth for now. She would understand when the time was right to let her know all of the legends and all about the elders. "I must go to find my father and rescue him from the lawmen who have imprisoned him. He will surely know of your father and may even know where we will find him.

"My love, you must remember that no matter how long I am gone, I will return for you. My only hope is that I do not find your father with your betrothed. I do not know if I will be able to give you up to him freely." He stopped. He had not meant to make her cry, but it was something that he could not hold inside of him any longer.

"Josh, I never suspected that you felt that way. You never said anything, so I assumed..." She stopped. He could see the love and passion in her eyes, even though they cried tears of pain. He could see that she had the same feelings, but she must accept the man that she was born for, because the legends would surely die if she went against them.

"I must go now. Please know that you are very special to me, and when the time is right, I will be able to tell you so many things." He bent to kiss her tenderly and passionately before he rose and left through the work room door.

She did not know what to do. She had never been without Josh since they met on the island paradise. She became very lonely almost immediately after he left. She tried to busy herself with little tasks, cleaning and taking care of the horse, mainly.

Ran and Josh arrived at the storekeeper's at the same time. They shook hands and greeted each other, eager to start the plan. They went inside to find Keiler working on the supplies and lists. He came to the front of the store and scolded the boys for not getting there sooner.

"I think that I have all the supplies ready. Let's go to the stockroom and we will go over all the lists. I will show you both how to mix the solutions with the rock. Josh, I have to speak to you alone for a minute. Do you mind, Ran?" Keiler took hold of Josh's arm to lead him to a small room where Ran would not be able to hear the conversation.

"You can tell me in front of Ran." Josh stopped abruptly. "We have had no secrets since the day we met. He is fully aware of most of my abilities, and I don't really think that you could tell me something that he does not already know, or will not find out soon enough." Josh was almost annoyed with Keiler for suggesting that he keep secrets from his best friend.

"Suit yourself, my friend. I know of the vision you had from the elder last night. I have made a few changes to the plan, and I wanted to talk to you about the vision." Keiler seemed nervous. He did not like talking about the legends in front of Ran, because he did not know that Ran played a large role in keeping the legends true to the tribes.

"Do not be afraid of what Ran knows. He is part of the legends. He is one of only a few left from his tribe. I believe that the elder I spoke with last night is part of that tribe, though, I do not know much about him. I did suspect that you would need to make changes. I will have to rescue Zerasha's father, then my own father. It will be up to you two to get the rock and solutions into the sky so that the white will nourish the lands again." He stopped. He could see the astonishment in Ran's and Keiler's eyes. They were not aware of Zerasha's father, and they certainly would be surprised to find out that it was Zac.

"Who is this other man that you must rescue? This is surely not part of the plan. Josh, you must stick to the plan, and leave the love of your life out of it. She will only be hurt in the end." Keiler was starting to show his nervousness, especially when Josh began to laugh.

"Keiler, Zerasha's father is a big part of this plan, only she is not to know yet. Zac is her father, and he came here, among other places, to find the man that he would have marry his lovely daughter." Josh's eyes glimmered with laughter while he explained to the other men.

"Josh, you mean that you have found the paradise? I never knew that such a beautiful woman could ever be..." Ran stopped. He could see the sorrow in Josh's eyes. It was a small secret, but a secret none-the-less.

"My mission is to find Zac, my father, and then the man that is betrothed to my Zerasha. I am to take them to the island paradise, then return for Zerasha and the rest of the tribes' people and take you all to the island paradise. Ran, I am so sorry that I have kept this from you. I have never kept anything from you, but it was a part of the legends." He looked to his friend for acceptance of his apology, but he did not expect him to really accept it.

"Josh, there is no need to apologize. I understand that the legends are important, though I know little about them. Let's get this plan rolling. The sooner we start the sooner Zac and your father are out of those pits. The sooner we are all off to the island paradise of our ancestry." Ran walked across the room and put his arm around Josh's shoulder and they walked together to the rest of the supplies and the lists that Keiler had left on a table in the back of the stockroom.

"I figured that Ran could drive the transport. He must be as good as you are, Josh, though he will need to know the worlds that he passes." Keiler started at the top of the list of changes.

"I know most of the worlds of this dimension. It is the only dimension that we will have to worry about, isn't it?" Ran looked to Josh to make sure there were no other dimensions that he must accidentally come upon to get to. It was always dangerous to go to different dimensions without someone like Josh.

"It is the only dimension that the Law could get to. The Enemy was unable to capture any of my tribe to go beyond this dimension. I will need you to tell me the exact location of Zac and my father and then we will all go our separate ways. Keiler, will you remain here at the store?" Josh was curious to know if he would be able to keep the Law at bay long enough to get the two important elders of the legends out of their prisons.

"I will remain here. I am able to pick up on some of the presence floating around these parts. I will be able to tell if the Law suspects anything going on, and you, Josh, will be able to inform either of us how things are going on at your end. Ran, you will have to rely on Josh to send messages through to me. He will keep in contact with us as often as is safe." Keiler was proud to be a part of the legends. He was even prouder to be alive still, without being detected as a tribesman or a part of the rebel cause.

"Josh, your father is in the same house as Zac. Zac was taken to a lower floor many weeks ago, to die. He did not divulge any information to the Law, so they tired of him. That was what the man on the one way communicator had meant when he said he did not care what was done with him. I have seen him only once.

"They had me take him some food and water shortly after he was taken down there. I assumed that someone else had taken over the duty when I returned the next time. You must go to the house with the supply trucks parked outside. It is not far from here by car, but you should go by horse or foot. It will take you longer, but it is safer that way. There is an entrance at the back of the house. It is below the level of the ground. You must pull the grate up and go inside the tunnel. Once you are there it is only a matter of time before you will see your father again. Zac is twelve levels below the ground level. Your father is at the end of the fourth level in a room at the end of a hallway. There are no other rooms in this hallway. You must be careful. There will be lawmen everywhere," Ran finished and told his friend to be very careful and use his abilities as much as possible.

"Keiler, will there be a transport available for Josh to fly the elders to a safe place?"

"Yes, I purchased one many seasons ago. I have kept it under cover in the back of Josh's land since his father left. Your mother and sisters and brothers will be very happy to see you." He grabbed Josh's hand and shook it strongly. "Go with the knowledge of the legends, my friend. Be safe. We will wait for your return. I will watch your woman for you and make sure there is no trouble there."

Josh took his small bag of supplies and left the storekeeper's. He figured it would take him at least three days of travel by horse, just to get near the house. When he finds it he will have another plan figured out on how to get the men out without being detected. He would have to wait until the last feeding of the day for his father. It would give him time to get Zac up and on his feet again. He knew that he was weak. He had enough food and supplies to get all of them back to the transport at Josh's house.

"Josh, my son, I see that you have initiated the plan. I am waiting for you. Please make sure that Zac is safe first. I will keep your presence with me, that way I will know how things are going and if there is any trouble." Josh's father had appeared in front of him on the first day. He looked well and ready to fight anything that might get in the way.

"Father, I am worried for Zerasha. She was not happy when I told her that I was going for you, her father if possible, and her betrothed." Josh wanted his father to give him information on the man that would have Zerasha for the rest of her life.

"Josh, there is nothing to worry about. She will be fine. She is a very strong woman and she has kept her deepest desires for the man that she will have. You will soon learn of him and where he is. Mother is happy to hear that you are coming. She is also a strong woman. She has been able to keep her chin up and the children occupied for all these seasons." His father stayed with him as he rode across the desolate land that would lead him to his family.

Josh had not seen any of them, except for his brothers, since the day the diseased white fell on the land where he grew up and killed all the living plants and animals. He had not even thought of any of them since he arrived on the island paradise. He wondered how beautiful his sisters had become. Were his brothers gifted like he was, or were they gifted with some other abilities? These were just some of the questions that he could hardly wait to find the answers to.

He rode in silence for a long time. His thoughts kept going back to the time of his childhood. It seemed like so many seasons ago. He had become a man that day at Zac's house. He could not even remember what it was like to be a child, carefree with no worries, just the time that every child needs, to play. He could see visions of his friend and himself making castles in the sand of Shurfate. Josh could feel the good memories flooding back to his conscious mind. He had shoved them so far back that he had trouble remembering them until now. It made him feel happier than he had for many seasons.

He found a place to take to sleep late on the first day. He had traveled very far the first day. He had not expected to get this far. He spent the second day talking with his father and sending his presence to Ran, Keiler, and Zac. He wanted to assure them that he was ahead of schedule and that it should not take him much longer to find the workhouse where he would find his father and family.

He rode all the way to a ridge where he could see the large house on the other side. He was happy that it had only taken him two days. He could see the supply wagons. There were only three, though Ran had told him that there were six total. So, if they were not all there they were making supply runs. It would be a good time to get inside. A lot of the lawmen would be on the supply runs for a break from their everyday routines.

Josh set up his temporary shelter behind the ridge, inside of a hole in the stone ground. That way he would be less likely to be detected. He ate cold jerky and rolls with butter instead of risking a fire being seen by the soldiers. He sat up and watched the guards by the entrance. They were sloppy soldiers. They did not watch very carefully for anything. It would be easy for Josh to get close to the house during the cool hours and be inside the grate on the ground before the sun would start to come high. He gathered what he would need to get his family and Zac out of the house that had imprisoned them for so many seasons, and set out across the rocky ridge and down into the center of the valley where the large house was located.

"Father, can you speak?" Josh had looked through his mind at the room and the hallway where his father was. He could see that there was no one around. "I am, well..., I guess I really don't need to tell you where I am. I am sure that you are well aware of that. I will get to the inside in a matter of minutes. When is your next meal?"

"Josh, it is so good to see you and know that your vision is almost close enough for me to touch. You have done well in your life's mission. Now, let's get the hell out of this dungeon and get on with the life that the elders have planned for many generations. I will be with you every step of the way this time, and whatever I do, do not let me send you away again. Do you understand, son?" His father's voice had become full of life and laughter.

"I understand fully, my father. Do not worry for me. I have learned a great deal since the last time I saw you in person. You will know me as a different person from this day on." Josh was proud to be able to tell his father that all of his early teaching had done him good in all of his travels.

"Josh, I can feel you. Where are you?" The voice broke the father son talk. "Josh, please tell me that you are physically near, and that I am not just feeling your presence."

"I am near, Sir Zac. I am just outside of the old house. I am lifting the grate on the ground and now I am climbing down the ladder and pulling the grate back over the opening." Josh's mood was very good.

His excitement and anxiety could be seen all over his face and showed in his quick actions. He moved quietly and quickly. It was as if he had eaten something that gave him extra energy, though he could not remember jerky and rolls giving him this kind of energy before.

He found the door that led to the second level of the house. He would have to find a way to the lower floors as fast as he could. It would be dangerous to risk being caught in the upper levels of the house. He used his abilities to help him, and he relied on the presence of his father. The halls that the stairs were located in were offset from each other but they were not unlike the underground tunnels of the house he grew up in. The only difference now was the Law and the soldiers. He glanced up at the wall outside the stairwell from the second level to see a picture of him with a warning posted below it, "Dead or Alive" was all it said. This would make it a bit more difficult at this point but Josh was capable of a lot of things that the lawmen and soldiers had no idea of.

He could feel the presence of the Law all around him. It was an evil presence, one he had not felt since his last days of soldiering. He was able to locate a doorway to the lower levels just before a couple of guards came for their usual check of those levels.

Josh had to get to the lower levels where Zac was before the soldiers cornered him. Otherwise, he would be unable to go any further. He was able to evade them until he reached the seventh floor. He peered out of the door in the floor to see two of them getting ready to come up right towards him. He scurried to the first available room and crept in, after he had checked for anyone inside the room. It was empty. He left the door cracked just enough to see the soldiers. They had just completed their rounds of all the floors, at least down to the eighth level. Josh assumed that they did not bother with the other floors, either because there was no one else down there or because they were ordered to leave the prisoners below the eighth floor to die.

Josh waited until the soldiers could be seen in his mind on the fifth floor. They joined up with the first two soldiers and headed up to the main floor. He would be safe now. It was only a matter of minutes before Josh had reached the twelfth floor. He could see Zac in his mind. He waited as patiently as an old man that had been left to die could.

"Josh, I can feel you again. It is a very strong and real feeling. Where are you?" Zac had become excited. He had not eaten anything for several days, or maybe weeks. It seemed like so long ago that the young soldier had deterred from his regular route of checking to bring him food and water. The darkness that surrounded him made it difficult to tell how many suns had come high which in turn made it hard for Zac to know how long it had been since he had tasted food or drink. The empty feeling in his stomach had gotten worse as the time passed so he knew that it had been quite a few high suns.

"Zac, you must keep talking so that I may locate you. Tell me anything that you like, though I would prefer that it be pleasant." Josh did not want to ruin this reunion with unpleasant talk.

"I can feel that you are nearby. Where is my Zerasha? I so desire to see her and tell her about her betrothed. Oh, I am sorry, my friend Josh. You did say pleasant, didn't you?" He teased Josh. "I remember when I left her for the first time on the island. She was but a few days old.

There were no men in the known tribes when she was born who would suit her for a companion. They were all either too young, or already betrothed to other women in the tribes. She was such a beautiful baby. Her mother had golden hair like hers when we first met. I still see it as golden as the first day even though it has grayed over the seasons. How is my dear wife? She must be worried sick about me."

Zac stopped. He had betrayed his wife and it made him sad to think that she may not ever have him again. He had given up on finding the island paradise just after Josh was born. He had not been able to find the secret passage back to the other dimension. That was when he came across Sharhi. She had comforted him and understood his loss like no one he had ever known.

"Zac, are you still there? Did you get lost in another time or world?" Josh stood before the elderly man, who had hung his head down to stare at his feet. Josh could see the shame in his face.

"Josh, my friend, I have missed you a great deal!" The elder stood and embraced Josh, now older in many ways. "Step back and let me take a look at you. You are surely a changed person since the last time that I saw you.

Of course, you were just a boy when you left here. Zerasha must do you good. You look well-traveled and very happy."

Zac sat back down on the bench. He was weak from no nutrition, but he still had a strong mind and Josh knew that it may be a few days before he would be able to find his father and a way out safely.

"Here, my friend, some jerky and rolls, and a bottle of the best sauce in all of the lands." He handed the food and drink to Zac. "We must make a plan to get out of here safely. Keiler has stored a transport on the other side of the ridge from my father's house. I will be able to take you and all of my family to the island paradise of our ancestry and the legends. We will do nothing until you have had enough food to get you back on your feet. I will leave this with you." Josh placed the extra bag of jerky and rolls at Zac's feet.

"I must find another way out. Ran thinks the fourteenth floor has a secret passage. It was used to bring the prisoners into the house so they would not know where they were." Josh stood and stared at the man from his childhood. He looked much older than his father now. When he was a boy, they looked about the same age, probably because Josh was unlearned and un-traveled then.

Josh sat beside the elder and talked with him about the time that he had found Zerasha on the island. He told him of the times that they had spent together. They talked about Sharhi and Zac's wife. Josh assured the elder that his wife was waiting for him and that she was aware of Sharhi. It was all part of the legends, and she was the only Queen left. Or until she found out about Josh and his family and the fact that Naihu had survived the war. Now there would be another Queen, Josh's mother.

Josh got up after some time and went to find the secret entrance that would get them out safely. He assured Zac that he would be careful. He would like to see his father, but it would have to be by vision only for now. He could not risk being caught by the soldiers.

It seemed like hours had passed since Josh had headed to the fourteenth floor to find the entrance. He checked all the hallways and was headed into the only room left to check. If the entrance was not here he would have to find another floor and search it like he had done with this one until he found the secret entrance. He stopped occasionally to send a message to Keiler and Ran, and to talk to his father. Sometimes it was not safe to talk to his father though. He checked carefully every time.

"Josh, the entrance you are looking for is under the bench in the room you are in now. If you did not know it was there you would never find it." His father's voice came to him as he entered the outer room of the double room. Like all the others it was dark, but it did not have a place for materials, only a bench.

Josh lifted the bench on the wall and could see the hinges of the door in the floor. There was no handle to pull the door up, so Josh assumed no one had ever gone out the door, just in. He took the knife from his boot and pried up on the floor boards. He finally found the one that would allow them to escape this horrible place. He walked to the end of the tunnel that led to a place not far from where Josh had left his extra supplies. His heart raced with desire and happiness. He had never felt this content in his whole life.

As Josh headed back to Zac's room, he ran a plan through his head. He spoke to his father. It was a time that they needed to catch up on all the things that had happened since the day Josh last saw his father. "Father, I am truly sorry that I did not return when I received your last letter. I knew that I should finish my mission first, and I felt very close to finishing it. Of course, little did I know at the time that I would fall upon the 'land of Naru' by accident? I had already given up by then. I knew I had shamed you, and I knew that the elders were full of something that did not exist until I met Zac's wife.

"She took me in like a son, though she was sure that the legends would die off, because they were unable to continue without her husband and the rest of the tribes on the island. She invited me to stay on the island for as long as there was life. Then I got the call from you, and I knew the legends would live on." Josh was proud to be able to discuss these things with his father. It was always kept a secret from him for the same reason it has been kept from Zerasha. She is too young to know, as he was when he left his family long ago.

"Josh, what took you so long? I feared that you had been caught by the soldiers."

Zac knew how the lawmen would be if they found Josh. They had given him up many seasons ago, because they did not need his abilities any longer. They had received a report that the transport Josh had boarded last was shot down and there were no survivors. If they found him now after his plan had gone wrong, they would surely execute him for treason and siding with the rebels. "I must ask you one thing. Please do not go for so long again without at least sending your vision to let me know that you are safe."

Zac treated Josh as one of his own. He had known him since the day he came into this world the first time.

"I am truly sorry, Zac. I was conversing with my father. I have so missed talking to him about my journeys and travels." Josh spoke with respect for the elder. He understood more of what he had learned from the other elders about the legends of the tribes. "Zac, do you know where Zerasha's betrothed is? Did you ever find him, and if so, where do we pick him up?"

"Josh, when the time is right I will tell you of her betrothed. Until then you keep all the good thoughts that you have ever had for my daughter in your head." Zac had grown tired and wished to rest.

Josh would keep an eye and mind out for any intruders to the twelfth floor. He passed the time talking with his father. The only missing part of the legends now was who the betrothed was to be heir to the tribal throne when Zac and his wife were gone.

"Father, do you know who Zerasha's betrothed is? I'm not sure that I want to know. I have deep desires for that woman and I do not wish to have to give her up to a man that I, nor she knows anything about." Josh could feel the concern in his voice. His father could hear the deep set desires for his lover.

"Josh, I never thought that I would ever have to say these words to you again, but you will understand and know when you are..."

"Older!" Josh interrupted his father. They both laughed, for Josh had not heard these words for many, many seasons. "Father, that is the only part of the legends that not even the elders are aware of. And, if they are aware, they are keeping it a great secret." Josh had become disgusted with the whole conversation. He was tired of not knowing. It was something that would make his and Zerasha's lives complete and the elders seemed to think that it need not be known.

"Have you reached the vision of the lost elder yet, Josh?" His father was curious to know where the elder was. He was also anxious to turn the conversation to a different topic. A topic that didn't require half-truths; Naihu had not ever liked them and his father was as good at them as he was to his own son.

"No, father, but I feel the same presence almost constantly, like he is keeping a watch over me, and all of you." Josh wondered why it was so important to contact this elder. He had already said that he would see him again. Maybe he held a key to the legendary tribes. Josh would know soon enough.

"Father, we will be leaving here day after tomorrow. Zac is almost fully recovered now, and he told me that if he had to eat any more jerky and rolls he would surely be sick. The plan is to move you and the family to the fourteenth floor where we will meet Zac. It must be done after the last meal and all the soldiers have gone to the main floor for their own meals. I should not talk to you again before I see you. There will not be much time. It will take half of the cool hours just to get to the door to the outside. Then it will take the other half to get far enough away that we are not found.

"I have mapped out a trail with several hiding places on it. We should be back to the transport on the ridge in a little over two days, then on to the most beautiful place you have ever seen," Josh finished telling his father the plan. Then he woke Zac.

He would have to get him to the fourteenth floor before the soldiers did their final check and feeding of the prisoners. Josh wanted to be on the fifth floor waiting for them to leave when they had finished and headed up for the cool hours.

"Zac, it is time to go now. How do you feel?" Josh was concerned for the elder. He had become so frail since they had seen each other last, but his strength had returned tenfold since Josh's arrival with food and hope.

"I am fine, boy. Let us start this journey. I am ready to end it already." Zac gathered what he needed and left the rest. Some soul would find it, if not in this generation then the next.

They both headed down the hallway toward the familiar steps and door in the floor. Zac could not believe that he was going still deeper into the underside of this house that had kept him prisoner for so many seasons. He had been captured with Josh's father, just after they had arrived at the transport site that would have taken them to a safer place, away from the Law.

"Wait here for me. I will send you a vision when I have found my father and the rest of my family. I hope to be able to get there just before they serve the hot plates. I will be able to get in, get everyone out and be long gone before they even suspect anyone is gone." Josh turned from Zac and headed for the passage that would take him to see his father and his family again.

CHAPTER TEN

Zerasha was very lonely. She waited for her Josh to return. She was grateful that the storekeeper came to check on her occasionally. It was nearly a week since she had said goodbye to her lover. She would never be able to be with him again, for surely he would find her father, and then she would be with a man that she knew nothing about. She only hoped that her new man would allow her Josh's company from time to time.

She spent most of her time sitting in the window in the sleep room. She had no desire to do anything without her Josh. She had not been without him since the first day they met. She spent the time making fabric with string. It was something that her mother had taught her, and she had never forgotten the importance of it. Someday she would have a husband and children who would appreciate the beauty of the old ways.

In her daydreams she always found herself back on the homeland. Sometimes she wondered if it was wise to follow Josh to this new land. He had come here to start a new life with her, and now he was gone, for he had found a part of his past that he so desired, his family.

Zerasha could never understand the pain he had endured without the knowledge that his family was well and happy. She had always had a family and though her father had been gone for much of her growing up seasons, she did not ever have to do without all of her brothers and sisters or her mother. They had always been there for her whenever she needed them, except now.

Her heart desired to go back to the homeland, where she could be with her mother and the comfort of the stories from the elders. She had even started to miss the younger children. When these feelings came, she turned her attention to the love of her life, Josh. Where could he be?

She had not even dreamed of him since he left. She only dreamed of the boat returning her father and the man that she would marry. The image of her father was clear but the man he was with was silhouetted behind him. She knew this was the way of the elders, but she still desired this knowledge.

The only thing that took her away from the window was the horse Josh had left for her to take care of. She had learned to ride it well, even when it ran. She dressed for the day and went out for her usual ride. She never ventured far from the house. She kept it in sight. She did not want to run into any soldiers on their routes.

Today was a nice day for a good long ride and time to clear her head. She had so much time to think.

As she rode over the ridge she caught a glimpse of a soldier, and before she could turn around and get out of his line of sight, he had raised his hand in greeting. She did not dare just leave, for he would think that she was a vagrant. She waved greeting back to him and finished her ride. She hoped that he would not follow her. He did not.

"Ran, my boy, what are you doing here? Josh will be here any minute to get us." Naihu was truly surprised that the soldier serving hot plates today was Ran. So excited, in fact, he forgot to check to see if anyone else was around. It was only the second meal of the day, which was usually when the guards changed their shifts.

"Be quiet, old man. I come only to feed you. You are certainly losing your head. Now you call me by the name of another soldier, and you talk of a man that is dead." Ran used his soldier tone well. Naihu understood completely that he was not alone. "Can you believe this old man? He has been down here in the dark for so long; he is seeing things that are not even there. When do you suppose they will send him to the lower floors? At least then we won't have to waste our time bringing food to him." Ran spoke to the other soldier like they had been friends for many seasons.

"I don't know. I thought I saw his name on the list. He is Nanhu, correct?" The other soldier asked Ran.

"No, Nanhu is the elder that is on the other wing. He is just as much a pain as this one is but he never says a word. It is almost like he has no tongue to talk with." Ran laughed. The other soldier took half of the trays and headed down the second hallway. It was faster this way and they could get out quick. None of the soldiers liked being in the dungeons; they were dark, damp, and eerie.

"I am on 'hot plate duty' today until tomorrow after the sun starts to go high." Whispering, Ran turned to the elder Naihu and explained to him. "It will give you and

Josh and Zac plenty of time to be back to the transport and just about on your way. I will report that all is well tomorrow and the next soldier will report you missing. The Law will assume that you left after the morning plates were delivered and they will spend the day looking through the rooms and floors of the house. This will give you all almost an extra day to be gone from this world. I will take Zerasha prisoner and meet all of you on Jemini." He spoke quickly and set the plate down, then left the room.

He rushed through the rest of the prisoners. He wanted to give a thumb up to Josh, and if he knew his friend he would not have any trouble knowing it was him.

It's Ran. Josh could hardly hold his excitement. He had been watching the soldiers since the shift change. He wanted to see what their route was so he would know when it was safe to get his father and family. He concentrated on his friend. It took no effort at all to reach him.

"Ran, you sly one, your pal is slow, or you're up to something I need to know about," Josh teased the soldier.

"I am on duty until tomorrow morning, I will give a good report and the next shift will report your family missing but not until they serve the mid-day meal. It should give you enough time..." he cut his sentence short. The other soldier was coming around the corner from his second to last hallway.

Josh watched the two soldiers for a few more minutes then he prepared to go for his father. Ran had given him the exact directions with a point of his finger behind his back. They would have plenty of time to get back to the transport. Josh had found a shortcut from the eighth floor to the fourth, and it had gotten him higher than he had planned so he would have had to wait until the soldiers had finished with the three floors below him or get in and get out before they got back. Now he could surely get in and get out without being detected.

He was truly astonished at his friend. This was indeed a nice change to the plan. He must not have had any trouble with the rock. He watched the soldiers head to the sixth floor.

Josh gathered his supplies and headed to the pointed out hallway. In seconds he knew which door his father was behind. Ran had left the outer door ajar.

Naihu jumped to his feet and prepared to slug the intruder good and hard. He knew that there should not be anyone else in the hallway. He had become so excited with Ran's news that he did not take the time to use his abilities. Now was the time to get out of there. He swung at the shadow on the floor coming through the inner door, only to find himself in a back arm hold with a large hand covering his mouth.

"Be quiet, old man. There will be a time for talk later. Where are the others?" Josh spoke in a faint whisper right into his father's ear. He had a very serious tone. He did not know that Ran had warned his father. It was hard to not jump and shout for joy, but both men knew the dangers if the other soldier were to hear or see them.

"They are in the next room. I am sure that Ran has told them. He was our server today." The elder spoke with great anxiety and happiness. He had not touched his son for so many seasons, and so much had happened since their last encounter. His mother had not seen him since shortly after he had left on his travels. She would certainly not be easy to contain. He was her firstborn and would always be her baby.

"We must be quiet. I have found a shortcut to the eighth floor, and we must get there while Ran is between here and there. They serve to the eighth floor. It is important that the children know this. It will be hard to contain their excitement." Josh was still whispering and holding his father.

His father nodded his head in approval and agreement and they went out to the outer room. The two rooms were adjoined to the outer room. Josh grabbed the handle and prepared again to duck the hostile hands of the prisoners behind the door. He pushed the door slowly and waited for the first swing. He quieted his brother with a finger, before his hand had come to the highest position.

Jhemel's eyes grew very large. He reached through the doorway and wrapped his arms, quietly around his big brother's neck. By this time the others had come to the opening of the door and received the same finger to the lips of their brother and son.

"We must go. We will have time later to exchange our kisses and hugs. Father, you go first, that way we can use the 'communicator' if there is trouble. I will follow behind, and make sure there is no trouble." Josh was still whispering. He could not risk being caught now.

Naihu headed down the hallway against the wall with his wife and all of his children behind him. He stopped at every corner to make sure there was no trouble. He slipped into the secret corridor and stopped to make sure the rest of them made it through. Josh pulled the sliding panel back into its place and motioned for the rest of them to go on ahead.

"Father, when you reach the end of the hallway, there is a wide spot that we can all fit into until I know the soldiers are headed back up to the upper levels." Josh spoke to his father with the communicator abilities of his mind. He was unaware that his brother Jhemel was able to hear the conversation as well.

Josh had not seen any of his sisters or brothers since he left his family for the Journeys of the Naihu-Shahi-Nehra legends. He did not know what abilities any of them might have or not. His mother was frail, but she had not aged much. She would soon be out of the darkness of the underworld and the sun would bring her back to life. Josh barely recognized his sisters. They had both grown to be very beautiful women. To whom were they betrothed? Was it already determined? He did not remember what the legendary stories said, if they had said anything. He could barely hold the excitement and turmoil inside of him. He felt like he was rescuing strangers for the good of the cause.

Josh could see the end of the corridor. He concentrated on Ran. He needed to see where the soldiers were on their route. They would not leave the corridor until it was truly safe.

Ran could feel the presence of his friend. However, this time he could feel another presence as well. He turned to check a hallway, and then headed for the entrance to the seventh level. He made sure that he slowed his steps. He did not want the other soldier to know anything was up.

"You go on ahead. I will double check the doors in the last hallway and meet you on seven." Ran told the other soldier who was his junior in rank. "I won't be more than half a minute." Ran waved the soldier up the stairs.

"Ran, I will keep my presence with you until you reach the sixth floor and then we will be gone from this floor and shortly after, from this place," Josh pushed the message to Ran, and then pulled the image back. Ran finished his so-called check of the last hallway and headed up the stairs to the seventh level. He could feel the excitement growing in the pit of his stomach. His friend and family were headed to a better place, and he would soon follow.

Josh could see that Ran was on the sixth floor, so he motioned for his family to go through the door of the eighth floor and head to the ninth floor as quickly and quietly as possible. Once they were on the tenth or eleventh floor they could stop being so quiet and take a chance to talk a little.

Josh's mother kept looking behind to see that her son was still with them. She did not want to lose her boy again. They stopped on the eleventh floor long enough to get instructions from Josh and move on. They were almost to the place that would provide the freedom that his family so deserved. He wondered when the last time was that they had seen the sun.

"Josh, I feel a presence, though I don't think it is a bad one," Naihu said to his son as they approached the fourteenth floor.

"Father, it is Zac. He is waiting for us at the entrance to your freedom!" Josh told his father. They did not need their abilities now. They could talk freely. "Head down the far corridor."

Zac jumped to his feet and grabbed the longtime friend from whom he had been separated from for so many weeks. "I am so glad that you are safe, my friend. How did your journey go?" He let go of his friend to greet the rest of the family.

"I am fine, but you... you look like you have not eaten anything for months." Naihu was happy to see his friend. They had been through a lot in the past seasons since he had sent Josh away. He was relieved to see that it was all coming to an end. He hoped.

They all sat around for the right time to go to the outside world, a place none of them had seen for many seasons. The children sat and asked Josh question after question and waited for each reply. They wanted to know everything that he had done in all the seasons he had been gone. The most important question they saved for the last.

"Did you find the 'land of Naru'?" Jhemel whispered to him, as he leaned closer to his older brother. He sat right there waiting for Josh's reply.

"We must get going. It will soon be the time that we must cross the barren land above us, and we must all have our wits together. Father, the time has come for us to go. I have contacted Keiler and he says the transport is ready. He wanted to know if the lady should join us." He looked to Zac for his approval. He wanted to see her one more time before he would not be able to hold her again.

"Ran will have gathered the rest of the elders from the other worlds and will take Zerasha with him. He says that he will meet us on Jemini. It is time the tribes are all in the right place." Zac seemed as young as he had been when he first met Josh.

"Well, then we should get this on a move." Josh led the way down the tunnel of earth and Zac brought up the rear this time. Josh was disappointed in Zac's answer. He was unaware of Ran's addition to the plan.

As they neared the end of the tunnel, Josh was getting a bad feeling. He wondered if his father felt it. He knew that he did. Josh stopped in his tracks and motioned for everyone to sit on the floor and not make a sound. His father had made his way closer to Josh.

"Did Ran tell you about patrols in this area?" Naihu sent the question without saying a word.

"No, but I will try to find him and see what in this world is going on." Josh closed his eyes and pictured his friend in his Law materials. He could see him, but he was around several of the other soldiers. Josh concentrated harder to make him feel the presence. After a few minutes the group broke up and went their separate ways.

"Ran, what do you know about patrols on the exit here?" Josh was scared now. There was no way that he would allow the Law to capture any of them again.

"I do not know, my friend. Let me go find out. If they go away, get out fast!" Ran turned and went inside the large house.

He checked the duty board. There was a group of soldiers out for the day. That must be who was out there. They should not be off the grounds of the compound, though. Ran had an idea. He would have to join the rest of them, and the plan would have to be expedited immediately.

He radioed the soldiers and wondered if one of them had a girl on the lower levels that he was romancing. It was something that the soldiers did with the prisoners. Some of the young girls needed the companionship and the soldiers were more than happy to oblige them. He got lucky. They all decided to come back. He would leave a message and be gone before they got there.

Ran arrived at the location of his transport and waited to get word from Josh. It seemed like forever since he had called the soldiers back, but it had only been a few minutes. Ran was due to be off duty for the night anyway. He had gotten the elders assembled so that they could take off as soon as he arrived at the transport site on Jemini. He would deliver the morning meal and take Zerasha from her home, then head straight for the small world that would reunite the woman and her father.

"Ran, what's going on?" Josh demanded of his friend.

"Coast is clear, go!" Ran did not have to say anything more.

Josh gathered his family and Zac. They left the underground prison through a small opening in the ground. They walked low to the ground. It was too barren of a land to just get up and run. As they rounded the top of a large hill, Josh stopped and waited for everyone. He knew that they would all be warm enough. There had not been any truly cool hours on this world since before the big storm that left the land the way it was.

He motioned them a little further, and then reached into the ground and pulled out a bundle of hides and some jerky and rolls. He was overjoyed to find the exit so close to where he had left his supplies.

"Josh, you have learned well, son. It looks like you have enough for us to..."

"Survive." Josh finished for his mother. "Yes, I have been taught by some of the best." He glanced at each of the elders that stood in front of him. "It will be another day before we can get to the transport if we stop and rest often." Josh put an arm over his mother's shoulder and waited to see what the elders of the group wished to do.

"We will take short breaks, my son. But I do think that we should keep moving. Is that good with you, love?" Naihu looked to his wife for her approval. He did not want to wear her down. She would get plenty of rest on the transport though.

"We will help you, Mother, if it gets too much for you." Jhemel looked with sympathetic eyes to his mother. The children had been ready for this day for a long time. Jhemel could remember the day his father had found Josh and was able to tell him to come home. Naihu had told him then that the elders had helped him with the vision.

"I will be fine. Just give me a few minutes every once in a while," she told her family, and put her arms around Josh and hugged him for the first time in many seasons. Tears threatened to roll down her face.

They all rested for a few more minutes, and then they were moving again. It would take them until the sun started to go low in the sky again, before they reached the transport. Josh could not wait to see Zerasha. He spent a great deal of his time watching her. His father had caught him dreaming of her on several occasions already. Zac still had not told him who her betrothed was. It was like he wanted to keep it a secret.

"Father, why does Zac hold the information of Zerasha's betrothed? I have become as curious as she has. She waits for us, you know. I can see her, sitting in the window in the sleep room." Josh walked beside his father.

"Josh, I do not like to tell you this, but you will have to wait. Zac will tell us when he thinks the time is right." His father had put an arm around his shoulder as they walked. "Son, it is very good to see you. You have grown many seasons wiser, and you have learned the legends from the elders. You were our only link to that dimension and I knew it the day you were born.

"I could not tell you the day that you set off on your journeys, because you needed to develop your abilities. I taught you the one that you needed to get there. You have learned the rest well, either on your own, or from Zac and the elders. I am very proud of you. Please, you must remember, when the time is right, all will know." His father looked at his son as he finished his conversation with him.

"I will go and walk with your mother. The children do not know that you found the 'land of Naru.' Why don't you see if they will bring it up to you again?" Naihu walked away from his eldest son.

"Josh, is she as beautiful as you look like she is?" Jhemel had been watching his brother. He was many seasons his junior, but he was very wise.

"Who?" Josh teased his brother.

"Who! Don't play games with me, brother. I am wiser than you think I am. I have been watching you since you came into the dungeon and rescued us. I see it in your eyes." Jhemel had missed his brother most. He could remember the day their father received notice of the transport being shot down. It had taken a toll on him. He lost transmission with him, and feared that he did not survive until an elder came to him in his mind and showed him Josh's image. His father had changed overnight. So had his mother. He should have known then that Josh was still alive.

"Jhemel, how did you get so wise?" It was a question that need not be answered. "Yes, she is beautiful, more beautiful than you will ever know. She is kind like

Mother, smart like Father, and playful like all you kids are." Josh ruffled the hair on his brother's head.

"Where did you find her? Did she live on Shurfate? Has she traveled with you? Will she really be at the transport when we get there?" Jhemel stopped. He did not understand why his brother was laughing hysterically at him. "What in this entire world is so funny?"

Josh could see the anger start to build in his brother's eyes. "You are not unlike Father at all. I remember when Zac laughed at me for doing the same thing. Question after question after question without even giving him a chance to answer any of them.

"I found her in one of the most beautiful places. She was with her family and she was beautiful. I decided that I had to meet her, so I went to her one night when she was alone and found out who she was. Brother, she did things to me that I still cannot explain today. Her beauty danced in my head every night and day. The only time she traveled with me was when we came here after Father's vision was seen.

"No, Shurfate is not the world I found her on, and no, her father has requested that she meet us at the transport on Jemini. There, are you satisfied now?" Josh spit out the answers to his brother's questions like he had rehearsed them.

"No, I am not! I, we, want to know if you found the land of Naru." Jhemel pointed to the other children. Josh began to laugh and looked to his father. He had been listening to the conversation as he walked with his wife next to the two boys.

"Jhemel, do not bother your brother so much. He has a great deal on his mind right now," Naihu chuckled.

He knew it would be good for Josh to tell the stories of the legends to his brothers and sisters.

"Father, the only thing on Josh's mind right now is a woman." Jhemel said it with as much respect as he could. He did not tease with his father like Josh did.

"And a fine woman she is, boy. Do not ever forget that," Zac interrupted the family conversation. "We should rest Josh. I am tiring a little, and I would like to hear of your journeys, also, more on the lines of my wife and qu..." He stopped. He did not want the children to know who he really was, yet.

"Okay, everyone gather around. We will rest for a short period." Josh sat on one of the hides and leaned against a large piece of the black rock. "Zac, your wife is one of the most wonderful people I met. She was truly a gift when she offered to guide me. She and I talked as much as Zerasha and I did. She is afraid that you will never return to her, because of the difficulty of getting back. I am proud to be able to be the one to return you to her. She knows of your Sharhi, and the children. She understands perfectly as she knows that you would understand also."

Josh stopped. He could not help what he was feeling. Zac had taught him so many things before he left the homeland. He would never be able to repay this man for all he had done.

"Who is Zerasha?" Chanti, the older of the girls, asked. "And, how do you know Zac's wife?"

"Zerasha is Zac's eldest daughter. You will all meet her at the transport site on Jemini. I know his wife, his love, and all the rest of his children. I came upon their house when I left on my journeys, but it was many seasons later that I found his wife." Josh had begun to daydream again.

"You still have not told us if you have found the land that you were looking for when you left," Jhemel interrupted his thought.

"Father?" Josh looked to Naihu for permission to tell the children of the real homeland. He continued after receiving the okay. "I traveled many worlds. I stayed on Shurfate for a long time. When I returned here to get you so many seasons ago, all of you were gone. I was so broken hearted that I would never see my family again. I boarded a transport on the other side of this world and headed out again. I knew that I must find the world the legends speak about or die trying.

I woke up one day in a small boat on a world with a lot of water on it. I had decided at that time that my family was lost forever, and it was best to forget all that I had known. I made friends with the villagers and stayed in a hut that I had purchased from them. They taught me their ways and their tongue, and there I stayed."

"So, you did not find the land of Naru." Jhemel sounded disappointed.

Josh glanced at his brother and continued, "The water was naturally as hot as a pot on the cooking stove for washing. The ground was sand. You could run it through your fingers. The water held many types of animals for eating. The trees all bore fruit and nuts. The sun would go away at night and return in the morning, but the air did not grow colder. It was a place that I intended to stay in for the rest of my days, until I got the vision from Father.

"I knew then it was a place that I could not keep to myself. I had learned that the legends were formed on this land, and I must return to my own homeland to find my family and return with them to the 'island paradise.' Yes, Jhemel, the land of Naru." He stopped. He could see the excitement in the children's eyes. They waited to hear more. Somehow the familiarity of the story Josh was telling sounded much like the story their father had told them all as young children.

"We must move on now. You will all see the land of Naru, but not if we sit here all day and talk about it." He got up from his seat on the ground and folded the hide. The rest followed suit, disappointed that Josh had not finished the story to their liking even though it was pretty much the same story that they had heard as they grew up.

"Josh, do you think you can find it again?" Chanti had caught up with him.

"I am sure that I can find it. I will be able to use the elders. With Father and Zac we will have no trouble at all. Why do you worry so?" He could see the shame in his sister's eyes.

"My betrothed is on the land of Naru. Father told me some weeks ago. He was so ashamed that he would not be able to introduce him to me. He told me it was a time that I should find a love that would care for me as my betrothed would. It was before he found you. Do you think that my betrothed will still be on the, what did you call it?" She waited for his reply.

"Island paradise. And I do not know who he is, so I do not know if he is there or not. Do not be ashamed of having a lover. Zerasha has a betrothed also, and I have been her lover for many seasons." He put an arm around her shoulders and hugged her.

Josh walked alone for a while. He wanted to contact Keiler and see if Ran had gotten out okay. He concentrated on the storekeeper and soon had him in sight. There were soldiers in the store, but he could see that they were just picking up normal, routine supplies. Josh waited until they were gone.

"Keiler, is the transport ready? We will be there shortly." Josh watched Keiler nod his head. He did not need to speak.

Josh picked up his pace a little. He could not wait to see his Zerasha again. It pained him to know that he would have to wait until they arrived on Jemini. He had never been away from her since the day that he met her. He knew there were things she would want to know of him, but every time he envisioned her she was dreaming of another man, her betrothed. Neither Josh nor Zerasha could see him clearly, however. It was like a faded vision, a silhouette of a man with no details.

Josh could not help but believe that this separation from each other would do them both good. He would concentrate on the mission and she would concentrate on her betrothed.

"Hello Zac. Are you tiring again? We can stop one more time if you like." Zac had caught up with Josh, but it was not to tell him he wanted to stop again.

"Hello, Josh. I thought we could talk, just the two of us. I have known of Zerasha's betrothed for many seasons now, almost since I came to this world. He is a very good man. You need not worry about him. I am positive that he will keep my daughter happy. I cannot tell you who he is until I introduce him properly to my daughter. It is the way of the legends and the elders. You know that, right?" Zac could see the torment that Josh was going through. He had spent many seasons with his daughter and they had come to know each other well.

"I know, Zac, but I cannot get her off my mind. It is like the time I first saw her on the island. She mesmerized my mind and body, and now she is doing it again. Only, now I can't go to her and watch her. I used to watch her day and night before I found her on the sand crying, because you had been gone for so long. I made one of the other villagers find out about her, who she was, why I had not seen her in the days before I discovered her.

"We talked about everything, except my past. She is well taught by the elders and her mother. I only hope that her betrothed will allow us time together. I think that is my only fear right now." Josh could see the spot where the transport was hidden. It would be only a matter of minutes before they would all be there.

"Josh, are we almost there? The sun has started to go low in the sky and you said that it would not take us more than a day to get there." Chanti had begun to tire like the rest of them.

"It is just over the next ridge, sis. I am tiring also. How is Mother doing? Will she need to rest again before we get there?" Josh was concerned with the frailty of his mother. She had been in that dungeon room for so long that she had become weak. She gave most of her food to the children when it was brought in. She knew they would need it to keep up their strength, not thinking of herself.

"I will be fine, Son, but you will have to slow your pace a bit. I am older now and I do not have the energy that you children seem to have found." His mother had been walking behind them.

"I am sorry, Mother. I needed to go through the plan in my head without interruptions from the other children," Josh apologized to his mother.

"You have also been thinking of a very special person. I can see it in your face. She will be all right, Son. She is a very strong woman, and she has endured many things in her life." Josh always thought of his mother as a very wise woman. "Did you get a chance to meet Ran's father when you were on Shurfate? He was devastated when he returned to this world to find all but his son gone." She remembered the day like it had just happened.

"I did. He had become much stronger after a while. At first he sat in the window and said very little or nothing at all. He is gone now, you know. Ran believes from age, but I am sure that it was from a broken heart. He never found a lover to spend the rest of his days with. I think that if he had, he would still be with us today." Josh remembered the time he had found Ran just before he quit soldiering.

The children ran toward the transport. They were excited that they would be able to go to the land of Naru. Josh saw Jhemel come to a dead stop. He had never seen a transport up close, not one this small. He wondered what it would have been like to soldier, though as he grew older he learned that the Law was bad and he despised the idea that his brother worked with them for so long.

CHAPTER ELEVEN

They boarded the small transport. Josh made sure everyone was seated and ready to leave. Naihu and Zac sat in the front to help guide Josh to the other world. They would stop briefly on Jemini and meet up with Ran and Keiler.

When they arrived on Jemini, Josh could feel his lover's presence. She waited anxiously to see her father. He could not feel any of her deepest thoughts, though. It was as if the only thing she desired was to see and touch her father.

"Father, I have missed you so." Zerasha ran to her father and wrapped her arms around his neck. She did not even wait for the rest of them to get off the transport.

"My sweetheart, I see that you have done well taking care of yourself. You are even more beautiful than Josh explained." Zac had tears in his eyes. He had left his daughter when she was just old enough to walk. He held her in his arms for a long time.

"Father, which of them is my betrothed?" Zerasha whispered in her father's ear before she loosened her hold around his neck.

"You will know soon enough, my child." Zac saw the excitement in her eyes.

Josh did not interrupt them. Maybe Zerasha had changed in the last month and found that she did not desire Josh as much as she had thought. He would be able to live with that. He would wait until she came to him, even though he was sure that she would not with her father there now.

He had forgotten what she did to him. His desires had returned stronger than ever. He wanted to take her behind the ridge and make passionate love to her like he had never done before. That would not happen again though, he was sure. He finished checking the transport and went to join the rest of the group.

"Has everyone been introduced?" Josh looked to his father.

"No! We all know each other. You and Zac and Keiler seem to be the only ones who know this beautiful outsider that has joined us." Naihu was teasing them for being rude.

"I am sorry, Father. Zac, would you like to do the honors, or should I?" Josh looked to Zac, without making eye contact with Zerasha.

"You might as well take them, Josh. You probably know her as well as I do, and besides it is the right time to let her in on some of the secrets of your past." Zac sat on a hide and waited.

Zerasha did not move from her father's side and Josh did not come closer to her. She did not understand why Josh had become so distant. It was like he had given up being her friend because the time to meet her betrothed was near. She hung her head in shame, for she did not know what else to do. She had so hoped that Josh would have been the first to the transport. She tried hard to keep her desires hidden inside. She too wanted to go behind the ridge and make love to the one and only man in her life.

"Everyone, this is Zerasha. She is of the tribe Shahi-Nehru. She is my lover and has been for many seasons." He winked at her, as if he had read her thoughts. He had! "Zerasha, my love and friend, this is..." Josh hesitated. He did not know exactly how to tell her about his family that she knew nothing of, much less about.

He bent on one knee and begged her forgiveness before he continued. "My love, I am so sorry that I have kept this from you. Please forgive me for what I am about to tell you. As you know, this is my father, Naihu. This is my mother, Chandelle, my sisters Chanti and Khami, my brothers Jhemel and the twins, Jhordahn and Hamel." He finished and hung his head in shame. He had kept his family from her, because he had put all of them out of his mind. "Will you forgive me?" Josh did not look her in the eyes. He was ashamed that he had kept the most important part of a man's life from the woman he loved and desired.

"My love," she knelt before him, "I have already forgiven you. I knew that you had secrets. I told you that when you feel the time is right you will tell those secrets to me. I know that you remember the promise we made to each other so many seasons ago. I have not forgotten." She held Josh's hands in hers. He could see the passion in her eyes. She did not care if the people around her could hear or not.

"Josh, I will always have a place for you in my heart. I have truly missed you in the last days. You should never feel shame about the things that you have not told me. I would wait all of my days, if necessary, to hear them from you, whenever you feel the time is right." She bent forward and kissed him on the cheek. She did not dare give him the kiss that would awaken the desires deep inside of her.

She finally rose and shook all of the children's hands. She told each of them how honored she was to meet such fine children. She then reached for Naihu's hand. "Naihu, I am so honored to meet you and your beautiful wife."

She did not shake the hand of the King of the legends. Instead she bowed to him and kissed the back of his hand. "My mother has spoken many times of you. The elders have taught the stories to the children and done as your father's father had told them before he left the island." She rose from her bowed position and repeated the gesture to Chandelle.

"Josh, why does she bow to them?" Jhemel had whispered to his brother.

"When you are older, you will understand." Josh repeated the very words of his father.

"You know, I hate when father tells me that. It seems to be his answer to all the questions we have ever asked." Jhemel was disgusted.

"I know. I hated it as well. How do you think I felt when he sent me on my journeys and told me, 'as you get older, my son, you will understand.' I knew that you would appreciate that type of answer."

Josh finished loading the supplies on the larger transport that he had bought on the island. "You will have to ask that question of father, and hope that he does not give you the same answer," Josh teased his brother. He turned to talk to Zerasha while the others got aboard.

"Zerasha, I did not know that you knew my father to be the king of the tribes. Why didn't you tell me?" Josh could not believe that she had kept something from his past from him.

"The legends forbid it, for one thing, and I did not know that Naihu was your father. Why didn't you tell me?" she teased him.

"I did not know that he was King of the tribes. I thought that you were the princess in this picture." He reached across to her and brushed the back of his hand across her cheek. "Besides, I think that the legends would have forbidden it, if I did know." He glanced into her eyes.

"Have you met my betrothed?" Her eyes showed the excitement that Josh was afraid to see.

"No, Zerasha, I have not. I suppose that he is on the other transport. I am sure that is why your father wishes to ride with you on that one." She could see the disappointment in his eyes.

"You both need not worry about it," Zac interrupted their conversation. "Josh, we will go to the other transport and sit with the others now. Your father should be up here in this transport with you." Zac took his daughter by the hand and led her to a seat with the other children on the other transport.

"Is everyone ready? We can finish all of our catching up while we are on the transports. The sun will soon start to go high again and we will want to be as far away from this world as we can." Naihu had gathered everyone and helped each of them onto the transport. Jhemel was the last one on.

"Father, why did that woman bow to you and kiss your hand? And if you don't mind, please don't tell me 'when I am older I will understand?" Jhemel waited for his father's reply.

"Jhemel, you will know soon enough. Now get on this transport so that we may get a move on."

Naihu had never told any of his children that his grandfather was the King of the Naihu-Shahi-Nehra tribes. Zac was the only one of the tribal names left to take the throne when his grandfather had vanished. The rest of the tribal members had been sent off to defend the lands from the enemies.

He was the last descendant of the Naihu name when he left the island. It was before his father had been born and the elders were unable to see the outcome of the wars.

"Father, the soldiers have discovered that you are missing. We must go! They are headed to Zac's dungeon now. It will take them the same amount of time to find that he is gone also, as it will for us to take off." Josh used the same business tone with his father that he had used in other business situations. "Will you join me up front? I will need your help when we get near the other side of Shurfate. We will not be safe until we are out of this dimension."

"Yes, my son, but there are things that the children need to know. I hope that you have had enough time with Zerasha. There are things that she needs to know, also. And the time has come for you to tell her if you have not told her already." Naihu took a seat with the others and prepared for the takeoff.

"Father, we have shared the secrets that we need to for now. She will ride with her father on the other

237

transport, I assume so that she can get to know who the man is she will be with for the rest of her days." Josh knew his father could hear the disappointment and heartache in his voice, but he did not care.

He prepared the transport for takeoff. His father came to sit next to him after he had told the children what they needed to know. They would surely die from excitement when they reached the Island Paradise in the other dimension.

They had not been in the air long, when they received a transmission on the communicator. "Naihu, you will not get away with this. We will find you and we will destroy your legends and tribes. I will have the worlds for my own." It was Har's voice. He had been trying to find the island paradise, so that he could drain all of that dimension's worlds of their precious trees and people.

When they reached Shurfate, Josh made everyone stay on board the transport. He would not risk having to spend time gathering them. Ran had arrived there only a few minutes ahead of them. He had made everyone stay on his transport as well.

Josh wondered if the man Zerasha was betrothed to, was indeed on Ran's transport. Zac and Zerasha chose to ride with Ran instead of Josh. He would need all he had in his mind to concentrate on the pathway to the other dimension.

"Ran, have you picked up all of your passengers? If so, as soon as I fuel up we need to leave. The soldiers have discovered that we are gone. Har has informed my father, by communicator, that he will not get away with this. They are aware that we are traveling by transport. I think we should change the identifiers on the transports while we are here. It will give us a better chance." Josh had been running the plans through his head since he'd heard the message.

"That is not a bad idea. I will get some new identifiers from the building. With the help of your brother Jhemel we will have them changed in no time at all." Ran headed to the building and returned with the new identifiers.

"Jhemel, will you please come out here? The rest of you, we will be leaving soon, so just stay put." He closed the door behind Jhemel.

Josh told his brother that the identifiers would need to be pulled from the electronic panels under each of the crafts. They were flat green boards that, with a slight tug, would come right out. This would identify them as a Law craft, until they were out of the dimension. Josh just hoped that Ran would have a plan to get permission to land with fake identifiers.

By the time Josh had finished fueling the two crafts of freedom, the other two had given the transports new identifiers. It would be very hard for Har to find them now. And he would never find them once they had gone into the other dimension.

Josh was preparing the switches for takeoff, when Ran signaled he was ready to get out of this dimension.

"Ready, over." Ran had put the speakers over his ears and gave the signal to Josh.

"Ready." Josh answered him back with a smile out the glass front. Josh lifted the transport straight up until it had enough clearance to jet forward in the direction of the new dimension. He would not have to go all the way around Shurfate. The dimension path was close to

Shurfate, but they would be able to see it before they were all the way around to the other side of that world.

CHAPTER TWELVE

"Josh, are we getting close? I feel that we are, but I am not sure." Naihu had joined his son in the cockpit of the small craft that would shortly spin them through an invisible hole in the darkness that surrounded them.

"We are, Father. I will start looking for the vision of the elders and then put it into your head. That way we will see the path together. There is no world blocking the path from this side, but there is a moon that we will have to veer around when we get to the other dimension." Josh could feel the excitement in his father.

Josh saw the vision of the elders and of Zac's wife. They all waited on the sand where Josh had first met Zerasha. He gave the vision to his father, and they scanned the sky together.

"I can see them. Josh, veer to your right. Can you see the path?" Naihu did not contain his excitement. He had never been to the paradise, and yet, he could see the vision clearly as if he had seen the place many times.

"Ran, over." Josh waited for his friend's reply.

"This is Ran, what's up, my friend?"

"We will be going to the other dimension in a few minutes. When we get to the other side, veer to your right immediately or you will crash land into the moon." Josh did not hold his excitement either. "Are you ready, Father. You have a great responsibility awaiting you."

"My son, I have been ready for that responsibility for many seasons. I am more ready than you are. I am so proud of you for continuing your search and mission. I was afraid to send my last letter to you. I feared that you would give up your mission and come to me right away. I needed you then, but I also needed you to finish your mission, so that the stories of the legendary tribes would live on. Let's go." Naihu braced himself in the seat beside Josh and prepared to go through the dimensional path.

The small craft shook violently and started to spin. The dimensional path was full of light spots and streaks. Josh controlled the craft well. He kept the spin to a minimum by adjusting the lever used to make the craft go in the direction that its driver wanted it to.

"Wheweee. That was a close one." Josh had made it through and could see the island in the water, though it was a great distance away.

Jhemel had joined the two men in the front of the craft. He could not believe what his abilities could see from this distance in the air.

"Josh, why didn't you tell me it was so beautiful." Ran's voice came over the communicator, interrupting the three men that had been mesmerized by the site as well.

"I am sorry, my friend. It is beautiful, isn't it? Can you believe that I spent all that time in this wonderful place?" Josh was so happy that he found the path once again. It was all because of his ability. He would be able to go between the distances as often as he wanted to. He was sure that his brother Jhemel would be able to join him.

"Where are the transport sites?" Ran could see that the tiny island did not have much room on it, much less enough room to land two transports.

"They are on the mainland. Follow me." Josh turned the smaller craft just enough to line himself up with the mainland. "This is JR2579, requesting permission to land with the King Naihu and the tribal elders." Josh waited for them to grant him permission to land. He knew that the people of the transport tower were expecting them, and not many people flew transports anymore. He had given out the original identifier of the transport and suggested Ran do the same.

"JR2579, permission granted, my friend." The voice came over the communicator.

"Malrui, is that you?" Josh could hardly believe his ears. "How are you, my friend? I have very important cargo to deliver to the island." Josh was as excited to see his friend as the people of the island were going to be when they were able to see the tribes together again.

"Yes, it is Malrui, and I know of both of your cargoes. The Queen is with me." Malrui was talking of Zac's wife. "Please land so that she will stop bothering me," he teased. "Ran, circle around one time, then you may land also." Malrui was relative to Ran, though they had never met.

Josh landed the transport and prepared everyone inside to unload. He allowed the children to go first. Zac was not sure he was ready for his wife to meet Sharhi. There were many plans to make, and at least two weddings to prepare for. Chanti would meet her betrothed and so would Zerasha. Josh was the last one off the transport. He followed Zac and Zerasha, his heart heavy with pain and sorrow.

"My love! Come here old man." The queen of the tribes waited for her husband to come down out of the transport. They hugged and kissed for what seemed like an eternity. "This must be your Sharhi. I am so pleased that you have come with him. I welcome you to our homeland and wish you to stay with us until we can have a suitable place made for you and your children." She greeted the lover as if she had known her all her life. She was not the least worried about her husband's intentions. She knew that she had been told of Zac's wife and that she would only be his companion until he could be returned to his homeland.

"Father, when will I meet him? I don't think that I can wait much longer," Zerasha interrupted the three of them.

"When we are safe on the island once again, I will make all of the announcements. First, though, I must confer with the elders and with Naihu. Can you wait that long?" Zac teased his daughter.

"And if I say that I can't?" she teased back. "The other women of the tribe were aware of the men they would spend their lives with well before they were even grown." Zerasha turned on her heel and walked away from her father, but not very far.

"Too bad, my sweet, you will have to." Zac put his arms around his two women and headed to the boat docks. They would board the boats and be on the island in no time at all. He could not wait to see the island of his homeland again. He thanked the young Malrui for putting all of the supplies aboard and gathered the rest of the lost elders to return to the island.

Josh boarded the other boat. He did not want to be near Zerasha right now. He had to learn to rid himself of the desires he had for her. The time was right for her to learn the ways of the legends and to learn of another man who would care for her. He spent most of the ride looking over the edge of the boat. He could not get her off of his mind, and he did not want his father to see him in such a state. He told him that it would only cloud his visions. Staying away from his family had not worked, though. Jhemel and Naihu joined him. He had been right about his father.

"Josh, you must get her out of your mind in that way. It will only cloud your visions," Naihu was teasing him. He knew of the turmoil that his son was going through.

"I know, Father, but there will never be another like her. Is there a betrothed for me on that island, or is she from one of the other tribes?" Josh could not help feeling the way he felt. He would need someone to keep his mind occupied.

"Josh, you have been betrothed since the day you were born. All of the tribal men are betrothed at their birth. I have not met her, but I am sure the elders of the island know who she is. There are many things that must be planned when we get to the island. There will be a ceremony to change the throne back to its rightful heirs. Then we will have to plan the two weddings and celebrations to follow. Of course, there will have to be the formal introductions first." Naihu was trying to get his son's mind off the beautiful woman that he had spent so much of his life with already. "We are almost there. I can see the people waving on the sand. Come, we will be the first off to greet them." Naihu took both of his sons in his arms, and they walked together to the entrance of the boat.

"Ladies and gentleman, I present to you Zachariah Shahi-Nehru, your King." Naihu made the formal announcement of the return of the King.

"Thank you, my friend Naihu, but I am not the true King of this island. May I have the honors?" Zac waited for the real King to grant him permission.

"You may." Naihu knew that he was the king of the tribes. His name had been taken from the tribal names because the elders did not know there were any Naihu tribesmen left.

"Ladies and gentleman, may I have the honor of presenting the tribal family to you; our King, his Queen, their children and heirs to the throne. King Naihu, Queen Chandelle, Princesses Chanti and Khami, Princes Jhemel, Jhordahn, Hamel, and Josh, our hero, for returning us to the land of the tribal legends."

When Zac had finished with the introductions the tribal people cheered. They came up the ramp of the boat that connected them to the land and carried Josh off to his hut. The rest of them made their selves comfortable until the ceremonies began.

"Josh, may I have a word with you?" Zac had come to his hut alone. He waited outside until he was invited in.

"Sure, Zac. Come in. Do you think that I may be able to stay in this hut? I have become quite accustomed to it. I will return Zerasha's things to her immediately." All of a sudden Josh was very nervous even though he had purchased the hut from the tribal people.

"Josh, you may stay wherever your heart desires, but I would think that you would want to stay with your family in the main hut. That is not why I came to you. I must tell you that the ceremonies will begin soon, and you will need to be there. I will turn the throne over to your family and you are a rightful heir to it. It is so good to have all the tribes assembled in the same place again. I have come to thank you and offer you anything that you would like. You are the only reason that all of us are able to gather on the homeland again. Your wish of anything on the island is mine to grant." Zac waited for the young Josh to reply though he hoped that his only wish would be for his daughter.

"There is only one thing that I wish for, and since I am unable to have it then I will be content to have just this hut for myself." Josh did not request Zac's daughter. He knew it was a request that Zac would not be able to honor.

"Be at the big hut in ten minutes then. The ceremonies will not start without you." Zac rose from the seat he had taken next to Josh. He was disappointed in Josh's answer because it would have made a perfect time to give him the answer to the question he had asked repeatedly for the last few days.

"Zac, will you tell me who her betrothed is before you go?" Josh waited.

"I will see you in ten minutes." Zac opened the cloth door and left the small hut. He did not reveal the secret he had held since he had met Naihu on the SuKhan World.

All of the people of the island had gathered in front of the large hut before Josh arrived. He was not ready for any type of celebration. He was losing the most important person in his life and he did not feel like celebrating. He felt as lonely now as he had when he left his family as a boy.

When he came through the crowd, they all cheered for him. He was truly a hero, even if he didn't want to be. He changed his mood to fit the occasion and continued through the crowd of people shaking hands with some of them and speaking to the ones he knew.

Zerasha was sitting on a bench outside the door of the big hut with her family. She looked at Josh, but he did not return the look. He made it a point to avoid her at all costs. He had been afraid of a broken heart, and now that he had one, he did not want to open the wound any further. He found his brother Jhemel and stood with him. All the rest of the children had joined the island children playing in the sand. His sisters were inside preparing to meet the men they would spend the rest of their days with.

"Are you okay, my brother? Maybe a little too much excitement for you!" Jhemel tried to tease his brother. It was no use.

"I am fine, Jhemel. It's just that we have had a long journey and I am ready to rest. I believe the ceremonies will last for many days. The people have a lot to celebrate. They are able to put the entire tribal name out to all who care, now. It has been a great many generations since the tribe has been called Naihu-Shahi-Nehra. This will be something that the elders will tell in the story hour for many more generations. Do listen to the stories the first chance you get. They are a wonderful part of the history of our ancestry." Josh wanted to tell his brother everything.

"Josh, did you think you would ever find us again?" Jhemel could barely remember the day that his older brother had left. He remembered the sickness and the white, though. It was a time so long ago, that most of the children had forgotten it or just did not remember it.

"When I got here to this island I lived on the other side of it for nearly two seasons. I spent that time erasing all the past that I could out of my mind. The only thing that I could not rid myself of was father's presence. Though I could not see his vision, I could feel him like he was standing next to me. I will show you the place where I lived. Once they have begun the celebrations we will have a chance to look around. Are you betrothed to any of these beautiful women here, my brother?" Josh wanted to know everything that his brother would tell him.

"I have not been told. I assume it is something I will learn and understand when 'I am older'." The two boys laughed at the cliché of their father.

"Josh, can you come in here for a moment?" Chandelle had come from behind the cloth door of the big hut.

"Yes, Mother." Josh gave a quizzical look to his brother and went inside. "What can I help you with, Mother?" He waited.

"Josh, I have someone that you should meet, and be formally introduced to. It has been a long time coming." Zac had pulled him aside.

"Can it wait, Zac? My mother called me in to help her with something." Josh waited for Zac to say something.

"It can wait only until the rest of the families are here together," Zac said impatiently. He tried not to show his excitement. He had been gone from all his possessions for so long. He just wanted to get things back to the way the legends told.

As Zac finished his sentence, Josh's family had gathered around him and Zac. "We are ready King Zac. You may go ahead if you are ready." Naihu gave the go ahead for the ceremonies to begin.

"Josh, normally it is the father's duty to introduce this person to you, but I have asked your father's permission to have this honor and he has granted it to me. Please bear with me until the throne ceremony is complete. Will you?" Zac waited for the young man's reply.

"I do not wish to be the King of the tribes, yet. It is my father who should have that honor first." Josh was confused. He may be heir to the throne of the legendary tribes, but his father deserved it more than he. "I will bear with you if that is what you wish." Disappointment spilled over his lips without any regard. Josh was not ready to end his life as he knew it with Zerasha, though he was sure that it had already ended.

"Josh, you will not inherit the throne, now. The elders wish for me to introduce you to your betrothed and as the hero of these ceremonies I have asked your father for the honors." Zac looked at Josh for his approval.

Josh gave it to him with a nod of his head, but he did not want to meet another woman right now. She would not mean a thing to him, not now. His heart had shattered when he had the conversation with Zerasha on Shurfate. They had not spoken to each other since. He was sure that he would not be able to spend time with her after the ceremonies, and all that he really wished for now was to go to his hut and stay there until his heart had healed enough to see her without his desires coming into the picture.

Zac went out the cloth door and started the ceremonies. Josh and his family followed the rest of Zac's family out to the pavilion.

"King of the tribes of Naihu-Shahi-Nehra, I hand down the throne to you and the rightful heirs of these tribes." Zac bowed in front of Naihu and handed him the crown of the tribes. "Your family has made it possible for the legends to live on. I make it possible for you to take the rightful position of your name. Please allow me to introduce a very prominent member of the elders. Sir Naihu, can you join us up here?" Zac waited for the hush of the crowd to quiet down. He could see the elder coming through the crowd. He could also see the astonished look on his friend's face.

"Father?" Naihu fell to his knees to worship the one and only true King of the Tribes. "How?" Naihu was truly stunned and amazed. He had not seen his father since before the first sickness. That was the image that Josh had felt. The senior man had been presumed dead, when there was no word or vision from him. That was when Zac had been given the throne. His tribal name was next to hold the throne and he was the only heir to it at the time.

"My son, I am glad to see that you have produced good members into the tribe. I was able to contact Josh shortly after he left this dimension. Though I was unable to tell him who I was, I kept my presence with him. I am honored that our name still abounds. I will catch you up in the days that follow." The senior Naihu had been on a world with no others since the first sickness had come to the many worlds of the other dimension. The enemy had caught him and left him there to die.

"The Naihu-Shahi-Nehra tribe will live on. All hail the King!" Zac was ready to complete the formal ceremonies. When the crowd finished cheering, he continued, "There are three people here betrothed to another that need to be announced. The one you all have waited for since I left this island many seasons ago, the one betrothed to my daughter. Formally they would have already been introduced, but since there are so many things to celebrate, we will introduce each of the maidens to her betrothed now.

Chanti, please meet Ranu. You have been betrothed since the day you were born, young lady. The legends wish you every joy you may come across in all of your days together." Zac placed Chanti's hand in Ranu's and sent them through the crowd. "Now the time all of you are anxious for, though not more anxious than my daughter. She has continued to ask me who he is since we saw each other in the other dimension."

The crowd laughed. Zerasha blushed. Josh wanted to run away. He did not want to be there. He could feel the pain in his heart leap to his throat. "Zerasha, my beloved daughter, I have searched many worlds for the man you will marry. He had not been born when you were, so you did not have a betrothed that was named to you upon your birth. The elders sent me on a mission to find him when you were still a baby in your mother's arms.

"I was able to return most of the time until I could not find the path, the last time I tried. Legend says that you will marry one who is kind and smart, gentle and loving, fun and happy. I searched many worlds to find that man. When I found him he was not ready for the news of his tribal ancestry. He was but a baby himself in his own mother's arms.

"I told his father, the day he was born, 'he is the one for my daughter." Only then I could not return to tell her. I have waited for this day as long, or longer than she has, so without further delay, Zerasha, if I may have the honor of formally introducing you to your betrothed?" Zac waited for his excited daughter to answer him.

"Father if you delay this much more, I will refuse him," she teased. Again, the crowd laughed. They knew the beautiful woman very well.

"Zerasha, meet Josh Naihu, heir to the Naihu-Shahi-Nehra throne." Zac placed their hands together. There was a great silence. Josh and Zerasha stood staring at each other, astonished.

"Zac? Father? Mother?" Josh did not know how to respond. The shock showed in his face as much as the excitement of having his real true love. "I bow to you all, even though you have kept this from us." He had begun to cry. He grabbed his bride-to-be and swung her in his arms and kissed her more passionately than he had ever done before.

"Let the celebrations begin!" He raised his hand to the crowd and waved it back and forth. "Zac, I am honored to be able to give your daughter all the happiness that she deserves."

Josh looked deep into her green eyes and held her in front of him. He wanted to see her true beauty. He could not wait to tell her of his desires. They had spent most of the last few days apart. They both had wanted it that way, then the hearts broken would not break so hard.

"My true love, if I had known this seasons ago. I am so happy I can't even begin to tell you how I am feeling. I have asked your father's permission to stay in the hut on the hill. It will be a perfect place for us. I will have to take all of your things out of the boxes and crates that I have spent the last few hours putting them in." Josh felt like his world had just begun.

He had so many questions for his father. "We will celebrate our King and the reunification of the tribes, then we will celebrate our coming together." He kissed her passionately until she pulled herself away.

"We must not do this now, my love. It will only land us in the hut alone, missing all of the celebrating." Zerasha knew the desires that Josh held for her, because they were her desires also. She had never been able to tell him exactly how she felt. She knew she had to save it for the right time and the right man, the man whose name had been held in confidence from her all her life. The one who was named for her shortly after her birth. "Always know that I love you, and know now that I have loved you and been in love with you for many seasons." She said it with such seriousness.

"I have loved you since the day that I laid eyes on you, and have been in love with you for many seasons." Josh kissed her again. He could not believe the passion that had built up inside of him.

"Ladies and gentlemen, I as your king have one more announcement to make. This will truly be a surprise to all of you. There is one more pair of betrothed individuals here today that we should announce, then we can begin the festivities. Marleigh, may I have the honor of formally introducing you to your betrothed?" Naihu waited for her shocked reply. Marleigh was Zerasha's sister.

"I would be honored, my king." She bowed to him, then replied in shame, "I did not know that I was part of the ceremonies, so I hope that he will not mind that I am not in my formal attire," she spoke softly. She had always feared that her man would never be found, so she never wore her formal attire.

"Marleigh, if it is your wish, I will grant you the time to go and prepare yourself properly." He waited for her reply. She shook her head and waited for the announcement.

"If there is any man here who would mind that Marleigh is not in proper attire, speak your mind." Naihu again waited for anyone to speak. "Then so be it. Marleigh, this is my second oldest son, Jhemel." He placed their shocked hands together and sent them into the crowd.

"Father, I did not know!" Jhemel bent in front of his father and kissed his hand. "I am honored to be a part of this family and celebrations." Marleigh was as beautiful and ravaging as her sister. Jhemel now knew how his brother could feel such desire for a woman.

"Then let the celebrations begin!" Naihu commanded the tribes. He turned to his loving wife, wrapped his arm around her and went inside the big hut taking her with him. "My queen, I have waited for this day for many seasons. I am so happy for my children. I only wish that the man for Khami could be here. He is the only tribal member that Ran was unable to find. I know that she is unhappy. I wish that we could have all of the weddings together." He looked to his wife and then kissed her like he used to before the wars had begun.

"Khami says that she understands. She will find a lover, or wait for her betrothed. Maybe we can have Josh and Ran go find him. He must be somewhere." She finished in time for Josh to hear the last of her sentence.

"Who must be somewhere, Mother?" Josh could not help being nosy.

"Josh, your sister Khami was to meet her betrothed here today, also. He did not return. I was just telling your father that he must be somewhere," she explained to her oldest son. She was so proud of him. She did not dare tell him the rest of the conversation for he was the adventurous type and he would be gone as soon as the ceremonies had ended.

"What is his name?" Josh asked.

"Son, his name is Malrui," Naihu said. Then, seeing the astonished look in Josh's eyes, "What, son? You look as if I have thrown you into a pool of cold water." Naihu saw the shock in his son's eyes.

"I will return. I must go to the other side of the island. First, though, where are Zac and his wife?" Josh waited for the answer then left in a mad dash out the cloth door.

"Zac, ma'am, I need to know why the villagers of the other side of the island do not join the tribes on this side?" Josh was out of breath and could hardly get the words out.

"Josh, they have lived there since the true King Naihu left the island many generations ago. They never understood how the elders could appoint another King without the true knowledge of their own King's death." Zac told him the answer he needed to know.

"I must find my friend. Malrui is betrothed to my sister Khami and he does not know that King Naihu has returned. Ma'am, is he still on the island?" Josh waited for the elder woman's reply. She knew Josh's friend, but she was unaware of his name and ancestry.

"He is. I invited all of them to the celebrations, but they assumed that the return of their King meant that they would be greeting Zac, and they have never agreed with that," she told him quietly, hanging her head down.

"Tell Zerasha that I will return. I must go find him." Josh left the celebrations in search of his first friend on the island.

He came over the hill from his hut and could see the villagers gathered in their usual afternoon spot. "Hey! I have returned to find my friend Malrui. Is he here?" Josh yelled to the people of the village as soon as he knew they would hear him.

"Josh, our friend. Malrui is getting food from the water today. He will return here shortly. Do you care to wait for him?" One of the elder women had greeted him. She was truly surprised that he had returned from the other dimension. It had been so long since anyone had attempted the dimensional transfer between the worlds.

"Do you know where he went? I have something to tell all of you, and I want him to be here. I cannot wait very long. I must return to the other village." Josh could not keep the excitement out of his voice.

"Is there a danger that we should know?" another of the members of the village came to him and asked.

"There is no danger. Where is Malrui?" Josh's excitement was starting to turn to anger.

"Josh, he is putting the supplies away from his small boat, down there." The young girl gave him a push in the direction of his friend.

"Malrui, you should not be looking for food on such a joyous day as today." Josh reached his hand out to the man he owed his entire life to for finding the woman of his dreams for him.

"What is more joyous today then yesterday?" Malrui finished pulling the supplies from the boat. "If you are referring to the celebrations of another King, then there is nothing to be joyous about!" Malrui turned from Josh in disgust and finished gathering his catch for the day.

"Do you know who your betrothed is?" Josh waited for Malrui to say no, but he didn't.

"Yes, I know of her, but she will never return to this island, because there is only one person who can get her here and he has not been heard from in too many generations. Why do you burden me with this today, my friend? I have all but put the idea out of my head. I am to live on this island alone, and our real King is never to return. The legends have told." He pushed passed his friend in disgust not paying any attention to the fact that his friend stood before him and indeed had returned from the other dimension. He took the food to the village.

"Malrui, wait. First, I want you to tell me how you think I got back on this island, and second, where do you think I have been for so long?" Josh did not wait for the answers. He could see the amazement in his friend's eyes. "If I told you that King Naihu was on the other side of the island celebrating as we speak, would you believe me?" Josh asked the question of his friend. "What is the name of your betrothed?"

"Her name was beautiful." Malrui gazed up to the sky, as he remembered the day he was told that she was on another world and would probably never make it to this dimension. "I wrote it next to mine for many seasons. Khami, isn't that a wonderful name?" Malrui had spilled the name like it was a feather he had spit from his mouth and it floated to the ground. "There is no Naihu King any longer. He was killed in the first wars of the Law." Malrui continued to put the food in its proper place, trying to forget the beautiful name and his King.

"Malrui," Josh begged, "you must come with me with at least one other member of your village, so that they will not think you do not tell the truth. If I do not tell the truth, I will not come to this side of the island again because of the shame I will have caused you and your people." Josh did not know what else to say to his friend.

"Josh, are you sure you know what you are saying?" Malrui was softening.

"As sure as my sister will be a maiden all of her life if you do not come." Josh gave it one more try, then he must return to the celebration with or without Malrui.

"Okay. Let me find a prominent member of the village and we will go and see. My friend, I do not think that you would tell me a lie." Malrui patted Josh on the shoulder and went into a small hut.

He emerged a little while later with an older man. He must be Naihu Sr.'s age, Josh thought.

"Josh, this is the man that I will take with me. He knew Naihu before he left the island. He is Jerad." Malrui introduced the two men. They shook hands and greeted each other casually.

259

The three men headed up the hill past Josh's hut and down to the celebrations. It took some time locating either of the Naihu Kings. Josh started out by the story place, then searched the crowd watching the dancers. He asked everyone if they knew where they were.

"Josh, we must go. It will be late when we finish preparing the food that I caught today." Malrui was getting impatient. He was starting to think that Josh had brought the two of them here to see what they were missing by not joining in on the celebrations.

"Wait there is one more place. Follow me." Josh headed for the big hut. "Jhemel, my brother, where is Father? Or better yet Great Father?" Josh found his brother with his new lady in front of the door to the hut.

"They are inside. Who are your friends?" Jhemel seemed very curious.

"I will tell you as soon as I find the Kings Naihu." Josh entered the big hut and found both of the kings deep in a conversation. "Excuse me, Father. I have someone here that I know you will want to meet. Great Father, I also have an old friend of yours here that believes you are no longer alive." Josh bowed to both of the elders as he spoke. He had asked the other two to wait outside, and for his brother to keep an eye on them so they would not feel compelled to leave.

"Bring them in, wise Josh." Great Father Naihu bid him.

"Malrui, Jerad, please come in." Josh showed the men in and introduced them properly, "Great Father, this is Jerad of Shahi, and Malrui of Shahi. They did not wish to live under a false king without the true knowledge that the

Great Naihu was truly no longer among the worlds," Josh finished the introduction.

Jerad fell to his knees in front of the Kings and begged their forgiveness for not believing. Malrui bowed to the older gentlemen.

"Josh, do you know what this means?" His father was astonished.

"Sir, I believe we have another announcement to make. And, a whole lot more people to invite to the celebrations." Josh waited for a reply.

"Oh wise Josh, you have brought the entire tribe back together and we will all be in your debt for all of our seasons." Great Father rose from his chair and bowed to Josh.

The two men of Shahi and the kings conversed for some time. Josh went to find his mother to have Khami put on her best. He told her to try and make it a surprise. His sister had been in her space alone, since the celebrations began. She would be ready for the announcement.

After he was finished with his mother he went to find his Zerasha. They had many things to do. They would be united as one in a few days, and there would be many things to take care of first.

"Khami, there is a boat coming in. Could you please put on your best so that we as the royal family can go and greet them." Her mother was very businesslike and would not take no for an answer.

"If I must, Mother." She dragged herself from the hides and started to put on the best materials that she had.

"You know that as a maiden in waiting for her betrothed you are to wear that dress until you have a companion or your betrothed is found and brought here!"

Chandelle repeated the legend to her daughter and left the room. She would go and do a little celebrating on her own. She wanted to meet Malrui, and she wanted Josh to introduce her to some of the Shahi villagers. It was truly a day of celebration.

Khami did not hurry to get her materials on. What was the sense? Her betrothed had probably been put in one of those dungeons and left there to die. She was feeling like her heart would just die. She had asked her mother why she was the only one that did not have a betrothed and got an answer that she did not like. She finished putting on her materials and fixed her hair and washed her face. She did not dare go out looking like she had been crying, though she had not stopped since she had found out there would not be anyone for her.

"Mother, I am ready. When does the boat get here? Khami used no excitement in her voice.

"It will be here shortly. Come out on the porch and sit with us for a while before it gets here." Chandelle had not used any excitement either, though she could hardly contain it.

"Ladies and gentleman, it looks like we have another announcement. Malrui, may I have the honor?" Naihu waited for his reply.

"Please, my king." Malrui bowed to him and waited.

"Malrui, may I present to you my youngest daughter, Khami. She was betrothed to you at her birth." The king placed their hands together, and winked at his daughter before he sent them into the crowd.

CHAPTER THIRTEEN

Josh was so excited. All of the tribes were reunited just as the legends had called for. His Zerasha was all he wanted before he left this world and when he came back. Now he would have her, and his whole family.

The next few days were spent celebrating, building, and conversing with all the new people of the island. The children sat every afternoon, like they had always done, and listened to the stories of the elders about the legends. Sometimes Josh and Zerasha sat and listened as well.

The ceremonies for all the new couples would take place in a few weeks, except for Josh and Zerasha. They were to wed at the end of the celebrations. They had already spent so much time getting to know each other as companions it was hardly worth making them wait until they got better acquainted.

Tradition was to let the bride and groom get to know each other before they were joined as one. For Josh, he just wanted to know more, all that there was, in fact. Now he would have all of his days to do it.

Josh and Zerasha spent most of the celebration preparing their hut and their finest materials. Josh would wear hides that his family had brought to the new world with them. Zerasha wanted to wear hides from his family as well, but her mother insisted she wear the traditional joining garments.

"Josh, my love, I am truly blessed to have you," Zerasha blurted out of nowhere. "There are so many things that I have held from you, for I was saving them for another man. I suppose you know most of them, just from watching me. The one that you probably don't know is one that we have never talked about." She hesitated.

"Zerasha, my only mission in life now is to make you happier than you have ever been. I am not sure that I will be able to do that, since we have already spent many happy seasons together." Josh wanted to pull her to him and forget about all the preparations. "I was truly surprised when I found out that I was the lucky man for you. I did not want anything to stand in the way of our friendship, and another man might have done that. Though I doubt that he would have stood in front of our friendship, I know that we would never be able to be companions again. Now that we are able to continue enjoying both, what more can I do to make you happier?" He waited for her to finish what she was doing and come to him.

"Do you want a family?" She spit the words out in shame. She had never discussed it with him. It was something that she should discuss with her betrothed. He had never said a word about having a family. In fact, he had never said anything about his own parents and sisters and brothers. He had blocked it out of his mind when he arrived on the island so many seasons ago. The news of him even having a family had made her shy away from the question, until now.

"I want to have as many children as we can, but they have to beautiful and intelligent and wonderful, just like you." He reached out to caress her face and neck.

"Josh, what will happen if they are like you?" She sounded surprised and scared.

"Then I must ask you to take them back. They must be like you, my sweet," he teased her.

Josh had not teased her since before he left in search of his father and hers. He had become very serious and separate from her even when they boarded the transport back to the island. The want in her eyes since the announcement was apparent as he watched her, but she had not come to him like she did before.

"Zerasha, do we need to talk some before the ceremony?" He seemed concerned with the way she was acting.

"I'm sure we will have plenty of time for talking after the ceremony. Was there something in particular that you would like to talk about now?" She was teasing now.

"Yes, I want to know why you haven't come to me since I left in search of our fathers. It seems to be the only thing I can see that is different." Josh had become very serious. He did not want anything to be different than it was before.

"Josh, is that what you are worried about! My love, I did not come to you again before the announcement, because I didn't want anything to stand in the way of our friendship and my betrothed. I have not come to you since the announcement, because I feared that you would not want to have children with me and I did not know how to approach you about it. Once a woman has been introduced proper to her man, then she no longer takes a root to keep her from being with child. I have been taking it since you asked my mother for companionship. She gave it to me so that there would be nothing for the elders to misunderstand, especially since I had not even met my betrothed. I did not..." She hesitated. Josh had held his hand out to her, with all the desires of his heart showing in his eyes.

"I want us to be one." Josh pulled her to him and kissed her lightly, but with more passion than he had ever given her. "I have loved you since before we left this island, and when I found myself falling in love with you I knew that I would have to back off or have a broken heart." He kissed her more, making sure that he touched every spot on her beautiful face. "I want to tell you all of my desires for you. I want to show you the true love that I have in my heart and soul for you. I want to be able to let every one of my desires and passions for you show." He had started to undo the ties on the chamille she wore. "There is one thing you need to know, love. I don't want to keep anything from you, and I don't want you to keep anything from me, ever again." He caressed her skin with the back of his hand.

"Josh, I will never hold anything from you again. There were times when I thought that I could not hold the desires for you inside me any longer. I wanted to give all of me to you, and I knew that I could not. I hid the fact that I was taking the root, so you would not suspect I was holding out for someone else. I just have never heard you say anything about families since I met you. I was afraid that you would not want me in the same way." She put her head down in shame for what she had said.

"I will always want you. It may not be in the same way as it was before, but the fact is I will still want you. I need you, Zerasha. I need everything that you have to offer me. I need you to love me as I love you." It was the first time Josh had said that he loved her.

"Oh, Josh, I love you." She did not need to say anymore.

They fell to the furs and spent the next few hours caressing each other and making love in a whole new light. Josh wanted to have children, especially if they were from Zerasha. He wanted the afternoon to be filled with the smell of their desires for each other. Josh had never put so much energy into his lovemaking like he had that afternoon. The passion he felt was steaming out of control. He wanted her, all of her! And he didn't intend to stop until he had what he wanted.

Zerasha could feel Josh's desires building in him. She had never been made love to in the way that he made love to her then. She wanted to touch him and hold him. The smell of the afternoon heat mixed with the smells of passion while she lay there under his command and let him treat her to his desires. She could feel the warmth of his tight stomach muscles against her as he slid up her torso to her breasts and caressed them with his tongue. The desire and passion flowed out of him. He gently kissed her and rubbed her skin all over. Then, he repeated everything over and over again. Zerasha felt like he could not get enough of her. When it was all over, she lay beside him in his arms and dreamed of the children that they would someday bring to this island paradise. Exhausted, she drifted in and out of sleep.

"Can I get you something to drink, my love?" Josh rose from the furs. All of the activity of the last hours had called on his thirst.

"Will you bring me some nectar from the feast table. I see no reason why we can't have a little fun and entertainment from this celebration." She had the same glimmer in her eyes that she did the first time she and Josh had made love on the sand on the other side of the island.

"This will not make you silly in the head, will it? I don't think I have ever known you to touch the nectar," Josh teased his wife-to-be, "though I am sure it will make me silly. I will be back. Don't you ever forget that, my love." He darted out the cloth door of the hut and nearly knocked his friends Ran and Shraze over.

"What are you doing away from the crowd? Did you need some time away from all those happy people?" Josh spoke load enough to warn Zerasha that they had visitors.

"No. Do you realize that we still have not been formally introduced to this Zerasha that you have spoken about since before the plan was started against the Law?" Ran stood with his hands crossed in front of him and his foot tapped lightly, though impatiently on the ground. "I figured if you were going to keep her in that hut all for yourself, then Shraze and I would come up and meet her on our own." He started to push past his friend.

"I would at least give the lady time to dress. I was headed for some nectar. Would you like to come with me, then you will be sure that I will come back and can properly introduce all of you." Josh teased his friend.

"I have taken care of the nectar for you." Ran held up a jug of the potent juice. "But, if we have come at a bad time,..." He stopped, embarrassed at what they had obviously interrupted.

"No, we were finished for now." Josh put a finger up signaling his friends to wait and went into the hut. "Are you decent, my wonderful lady?" He could see that she was. "I have some old friends that I would like you to meet. Come on in, guys," Josh called to them. "Zerasha, my lover, companion, friend, and soon to be wife, this is Ran and his wife Shraze. I have known them both since I was very small. We lived and worked together on the hom... another world before I came to the island the first time."

He did not like to refer to the place where he grew up as the homeland. Besides, Zerasha did not know that the place they had rescued their fathers from was his homeland. She just suspected that it was where the Law had taken them after they had been caught.

"It is sure a pleasure to meet someone that Josh had said so much about. He told us about you when we ran into him at the house. The only thing he told us was your name, and that we were not to tell you that we knew him from before the wars." Ran held her hand to his lips and kissed the palm. He had never seen such ravishing beauty in all his days. Why had she been hidden from the rest of their dimension for so long?

"Hi. Josh has not said anything at all about you except your name, and I would have to say that slipped out of his mouth." Shraze curtsied to the royal princess.

"Please. You are Josh's friends and I am sure that he does not wish for you to bow to him, so I do not want you to bow to me. I want to be your friend also." Zerasha blushed at the insinuation.

"Oh, my love, you are wrong. I want most of all for Ran to bow to my every wish and command." Josh rolled over to miss the swing of his friend's fist. They all laughed at Josh's statement.

"Josh, you know that Shraze and I will return to the other world. We will leave following your ceremony. I must check to make sure that the white has begun to fall on those worlds in the other dimension. I wish that you would come with us. I could sure use your help." Ran broke the news to his friend. He had pulled him aside while the two women talked.

"I will have to talk to Zerasha. Surely she will not want to return to that place, but I am sure the elders will wish that I go with you. I will surely miss you. You will not be able to return here after you have left, unless one of the Naihu with great ability come for you." Josh was referring to himself.

Zerasha and Shraze talked between themselves of their true loves and their desires. Shraze did not tell Zerasha that she would be returning with Ran to the other dimension. She did not want to think that she would never see her new friend again. Besides, she did not want to think that she would never be able to see her old friend Josh again, either.

Josh and Zerasha stayed in the hut for a short while after Ran and Shraze had gone. They prepared their things for the big ceremony. Josh wanted to make sure everything was perfect. When they had finished most of the preparations they ventured down to the rest of the villagers and the celebrations.

"Josh, Jhemel, my sons, there are some things that the elders and I would like to talk to you both about. Can you come inside for a little while?" Naihu had found his sons outside with their brides-to-be.

"Yes, father," Josh replied then turned to Zerasha.

"Can you live without me for a short period of time, my sweet?" He kissed the palm of Zerasha's hand and left her outside with her sister.

"What is it, Father? Is there trouble?" Josh did not seem too concerned. The elders were in good spirits.

"Young Josh of Naihu, we need you and Jhemel to go and inspect the worlds of the other dimension to see that the white falls properly, now." The senior of the Naihu name spoke first. "You are the only Naihu tribal members who can find the path back to this dimension and are young enough to make the transfer. Now is a good time to tell Zerasha all about you, the things the legends have forbidden and the things you have chosen on your own to keep from her," he finished and waited for Josh's answer.

"Ran has spoken to me of his return to the new world. I desire to go with him, but I would like to make sure that it is okay with Zerasha before I take her back to that barren place again." Josh asked the elders for time to talk to his love before the ceremony tomorrow.

Jhemel was astonished. He had no idea that he would play such an important role in the rejuvenation of the other worlds. He had not replied. The elders waited for him to say something. They would grant him the same as Josh. He could speak with Marleigh and then make his decision.

"You may have the time that you need. She is a wise woman, but she needs to know of the place that you are from and she needs to know the abilities that she shares with you. Her green eyes need to practice what yours have practiced for many generations. She has some of the special abilities of the Naihu, but she also carries abilities of the Shahi and Nehru tribes. She must have the time to find and use these abilities," Naihu finished the conversation with his sons. He bade them farewell until later.

Josh was anxious to find out how Zerasha would feel about returning to the new world. He searched the crowd for her until he found her on the sand where he had first talked to her. She sat there alone watching the sea, but this time she did not cry.

Jhemel stood in amazement for a long time. Then he, too, went to find his woman and explain to her what the elders desired of him. His only hope was that she would want to go on the journey with him.

"Zerasha, I am so happy to see you here in this special place. Are you ready for our ceremony?"

She nodded her head.

"There is something that I would like to talk to you about before the ceremony. The elders have asked me to return to the other dimension and check the progress of the white." Josh could see how excited she was. He continued, "If you would like, we can go together and learn the things that we have kept from each other. We can even stay in the same house."

"Josh, I would be honored to go with you. My father has just spoken to me of the same journey. He said that we would not have to go for a few weeks. We need time to finish the celebration of our unification." Zerasha stood and put her arms around Josh.

She kissed him lightly then dashed off to the rest of the villagers and the celebration. She would wait long enough to let Josh get close to her, then she would tease him and run off again. She enjoyed the game as much as he did.

Zac had also spoken to his daughter Marleigh. She had not been as excited about the journey. It frightened her to think that she might never return to her island homeland. She was not as adventurous as her older sister, but she did not want to let Jhemel go without her. If she did not make a decision she would have to wait for his return for their unification.

Jhemel looked all over for Marleigh. When he did not find her right away, he decided that he would sit and think about the decision he had to make. His only hope was to have Marleigh join him there and learn of each other in a different place. When he finally found her he could see that she was less than receptive of the idea of leaving her paradise home. He assured her that there was only one thing that would not permit them to return here, and it had nothing to do with finding the dimensional path. He and his brother would be able to find it without hesitation. The Law would be the only thing that would come between them and the dimensional path to return, and Jhemel as well as Josh had no intention of letting the Law find them.

It took a lot of convincing on Jhemel's part as well as Zerasha's to get Marleigh to agree that it would be a fun adventure for all of them. Zerasha was the deciding factor. She convinced her sister that, though this place was barren, they would have plenty of time to get to know each other again and enjoy their men.

Marleigh, finally convinced, turned to Jhemel and agreed to go with him. She hoped she was making the right decision. The decision meant they would have to have their ceremony at the same time as Josh and Zerasha. It would change a lot of things for their lives, but Marleigh thought that she was ready for it, and she knew that Jhemel was ready.

After the decision was made, Jhemel and Marleigh made the necessary arrangements for their ceremony and prepared their belongings for the long trip that lay ahead of them. While they prepared things, Jhemel shared things from his childhood with her, and then she with him. It was a happy time for them, and Jhemel made sure she understood that he would always take care of her no matter where they lived.

The ceremonies were short. The two couples exchanged their promises again to each other. Then they went to their huts where they finished preparing things for their new life in the other dimension.

Josh did not get the chance to tell Ran that he was going to join him, so it would be a surprise when they showed up. Josh knew that he must tell Zerasha the stories of his past and the true place where he had grown up.

He just could not find the right words. He did not want to burden her with all the knowledge until they were safe on the other world. That way if she became angry with him, she would not be able to run far, though he was sure she would never run.

"Zerasha, will you be terribly upset if I do not share some of my past with you right away? I know that these next two weeks should be spent telling you everything, but I want to wait." Josh broke the silence that had fallen between the new couple.

"No, Josh, I will not be terribly upset. But, if you insist on keeping all of these things from me, then I will be forced to return here without you and never allow you my companionship again." She teased the man who sat beside her.

The next two weeks were grueling for the two couples. Arrangements had to be made for their return to the harsh climate they had just returned from. Jhemel was concerned that he would not want to be there once they arrived. He spent most of his childhood and early adult life in a darkened room, with little to eat, and no sight of the outside. He worried for his new bride, but he made sure her sister filled her in on all the things she needed to know to be comfortable.

The four of them made their final preparations and prepared to board the boat that would take them to the familiar transport and the other dimension. Their families had joined them. There were tears in the elders' eyes as well as excitement. All of the villagers from all three of the legendary tribes had gathered to see the four voyageurs off on their new journey to the other dimension beyond the sky.

"You must return as quickly as you can, my son. The younger children's ceremonies will not start until you have returned with the news that we will wait patiently for." Josh's father bade him farewell one more time, though this time he did not fear that he may never return. "I am sorry to have to send you away again. I have said that I did not want this to happen again, but it is and I can do nothing to stop it." Naihu was sad. He hugged his son and turned away from him so he would not see the tears that had formed in his eyes.

The rest of their families bade them a safe journey and allowed the couples to board the boat. It would not be long until they were alone together again. Josh put his arm around his wife and waved to the crowd as they pulled away from the island.

Jhemel and Marleigh stood beside their sister and brother and waved to the crowd as the large floating room moved away from the dock and headed to the mainland. This would truly be a different adventure for Jhemel but with Marleigh, Josh and Zerasha beside him it would truly be an exciting one.

CHAPTER FOURTEEN

The trip to the new world was uneventful. Josh set the transport down in the field behind the old house. He would see Keiler in the morning.

Keiler had returned with Ran shortly after the ceremonies to help him get settled and to finish closing up his shop. Keiler had decided, after seeing the paradise that he would not stay on SuKhan. The Law had taught him plenty. One of those things was that this was a place that he did not wish to be in with the Law around, at least for the time being. If they ever found out that he was part of the rebel cause that had not destroyed them, but put a big dent in their operation, his life would be worthless or ended.

Josh had seen the storms on the horizon when they arrived on the barren planet. He was pleased to know they had started producing white again. There was something different about the land. He could not figure out what it was. Maybe it was the fact that the days did not get cooler yet, as they should during the season of white. He wondered why the white fell, but never reached the rock hard ground of this barren land.

He could see the storms. They moved, but by the time they reached the land, there was nothing coming from them. He did not understand. Maybe the air was too hot for them to produce. They had not figured that into the plan though none of the other barren worlds were having problems with the white. He noticed that Jemini had started to grow vegetation again, something he did not know that world could do. The thought of SuKhan not flourishing bothered him deeply.

Josh kept in contact with the elders and his father in the other dimension. It was hard sometimes to reach them because of the distance the thoughts had to travel. Zerasha practiced with him. She was good with that ability. It made it a lot easier to have both of their minds together when communicating such long distances. Jhemel joined them sometimes and though the four of them shared the large house, Jhemel spent most of his time with Marleigh.

"Father, the storms come, but the air is too hot to produce anything. It may be a few more seasons here before the white falls. Will all of the children still wait for their ceremonies?" Josh could see that his father was disappointed.

"Josh, you must stay there until the white falls and the plants have returned. We must know that Har has been defeated for good." His father told him goodbye and left the ridge that he stood on.

The two couples spent the next two seasons on the new world. Josh was away from the world they lived on much of the time. He took the transport to the other worlds and checked to see if the white was producing the nutrients the lands needed. It was a wonderful sight to behold a world that had begun to flourish again. The black ground turned light green and then the animals returned like they had been hiding in the underground until the food they ate grew again. Josh returned to the new world in time for the new season to begin.

Most days, like this one, were cold. The sun was rising late in the sky. Josh could see a storm coming through, but most of the storms passed by without incident. He had seen them go by this world time and again in the last two seasons. He hoped this season would be different. The times of three and four day blizzards had gone from this place many seasons before. It had been a mild year so far and it didn't show any signs of change. As the sun rose, the temperature also came up to its regular daily number which until recently was nearly the same when the sun was high as when it was low.

Josh arrived at the large house of his childhood to find his wife sleeping soundly on the furs by the window of the sleep floor in the spot that he had made his room as a child. He undressed and joined the woman he had shared his home with for the last three seasons though she spent more time in it then he did.

It seemed to be the best time of the day. He enjoyed lying there with her in his dark arms. She did not know he had returned. She rolled over and looked into his morning eyes and whispered to him. "Good day, my love." She had been dreaming about the paradise.

"Good morning, my most beautiful love of all the worlds." His eyes glistened as he spoke, in a deep, heavy accented tone. He had missed her more than normal this last trip. He could tell that she had been dreaming of the paradise. This was the land and world that she had always considered her homeland.

"Shhh." He held his finger lightly to her lips and kissed her. "We must remember that this is the homeland now. Someday, we will be able to return to the paradise, but for now, it should not be kept in such a beautiful head." Josh hated to tell her those things about the beautiful land that the legends had taught them about. He just didn't know how long it would take before they would be able to go back to it. Trying to keep her mind occupied with the idea that it might be some time, didn't usually help.

The people of the town knew that they were strangers from a place they did not speak of. They had to be very careful who knew about the paradise, and more importantly, who they told about their abilities and the other dimension, the place that they had considered home for a long time. Josh was not sure how many of the people who had returned to their homes, after the fall of the Law, were still with them.

Most strangers could not deal with the harshness of this land and they left within a short time of their arrival. The only people who stayed there were ones that had never left. They had just been held captive in the arms of the Law where they worked and were fed.

There were very few places that even had precipitation, and that usually fell as if the sky had opened and drained all that it held. These places were so far away. The only people who could afford to go to these places were called Well-to-do's or the Law, and the small town visitors. They could afford almost anything.

Why did they come? Why would they want to live in the Harshlands? Keiler and Ran were the only ones left in the small town who knew Josh, Zerasha, Jhemel, and Marleigh. He also knew the reason why he returned. The rest of the people would just have to think of them as strangers.

"Come, my love, we should go to the small store and get what we need. I have seen a large storm on the horizon. It was quite a ways away still, but it moved fast. I think this one will come. Somehow it is different from the last ones," Josh coaxed her from where she lay on the firs.

"Do you think this one will come for sure?" She could remember all of the other warnings that never produced anything, not even a gust of wind.

"I don't know. All I know is if we don't get what we need, then we will end up stuck here with nothing," he teased her with his finger on her belly. "Now, get dressed." He smacked her bottom gingerly. "Wear that long, warm, sexy outfit. You always look so beautiful in that." He put his arms around her waist and laid her under him on the fur that made up their bed.

He caressed her fair, olive skin all the way to her ankles. She felt exhilarated, as the rush of love ran across her skin. He didn't stop this time, as he usually did. His travels had kept his mind occupied, and they had little time together since they had come back to this world.

Josh knew that there was little time before the storm rolled in, but he needed the love of his wife one more time. He was unaware how big the storm was, but he knew he would have to travel again soon, if this one did not produce.

They had not been together since the day that they arrived in this place again, nearly three seasons ago. Josh had asked her to be patient with him. He wanted to finish his missions and be able to give her his full attention. He needed his entire mind to concentrate on the storms and the well-being of the rest of the worlds of this dimension.

All the times in the past three seasons had been interrupted by another storm that needed his attention. He rolled her over on top of him and as he caressed her back and muffled her gorgeous blonde head, he made passionate love to her. The smell of his flesh, the sound of his deep voice, sent shivers of passion through her body. She returned the passion to him. She always liked the things that he did to her. She felt the pleasure in her female anatomy light up. She feared she would not be able to hold on to the desires she had waited for so many seasons to show the man of her dreams. Maybe this would be the time they would be united as one finally.

Zerasha had wanted it from the time of the ceremony, only he had stopped coming to her. She did not question him though. He would explain things to her when the time was right and she was prepared to wait as long as she had to for that time. His desires exploded inside of her. She had not felt such power come from him in all the times they had made love to each other. He touched her breasts and caressed the hardened nipples. Reaching between her thighs, he could feel that she was ready for him. Exploring with his fingers, she moaned her ecstasy in his ear. Needing what he was offering her, she took it graciously and surrendered her body to him.

"It looks like it will be the same kind of day today as all the rest of them. Why do we have to...?" Zerasha sat on the edge of the furs and looked out the window at the new day unfolding. Their lovemaking had made her wants and desires apparent. She did not want to end it, but Josh knew that they needed time for preparations.

"Please, my love, let's go and get what we need. Then we can spend the rest of this day…"

"We will spend the rest of the day, getting things ready for the storm." She stomped her feet in her protest and went off to finish preparing herself to go.

Her only desire was to spend the rest of the day in the arms of her lover and husband. She had been away from him so much in the last three seasons. She found it very unfair that she must now share her time with some stupid storm that would probably fizzle into nothing.

The town looked as busy as always: One man on the bench, outside of the store, and a few people mulling around the corner. Probably discussing the storm, or possibly they were talking of the strangers. They all wore the same clothing style, overalls and heavy shirts. It seemed to be the most practical for this harsh land. Most of their clothes were handmade from hides that were cured for many seasons.

The strangers waved, as they always did, and said good morning to the man on the bench.

"Have you heard any more about the storm? I did not see anything menacing on the horizons as we rode." He questioned Keiler, as they stepped up to the counter where he was placing jars into a box for transporting.

"Nothing," said Keiler "Are you here for the usual?" Somehow, Keiler knew something was going on.

"Yes, only today I would like to have double." Josh poked around the half empty shelves. "If you think that you have enough," Josh teased. He knew what was under the large store and there would never be a need in this part of this world.

"You know something we don't, about this storm?" Keiler continued to fill Josh's regular order while he waited for his answer.

"I know that this one, somehow, feels different, a feeling I have not felt for many, many seasons!" he ventured as he glanced at his beautiful love to see if she was listening to the conversation. She was not. She was at the other counter eyeing the fine threads that were kept under the glass. "Please give me two balls of your threads over there. Let her choose the colors."

Zerasha eyed the threads like she had never seen anything so beautiful. She acted like a spoiled child any time he gave her anything. As the storekeeper approached, she shied away, only to learn that it was okay this time. There were a lot of things different this morning. She could hardly get him interested in the things she wanted, when she wanted them. He always showed up later with it, surprising her every time. She glanced at him with questioning eyes, as if she were asking his permission. He nodded his approval, and the child in her eyes appeared as she pointed to the ones she liked the most.

As they climbed back on the bare back of their transportation, he seemed distant. He knew that she would catch on to the storm, if she had not already caught on.

"Why did you buy these for me?" she asked, carefully, so she didn't let on that she knew there was something different.

"You don't like them? We can take them back," as he whirled their transportation around.

"NO! I mean, no, I love them." She knew he was teasing her. She just wasn't sure why. Maybe it was the thought of the storm leaving them alone. Maybe it was the passion in their lovemaking from earlier. No, there had to be something else. She never had a problem talking to her love. Today was different.

The storm arrived as promised this time. At first it looked like dirt was falling from the sky. Then, everything was white. It lasted like this for five or six days. Josh had warned the people of the village, and he had told Keiler in confidence that this would be the season. The time was hard to keep track of when the sun did not come up.

On about the fourth day, he came to her again. He wrapped his arms around her and held her like he had not held her before. His deep green eyes had darkened in the last days. He spent most of the storm sitting in his chair watching the white fill the window. As the window filled, he turned his attention to her. She lay on the bed with her threads. She made some of the most beautiful things though he had never seen anything like this one. She knew. Somehow, she knew. He didn't dare say anything yet.

He did not know how long the storm would last, but he did know that it would be big. He walked over to her on the bed, pushed her threads to the floor, and lay down beside her.

He wasn't sure if she was reading him, or just glad to have his attention. She took the buttons of her chamille and delicately unbuttoned each one until her breasts fell from under the soft material. She glanced at him as he lifted his dark hand to feel her soft skin. He caressed her chest as she finished taking off her clothes. Slowly and deliberately she stripped each piece of material from her skin. She knew that he wanted her, again.

He did not undress, though. He just lay there and watched. As she lay back down beside him, he knew what she wanted, but he was not sure that he should give it to her this time. She would know for sure, then.

"How long do you suppose we will be here?" she questioned innocently.

"I don't know, my love."

"You knew it was coming, didn't you?" she said, almost accusingly. "Why didn't you tell me before the day it came?"

"I didn't want to frighten you, love. I knew for a few days. When I was out hunting, I crossed a ridge and could see it there. I didn't want to alarm people, especially these people!" he swung his arm, gesturing the people of the small town.

"What do you know about these people?" She was finally curious. "I was sure that this was just a spot in the new world that would bring us together. It is just a spot in the...?" She noticed the shift in his eyes. He was no longer looking at her. He acted like he had just shamed her. She took her long finger and placing it under his chin, raised his gazing eyes to hers. "You have only kept one secret from me, and that is a secret that I can live with." She started to weep.

"Please, don't. I am not ready to share this with you. I know that you are aware of it, but..."

"I would never push you." She caressed him, and then lightly unbuttoned his shirt glancing at him to make sure this was okay. He helped her finish. She could feel the love inside of him. She always could.

His mouth covered hers as he embraced her. The smell of love had filled her whole body, again. She tingled inside and out. As they made love again, her mind floated off to the homeland. She remembered the days of lovemaking, and all the fun. She had never laughed so much. It was a time of carefree living.

Her family had always lived on the homeland. She was always well off. She never longed for anything. The only dream she had ever had was to find a man that would love her, her beauty, her talents, and her knowledge. He was the man. She snapped back to reality. Her whole body limp, she felt different.

"The white has stopped!" he exclaimed to her.

"How do you..." she stopped. She knew his answer would be the same. 'I just know' is what he would say. "Well, Mr. Know-it-all, what do we do now?"

"We must check on the town folk. Prepare some food to take with us. We may be gone for a few days. I don't know if we will be able to take the roads or not. While you are fixing something luscious, I will try to..." He pulled the door open, only to find white everywhere. "I don't think that we will be going for a while."

"Wow! Did you know this, also?" she demanded.

"No. I knew that it would be big, but this could be the biggest storm in these parts since..." he broke his sentence off. "I better see if I can cut a hole in the roof. If not, we will have to dig our way out." He grabbed the saw from the closet and a ladder. He seemed to know exactly what to do, like he had done it a hundred times before.

"Can I help with something?" she asked, even more carefully than usual. "I have bread and rolls in the oven, and if we get out, there is jerky in the smoker."

"Can you call Jhemel in here. Have Marleigh help you with the biscuits and jerky. Also, get me the flat pan under the work shelf." He would need it to get through the white. As he cut the roof, neatly, so he could replace it, the white came through like it had fallen from the sky for so many days. You could hear him mumble something under his breath. "Well, I can see the sun, again, but we won't be able to go this way, the structure is weak and may collapse on us."

"I want to see. Please," she begged. Malreigh had joined in her begging. Neither one of them had seen white much less so much of it that it covered the whole ground. Jhemel stood with the flat pan in his hand and waited for Josh to start the machine for tunnel digging. He had not been part of the last time the storms were this large, though, he remembered the devastation that came with it. He silently hoped that it would be different this time.

"Okay, but be careful." Josh reached for Zerasha's hand to guide her up the ladder. "Don't touch the roof. It may all come down." He helped her on the ladder, knowing how frail, but strong she was. These were the traits that had drawn him to her those many seasons before.

"It is so beautiful, just like the homeland." She could remember this type of storms from her childhood. Not many, though, because she lived where it was warm most of the time. The storms from her childhood were like this one, but they were always gone before you could behold the beauty of them.

The white in the homeland fell in the high country. The trip took so many days, and by the time you could get close to the stuff most of it was gone. She would only see it from a distance. Her father had taken her one time, but she was so little she could hardly remember what it was like. She stared at all the white silhouettes. Everything had white on it. Marleigh had joined the two of them in the large room. She anxiously awaited her turn to see the beautiful cold white that seemed to be the only thing that Josh and Jhemel had talked about for the last week.

Zerasha could not see the smokehouse, even though she knew exactly where to look. "I guess I better put something else on to eat. Looks like the smokehouse has been buried."

"Let me help you. We will not be going anywhere for a few more days. This will take Jhemel and I a while to get through." He gazed into her eyes, with all the love that they held for her. "I will need your help, also. There will be a lot to be done, and the longer it takes, the longer 'they' are out there." He referred to the town people some of which had never seen white nor would they know what to do with it. Fortunately the chimney's had all been strengthened against storms of this size so their work would be simpler this time.

It had been so long since he had cleared white. It was when he and his family lived in the big house that he shared with his wife, brother and sister-in-law now, not far from the small town. The white had fallen then, like it did this time. It covered everything. He remembered it like it was yesterday.

His father had done the same things. It took them many days and nights of digging in the white to get to the sunshine. They did not have a strong enough roof, then, to cut holes into. The temperatures were different then, also. There were layers and layers of materials to be thrown over the body to protect it from the cold, harsh winds. The wood stove was always on, and it seemed like there were times when it just would not warm the place enough. That was one of those times.

He remembered asking his father, "Why do the chimneys stick up so high?"

His reply was because the storms from the old world would cover the stacks and put the fires out. If there was no one on watch they would freeze from the cold.

"Is everything okay? Love?" He did not answer.

He was lost in the ways of the old world. People did not think that way anymore. The storms had not come for so many generations. Would this be a new beginning? Would the land become fresh again? He dreamed of the times when the flowers and trees were everywhere, when there was happiness, and glee everywhere. The storms would come and go, until...

"Can you look out the roof and see the chimney?" he called to her, as if he had not left the room with his mind. The thought seemed to terrify him. He frantically started to get tools and supplies together. He was glad that Jhemel was there to help. The cleanup would go much smoother than without him. Jhemel was older than Josh had been when he first cleared the white from the doorway creating a tunnel to get out of the large buried house, but this would be his first time.

"I can see the chimney, and I can see smoke on the horizon, over the hill." She loved the coolness of white. It made her eyes hurt with the sun on it. She came back down, only to find him rushing around the place, scurrying about knocking things over. She had never seen him like this. He knew something, and she wanted him to tell her, but she knew he would share his secret when the time was right. Obviously, not now, she thought, as she climbed down to find out where the fire was.

"What are you doing?" she asked him, as she grabbed his arm in mid-flight around the room.

"Nothing. I just have to get this done." And he scurried off.

Something had thrown a scare into him. Was it a vision from his past? She pulled some meat from the freezer and put it on the stove to cook. She pulled the bread and rolls from the oven and spread creamy butter all over them. Marleigh helped her.

The days seemed to flow into each other as time passed. The tunnel went on for what seemed like miles. Jhemel and Josh took turns every few hours digging and Zerasha and Marleigh did the cooking. The tunnel was started with a bucket of water. This hardened the white crystals and formed the entrance at their doorway. As the tunnel got longer the white was melted and placed on the walls to support the tunnel from caving in. There was only enough heat in the little machine to melt the white, then it had to be placed on the walls and ceiling quickly before it hardened. Josh did the forming better than Jhemel could, but then he had never had to dig out of the stuff before.

Zerasha and Marleigh wondered how they had so much knowledge. They knew that the men had seen white in the wars, but...Was this a part of their past that they both so desperately wanted to know about?

The sun continued to shine in the hole in the roof. Their supplies were holding up fine. There would be plenty for many more days. The seclusion didn't seem to bother any of them.

After the fifth day of sun the roof started to drip. She remembered a time when this was caught in buckets for drinking and washing. Now she did not know. It had been such a long time ago. She looked to the tunnel to see if he could be seen coming out of it, yet. The time seemed to just flow - not fast, not slow. This time seemed longer.

She didn't dare go through without him being back. She climbed to the hole in the roof to see if she could see anything going on. Nothing. Where could he be? She did not want to get frantic, yet. She knew he would return. He always returned to her.

The smoke on the horizon was still there, just like theirs. She knew a few hours had passed and the worry on her face started to show. She pulled out the special threads and started to work on them. This would keep her mind occupied. Marleigh joined her. They sat in silence as the time drew into the cool hours. Jhemel had climbed the ladder to put a cloth over the hole in the roof. He could feel the coolness returning to the cool hours, just as it should.

The hours seemed to pass quickly now. Josh could see the sun through the white. Every scoop seemed to make the whole tunnel glow. He fought furiously to get out like a mad animal in a cage. He was on his last roll and jerky. He had never spent this much time in the tunnel. He just knew he was almost out. He had to get there.

His thoughts raced back to his childhood, then to the homeland. How had he kept all of these thoughts from her? She was smart, and there were many times when he thought she had figured everything out, only to find out that she was as secretive as he was.

Never before had he had feelings so deep. They stirred the blood in his groin. He intended to stay in this new world for a long time. He certainly had not planned on returning to the harshland, the homeland.

However, the urge kept drawing his thoughts to the "Harshlands" he had left. The Harshlands brought him back to reality. How long had he been in the tunnel? She was probably frantic. He packed up the tools and headed back. The top of the tunnel had started to drip, just like the roof, which he was unaware of. He did not like the time it was taking.

The tunnel had to go up at a very small angle, otherwise, the white would cave in behind him and leave him stranded. This time was different. He had only seen the tunnels drip one other time. He started to run. Questions raced through his mind. Was she all right? What about Jhemel and Marleigh? Would he be stranded? What about the others? Were they digging, or were their chimneys covered? Why did this happen?

He reached the end of the tunnel, panting. She jumped to her feet. "Did you get through?" The excitement in her voice was drowned out by his panting as he embraced her.

"No, but almost." He was so glad to hold her. She sat him down and fixed him a hot plate.

"What was taking so long? You are supposed to take turns with Jhemel, so that you do not wear yourself out," she scolded him, as she took off his sweat soaked shirt to dry by the fire. "I was starting to get worried. I wanted to come find you. The roof has started to drip."

He glanced up. "We must get this tunnel finished. It has started to drip, also." The fear in his voice was apparent. She could sense it even though he tried as hard as he could to hide it. "If the tunnel collapses we should be on the other end of it. We don't have enough supplies to spend the time digging out again."

She jumped to her feet and proceeded to fill the sled with as much food and supplies as it would hold. It would take all of them to move it, but that is what he wanted. She piled the furs from the bed on top neatly, so they could have warmth, if the tunnel should collapse. She never questioned him. He was strong, and wise. He knew of things she had never heard of. He told her of places that other people dream about.

She suspected something was wrong. She had known it since the day the storm came. He would tell her. She knew he would, when the time was right. Until then, she needed to finish getting the supplies, and make sure that they had plenty to survive on. That was something he had taught her early in their relationship. Always have enough to survive on. She put the rest of the supplies in the sled and covered them with the furs.

He pulled her to him and pressed his lips to hers. The passion was hot and steamy, enough to make her want him. She pressed her bosom to him and returned the kiss, with as much if not more passion than he had.

He gazed in her eyes and told her reassuringly, "Don't worry, my love. All will work out fine." He took her by the hand and tugged the rope on the sled. It moved more easily in the tunnel. The floor was smooth and slick. The dripping had stopped, but only for the time that the temperatures had dropped. At least the temperatures were dropping this was a good sign.

When the light at the end of the tunnel got bright again, the dripping started again. There would not be much more time to get out before the white caved the tunnel in, stranding all of them in cold and almost darkness.

She could hear his breathing. It was even, almost as if he were sleeping. She handed him the scoop, and watched as the white fell to the floor, covering all they had with them.

"Wheeewee! That is some of the coldest white I have felt," he shivered as the powder fell from the opening, down his open shirt collar. They were out.

He took a deep breath and looked around, their heads sticking out of the new opening like two animals seeing the world for the first time. The land was completely covered with white. The only man made thing that was visible, was the tall chimney from the place they were living in.

The smoke could still be seen on the horizon. It was a chimney burning, while a family struggled to get out of the cage that had trapped them so many days before.

"We have to try to get to that place. I don't think we will be able to get to the vehicle, or the horse. We will have to trek it by foot. Do you have the shoes? We should gather wood for the cold part of the day. We will also need to check on the storekeeper. Is there any wood on this sled for cooking? If not we will have to get to the storekeeper's first." He was rambling off statements and questions at her as if he were checking off a list in his head, one that he had not used in a long time.

"We have wood for cooking and for warmth. No vehicle, no horse. Yes, we have the shoes. We will not need to gather wood or go to the storekeeper's first, because we learned from you many seasons ago to take what you will need to..."

"Survive," he finished for the women that had made the last statement in unison. He placed his hand on her beautiful cheek. "I knew that you were a smart, though beautiful, woman." He embraced her again. They lost balance, and laughing, crashed to the white ground, happy to still have the one thing that was most important to them, each other.

"Come on now. We should see if those people need our help. Their tunnels are probably dripping just like ours is." He took her by the hand once more and, pulling the sled, they all headed toward the smoke on the horizon. The white made the sled move easily, much easier than without it.

"Have you ever seen the white drip like that?" she questioned, knowing that he probably had.

"Only one other time. That was so long ago, that I had forgotten about it. This is the first time a lot of the folks have seen white. We should probably get as far as we can before the coolness is upon us. I don't know how long these tunnels will hold up."

They walked for hours in silence. His thoughts were laden with the wars of another time when most people in these parts perished, for lack of supplies and sickness. Most supplies in those times were reserved for the soldiers, the men who destroyed all that he could remember. His family, his home, everything.

Most of the families in the Harshlands today were there for no other reason than because they had not ever been anywhere else. The men had all gone off to the wars and other lands to find suitable places for their families, only to never return, or to return to nothing, like he had.

The only sounds that were heard were an occasional creaking, coming from the ground that they walked on. He assured her that there was nothing to worry about. He remembered the sound from his childhood.

They stopped in a crook in the land where they would be safe from the cool air until the sun came high in the sky again. She prepared the cook fire and the warming fire, and busied herself with a hot meal for all of them. They would need to keep their strength up. She unrolled the furs and placed them on a smooth spot on the ground. Marleigh assisted with the furs and the meals.

As she lay the last one down, he put his arms around her and turned her to him. The passion in his eyes and his touch was different. He lightly caressed her face, then worked his hands down to the opening of her shirt. He started to unbutton and undress her beautiful body. As the layers fell to the bed she had made, a chill ran up her body.

He quickly put her on the bed and covered her up. He lay down beside her. He felt something inside that he had not felt since the first day he laid eyes on her. His desires were apparent. The couple had not had much lovemaking since they had come back to the harshland this last time.

Her body ached with desire. She caressed his smooth dark skin. He put his lips to hers and plunged into a long session of lovemaking. Her desire for him increased with every minute that passed. She woke to the sun rising high in the sky, more refreshed than she had felt in seasons.

As the sun came high, the temperature seemed to climb rapidly, faster than either of them had felt before. The smoke was still visible and that was a good sign. Maybe the folks inside did not start a tunnel. Maybe they were just waiting for the white to disappear, as it had done around the hole in their roof.

He was right. Most of the people had never seen white. They were all too young to remember it, and those that could remember it didn't want to. Ran and Shraze were out there somewhere. Josh did not worry for Keiler; he had been through many storms and would know what to do.

"Come on love. Let's get this packed up and get moving. With these temperatures, we will have to hurry before any tunnels cave in." He gathered their bedding and piled it neatly on top of the rest of the supplies that were already on the sled. In no time, the place was cleaned up and there were no signs that anyone had even been there.

As the day grew longer, the materials were stripped from their bodies, until they only had one layer left. The heat seemed to be unbearable. How could this be? She ran the scenario through her mind many times. The last time she had felt heat like this was on the homeland.

"Why is it getting so warm? I have not felt heat like this since we lived..." She was careful not to say it this time.

"I wish I could tell you. I have never felt heat here like this, ever, not here in..." He stopped. She was waiting for him to finish. He never did. It was as if the time was not right. Was the time ever going to be right? The question popped into her head again and again, especially these last few weeks.

Why did he feel that he could not tell her this? There wasn't anything that they kept from each other. Only this! It was something that he promised he would tell her when the time was right. She has always accepted this from him. It was part of the promise she made to him so many seasons ago, one that she would not question, at least not insistently.

There has always been a place where he goes to in his mind, a place that only he knows. He has never shared this place with her, or anyone that she knew of. He tells her that it is a place that she does not need to know of yet.

They cleared the top of the hill, and could see the chimney. It was the only thing they could see, except white. He stopped, scanned the horizon, then started to pull the poles from the sled and make a temporary hut to stay in. They would stay here until the people under the chimney had been rescued.

She did not know if she knew the people or not. She stayed to herself most of the seasons that they had spent here. The only time she came upon people was when they would go to the store for their supplies. She did not know where any one lived or what their names were. After all the supplies were taken from the sled and set up, she started the cook fire and the warming fire, and he took off for the direction of the tunnel, if there was one.

These folks had not cut a hole in their roof, so it was difficult to tell where the hut was except for the chimney.

"This must be one of the few old houses left standing from before," he said. "The chimney is high enough to keep the white from covering it. I will start there. I may be able to find the edge of the roof and I can cut a hole in it if the structure is strong, unlike ours is." He glanced in her direction and blew her a kiss. "I will return before the cold sets in. If you get bored, come on over, I might need your help."

"I will finish the meal preparations and be right there. Do you think there is anyone in there?"

"He is in there. The smoke would not be coming from the chimney if he wasn't." Though he knew of the dangers of collapsed tunnels, he did not let on to her that there was always the chance that the tunnel caved in, especially with this heat.

He had only felt it like this one other time that he could remember. It was the last time he saw white this heavy. It was the time that he last saw his family, together, before he had rescued them and taken them to the Island Paradise. His father and he had dug themselves out. When the tunnel was complete, his father urged him to find a place where they could live without this incessant white everywhere. That was a time shortly after the wars had started.

He was a young man and ready to do whatever it was that would make his father proud. The heat that day was almost unbearable. He searched and searched for that land of Naru, the place his father spoke of. The wars dragged him away to faraway places, only to find most of them had white. He fought and looked everywhere he went. The white had devastation all over it, wherever he went.

He visited his father two times every season since the wars started. His father was kind. He only wanted the best for his son and the rest of the family. As the time grew the trips were harder and harder. There were a few seasons that he could not make it to the Harshlands. People insisted that he did not want to return there with the wars so close to that land. That was where most of the fighting was.

It worried him to think that his family may be closer to the war than he was. The soldiers had overcome and taken the lands from the people. The women and children were taken from their homes to work and sleep in the big places where they supplied the soldiers.

The men were trained in their own towns and sent to the front lines. His brothers and father were some of the last to go. They had an important business that would supply the war for many seasons, so they were allowed to stay for as long as they were not needed.

When he finally made it back to the Harshlands, there was nothing left. The wars had ended pretty much and most people were being allowed to go back to their homes and collect whatever it was that people collected from their homes after wars.

It was as if the people had seen the devastation and their warnings were for his own good. The few folks that remained were mostly small children and girls who had been too young at the time to work the supply houses. The town had not been destroyed. It was simply empty.

The family business had been boarded up and shut down. It looked like it had been abandoned shortly after his last visit there. This was a time that he wanted to forget. He longed to see his family, his mother, sisters, brothers, but mostly his father again. He had become sad that he had left them again so soon after finding them. He was lost in a world that he needed to tell Zerasha about, but he did not know where to start.

"I'm sorry, love. Did you say something?" he said as he came out of his daydream.

"Are you okay?" She looked at him, confused. "Where did you go?"

"To a place from long ago. When we are done with this rescue stuff, the time will be right to tell you. Until then, we must get busy. The cool air is coming and we haven't even begun." They both walked, arm in arm, to the chimney together. As they approached, a man's voice could be heard, screaming at the top of his lungs, "Is there anyone left? HEY, is anyone there?"

"Where are you?" they called together.

"I am south of the chimney. Please help. My wife and child have been without food for several days."

As they reached the man, they saw that he had not prepared for this many days of being stranded, though he had been warned before the storm had hit. He had not prepared for this big a storm, probably because he was tired of all the false alarms. There were so many.

"I think that my tunnel is about to cave in. My wife and child do not have the strength to come out. Please, please, you have to help her. The tunnel started dripping very heavily this morning. I broke through just minutes ago."

He turned to look at Josh. "I have not seen this type of weather and white since you and I..." He stopped as if he had started to say something that he shouldn't have.

"Go back through the tunnel and load your sled with all the supplies it will hold. Then put your fire out. The heat of the sun will keep you warm. I have to cut a hole in your roof, so that we can pull your wife and child out. Is it strong enough?" Josh did not wait for the answer. He knew this house from before the wars.

"You will not be able to use the tunnel. It will surely cave in, hopefully not before you get back to your family. Here, take some of these rolls and jerky with you." He handed the familiar man a satchel of rolls and jerky and sent him on his way.

"You spoke to him like you knew him. Have you met him before?" Zerasha could not see the man that Josh spoke with. She could only hear the conversation that the two men were having.

"Yes." Josh hesitated as he remembered the meeting of his old friend Ran just before the storm came. He hadn't seen him or Shraze since he and Zerasha had arrived. Neither one of them had seen him since the ceremonies on the island. "He was on the ridge with me when I saw the storm. He is one of the only people left from my past. I ran into him that day on the ridge for the first time since..." He hesitated, not sure if he should tell her who he really was. She had not recognized him.

She, again, like so many times before, waited for him to finish. She was almost sure that he would this time. He had already admitted to knowing this man and his wife. Would he tell her little bits at a time?

"It's Ran and Shraze. You remember them from the ceremonies, don't you?" He gazed at her as she nodded her head. Neither one of them had seen them since the ceremonies. Josh had inquired of Keiler upon their arrival but Keiler had only seen them the one time.

After he finished, he called to her, "Come, we must get back to the roof and chimney. If the wind did not blow much during this storm the white on his roof shouldn't be any deeper than it was on ours." She reluctantly followed, though she really wanted him to stop and finish the rest of his story.

The roof was easy to find. It was about a foot higher than theirs so there was not as much white to deal with. The structure was sound, just like it had been the day it was built, before the wars. He grabbed the saw and yelled to stand clear. He cut the smooth hole in the roof and pulled it out.

The man's wife lay on the floor with their new child, next to the fireplace. She was thin and looked too old for her age. Her black hair was stringy, and lay in a heap on her head. The child lay there motionless, though with good color. He was sure it was just sleeping. There was no sign of his friend.

The ground creaked, like it had for the last two days, then it rumbled. Before they could move from the roof, the whole tunnel collapsed sending a spray of fine white powder through both holes of the tunnel. Was his friend all right? He waited. As the powdery stuff settled he saw, at the opening of the tunnel inside the house, his friend. His eyelashes were white, and he just lay there.

"Hey, are you all right?" they called out to him from the hole in the roof. After a short while the man moved. He looked up to find his wife on the floor and his friend from a long ago time looking at him through the roof.

"Hey, I'm so glad that you showed up. I was about to quit and join my family in their bliss, when I got through. Where did this stuff come from? I haven't seen this stuff since the day you and I left here so many seasons ago. What happened to you? Why did it take you so long to get here? When did the storm stop?"

"I have been digging a little every day since a few days after it started. Who is this ravishing woman by your side?" Ran did not recognize Zerasha, either. He had not seen her since the day of their ceremony. He had so many questions.

So did she, now! How did this man know Josh? Who was he? The thoughts ran through her mind so fast, she nearly lost her balance. He gazed at her. His eyes were very dark. He knew he had a lot of things to tell her, but now was not the time.

"Please, not now." He gazed into her eyes. "Let's get these people to our temporary hut and get them fed and warm." Her look told him that she was in no hurry to hear these things yet. She just wanted him beside her. He kissed her, thanked her for all of her understanding, and went to work.

He lowered a strong rope down to his friend and tied one end around the chimney. His friend took the other end and ran it through the rails of the sled. This would hold his wife and child. Then they would fill the sled again with all of his supplies, which was not much. His wife was dull of her senses and probably in shock for lack of nutrition. The child seemed to be fine. She had spent the last of their supplies feeding her husband and the baby taking only enough for herself to barely keep her strength up.

The men pulled the rope until the sled cleared the hole in the roof, with the woman and child inside.

"Take them to our hut. I will use our sled to load his supplies. Then we will come." He reassured her that everything would be just fine.

"Do you think that she will be all right? She has lost a lot of strength. I don't think that she has eaten anything at all for a few days. I will get her and the child warm and fed. Don't be long." Her voice cracked as she swallowed her words. She did not wait for the answer to her question. She pretty much knew the answer if she kept the woman out too long.

As she pulled the sled to the temporary hut the woman spoke to her, "Thank you for rescuing us." Her voice was faint, almost a whisper. "I am so glad that your husband found mine that day. If he hadn't met up with him, we surely would have died days ago."

"Shhhh." She calmed the woman and told her to save her strength. She would need it in the days to follow. She opened the door to the hut and helped the woman and child in. After she got them both settled, she went to heating the food that she had prepared earlier.

The men were due back, and she wanted to have hot plates ready for them. The cool air was seeping into the day. The heat of the day made everything creak as the cool air settled to the ground.

"Whewee," was the sound heard from outside when the two men had arrived. The men had returned with all the supplies that the sled would carry. He came in and reached around her waist and whispered a quiet thank you into her ear. She blushed and shooed him away.

He was in an extremely good mood, one that she had not seen for many, many seasons since everything in the world was carefree. She wondered if there were ever going to be times like that, again. All she could do was hope. When the meal was finished, the men went out to build a make-shift room for the other family to sleep. There just wasn't enough room in the one for all seven of them. The woman had regained much of her strength back after the meal, and helped to put the rest of the supplies away.

When the men returned, Zerasha asked her love, "Will we be here long, Josh, or are we traveling again?"

"We will have to stay a few days, just until she can get all her strength back. Who knows? By that time, the white may be gone and we will be able to return to our homes. Tomorrow Ran and I will make our way to the store for more supplies, if we can get to it. It will be the only building in these parts that has a chimney high enough to keep the white out. That will certainly make it easier to find." He looked at her with his dark, drawn eyes. Something in them was sad, something she had not seen before. She brushed the thought from her mind.

"How long do you think it will take you?" She worried every time he left her, even though she knew he would always return.

"Well, it took us two days to get here. We should probably follow our trail back, and then we will head the direction of the store. That should only take us a couple more days. You have enough supplies here to last you a week. We will be back by then."

"If you are not back, should we come for you?" This was the first time she had ever questioned him coming back. She was almost afraid to look at him when she asked.

"If we are not back in seven days, head down the trail to our house. By the time you get there, you should be able to see the trail to the store, but I don't see any reason why we would not be back in four or five days." The look in his eyes had changed. It was colder than she had ever seen it, even more than the first day she met him all those seasons ago. She hung her head in shame for even questioning his return.

The following hours were very hard for her. The other family had retired to their own hut, and they were left alone. She wanted to ask him so many things, but his mood had changed since they had eaten. He became very distant. What was he thinking? Was he mad at her for her question? Was he trying to find the right words to tell her the secret? Did she dare venture into a conversation with him?

"You know that I have never loved any one so much as I love you." He started, "There was a time when all I wanted was to make my family happy, and to be able to take them to a world where white was not. When I returned here, before I even met you, my family was gone. Part of my secret is that this is my homeland.

"My father, Naihu's, business was boarded up. Like most of the buildings, they were abandoned shortly before or after the end of the wars. The building where we live now was my childhood home. Now you know that the time we returned here for my father, we lived in the same house."

Josh could see the astonishment in her eyes. She had always thought he was from the island homeland. He continued, "There wasn't any one left who could tell me where my family and friends had gone. I concluded after two seasons of searching, that they had gone off to find the 'land of Naru' that my father spoke of." The tears streamed down his cheeks, almost faster than he could get the words out.

"Now I know where I know that couple from! They are your friends that helped rescue our fathers." She had almost forgotten them. "You don't have to do this if you are uneasy with it." She tried to comfort him.

"There are things that you must know, before Ran and Shraze tell you. This is the time that we need to really understand each other and our pasts. The only way I felt we could do this and check on my homeworld was to tell you that we should go back to the big house. I knew when we left the island that I was on this mission. Ran also knew that when he returned here with Shraze." Josh was careful what he told her. He did not want her to know it all yet.

"When I found there wasn't anyone I knew left in the small town that I had grown up in, I took my search to other places. I was gone for the last two seasons of the wars, unable to return because of the lack of transportation. The only transports available then were ones to carry the soldiers to the wars. I had not been a soldier for two seasons, so traveling was difficult at best. The inability to get a transport made searching for my beloved family very hard. Even though I had plenty of money, I could not buy a transport to anywhere." He glanced up to see if she was still interested.

Her eyes held his for a short time. He could see the questions, but most of all he could still see the love in them. He waited to see if she wanted to speak out.

"Why didn't you tell me of your homeland before? I was sure that you were from the other side of the island. You never spoke of it. How do you not speak of your own homeland for so many seasons? I have so many questions to ask you. I just don't know where to start, or if I should even start." The tears had started falling down her cheeks. There were many parts of his life that she longed to know for many seasons.

He had always told her 'when the time is right, you will know all there is to know of me'. She had made the promise to him on their wedding night not to question him about certain things. Now must be 'the right time'. She let him continue.

"I received a letter from my father just before I ended my soldiering. He said that if I could get a transport back, now would be a good time to visit. He did not know that I was ending my soldiering, so that I could find the 'land of Naru' he sent me out for that dismal day. I had a choice when I left soldiering, to go back to my homeland, or somewhere else. Even though I had received the letter from my father, I chose to go somewhere else.

"The place that he told me of when I was a boy had to be out there somewhere. I had to find it. After two seasons of searching, I still had not found the place. I decided to go back to the homeland. I longed to be with my family again. I wanted to see them, and that was the only 'land of Naru' I cared to see. I finally was able to get a transport back, only to find all of the townspeople gone.

"The few children that were left behind had been too young to remember where everyone had gone. One of them told me that the transports had stopped many seasons ago. They did not come to pick them up as they had promised. They had taken all of the men and women who were old enough to the supply places. She did not know where any of these places were though. They had taken the last of the mail over two seasons before that, and only returned in the sky once a month to drop supplies. They never landed, they just dropped the boxes of supplies out of the transports and left.

"She said that my family must have left in the cool hours of the day, because she had not seen them go. The only ones left were my father, who was too old for warring, and my two younger brothers who were too young. My mother had been sent, before my last visit, to the supply places with all of my sisters. Not even my father knew which one she was at. She was allowed one letter a month, and she could not divulge her location.

"My father left shortly after he sent the letter to me. I don't know why it was so important that I come and visit then, but I chose not to. From then until our last visit to this world, I had been on a forever search for them. I left the harshland, which is what it came to be known after the wars. The Law and enemy had changed all the weather patterns, and the only thing left was what you see now. Or, what you could see before the white came. I am sorry that I have not been able to tell you all of this before, but after all the seasons of searching, when I met you I had already come to the conclusion that my family was lost forever, and I would never find them.

"I found the 'land of Naru' on your island home by mistake actually. I had never heard of a place with a sea. It just couldn't be true. Maybe I would find my family there. I searched for another year in the Harshlands. I wanted to make sure that the supply places had all closed down. I found one, just before I left for what I thought was the final time, that was still open. A few people still worked there, though they were not being held there against their will any more. They just chose to stay, because it was a place that would shelter you from white and you still had plenty of supplies even if there was no white to fear.

"I asked about my family. They would not be hard to find if anyone at all had seen them. My father was a big man before and during the wars. Most people had at least heard of him. Even people from as far away as the other world. I finally found a woman, about the age of my mother, who remembered my family very well. She told me that my father came for them some three or four seasons before I arrived. She could not remember exactly. I asked if she knew where they were going. She said everyone went to the new world, or they were caught by the Law.

"I gathered my things and spent over six more months trying to find a transport landing site. The wars had been over for so long now that most of the landing sites had been abandoned just like everything else. By the time I finally found a transport more than another half a season had gone by, and the storms were being forecast again. They were not going to let any transports out until after the season. It was too dangerous. The last one was going out at the end of the cold hours, and if I was going to be on it I had better be there. I found myself waiting until the hour came when the transport was ready to go. I got on it, and found myself floating alone, in a sea that was not kind.

"I was lost and had no idea what happened to the transport."

"It was shot down above my world nearly two seasons before you showed up." The love of his life told him something that he had never thought of.

"How do you know that?" he questioned her.

"It was all over the village. There was a transport shot down, and all aboard were lost." She acted like it was everyday news. It was, ever since the wars. The wars never reached her tiny village, but the news flowed in and out daily. Enemy transports were shot down before they cleared the dimensional pathway.

"I suppose if my family heard about it they figured I was gone right with the transport." He cried again. "I gave up my search when I reached land. I knew that there were so many worlds to search, and for all I knew my family had gone back to the Harshlands. I made the hut on the beach, on the other side of your island and spent many months there. I didn't want to be known by any locals or anyone for that matter.

"I had deserted my soldiering for a place that I was sure I would never find, and a family that I was sure thought I was dead. I learned to find the animals in the water that were good to eat, and spent all of my time trying to forget a place that was true to my heart, and a family that I would never find. After I had all my thoughts cleared from my head, I ventured around the island. I found a few villagers that were kind enough to point me to a place that I could buy if I was interested.

"I was. I needed a place where I could start over, a place where I was not known. This was the place. I headed away from the sea, up the trail that led to the hut I was going to buy and live in forever. It was a bit close to the village, but it was cozy and perfect for one. After I settled in, I went to the village and sat and watched the villagers from a distance. I did not know if they were friendly or not, and I just wasn't up to a confrontation. I always remembered that I was the stranger, not them.

"The day I saw you, I almost did not return to the village. I was afraid that you would want things from me that I was not willing to give to anyone. As the time went by, I found myself searching the island for you. I could not get your image out of my head. I dreamed of you while I slept, and I had to see you as soon as I awoke. I spent two seasons watching you and every move you made.

"I soon learned that you probably had more money than I did, and if there were things that you wanted, I would probably not have to give them to you. You could get them for yourself. This is something that I could see, the

313

more I watched. I wanted to reach out and touch your smooth olive skin every time I saw you. The longer I watched you the more I wanted you. I knew, after some time, that you were a very prominent member of this village I had come to call home. I had to meet you, but I was unshaven and probably would have been thrown off the island, if I had approached you.

"I spoke with some of the villagers who had become my friends. They continued to tell me that you were alone. You lived there with your family, and your father was head of the village though he had not been on the island since the wars started. When I finally got the nerve to approach you, I found myself afraid of the rejection, and it took much longer than it should have." He took a deep breath and gazed into her luscious green eyes.

She was taking everything in. She remembered the day they met, like it was yesterday. The deep, dark secrets of his past showed in his eyes then, like they did now. She remembered the first time they embraced, only to be laughed at by the young children, and teased. She also remembered the places they used to go, the quiet places they went to be alone. Those were the places where they spent many hours, looking into each other's eyes and making love on the open sand.

He had told her then that he lived on the other side of the island for many seasons, until the wars had called him away. He had just recently returned, only to find that the villagers he had left behind had aged. Some were gone, he assumed to the war worlds. Some were grown up and had children of their own. She was young enough that he knew she was but a child when the wars began, and she would not know that he had come upon the island by accident.

She was content with all he told her at that time. Now she was starting to put the picture together.

"I am so shocked at all that you have been able to hide from me for so many seasons. I can see why you could not tell me these things before our ceremony. If I had found out from you, through the legends, that you were my betrothed, we both would have surely been banned from the tribes." She waited. She knew there was more.

"I met your father for the first time when I was but a boy. He arranged for a transport to take me to all the worlds that I would see until I found the paradise. I did not know that he was your father until I spent many hours talking with your mother. I did not know that I was your betrothed until your father properly introduced us. I do not wish to spend my days on this world with you. I plan to return to the Island Paradise and enjoy the fun and laughter that we had before we found our fathers.

I am a prominent member of the tribes and the legends. I have known this for many seasons. Your mother told me many things that I have had to keep from you. I brought you here the first time to see your father, only I was told that you should not know that until I had actually laid eyes on him." Josh finished. He waited to see if she had anything else to add.

"Josh, I have known about your abilities for a long time. I have some of the same abilities, but I have some that are really different. I do not know how to use all of them, because my father spent most of my growing seasons away, on this land. I knew about the loss of your family when we came back to this land three seasons ago. I could not tell you, because I knew that it would have to come from you. I also knew that when you found my father that I was not going to meet my betrothed.

"I had decided after spending the time with you that I had, I would rather live as a lover and companion to you than be left with a man that knew nothing about me. I told my father and he forbade me to tell you this. He knew that you would not go along with it, and he did not want to hear another word of it. He did not tell me at that time that I would have nothing to worry about, that the man that I had been living with and loving for many seasons now, would be the man that would spend all the rest of my days with me." She stopped. She could see the happy glow return to the face of the man she truly desired and loved.

He finished telling her all the things he could think of about himself. He listened to the few things she told him about herself that he didn't already know. He had become very relaxed even though he knew his mission was not finished. He pulled her close to him and gave her more of the lost desires that he had been holding from her. She did not resist.

Zerasha became very relaxed. She wanted all of Josh and would not stop until she had it. He caressed her skin and kissed and loved her all over her body. The shivers of desire melted her body as she lay beneath his strong frame. The want inside of her did not stop. She had to have him all night. There would be no stopping the unity between them now. They had no more secrets.

***

Josh, Ran, and Jhemel started out before the sun began to get high. The heat of the day would slow them down more than the thick blanket of white that still lay on the ground. Josh did not say much during the first part of their short journey. He kept his mind occupied with the woman that he wanted to spend every waking minute with. Ran did not question him. He knew the secrets had been told the night before. He assumed that Josh had just not gotten enough sleep and left it at that.

Zerasha, Marleigh, and Shraze occupied their time with the new baby and talk. They were not able to get to know each other until now. There was plenty to catch up on. It had been three seasons since they had even seen each other. And, they barely knew each other then.

"Will you and Josh have a family?" Shraze asked carefully. She did not want to stir any bad emotions. After all it had been three seasons since the two had been united as one, and they still did not have a baby.

"We will when the time is right. That may have been last night." Zerasha blushed.

She could feel the difference in her body from the last few times they had made love to each other. It was all the lovemaking that they had had since they arrived here after the ceremony. She did not dare tell Josh yet, or they would have to remain on this world until after the baby came. If they did not leave soon, they would surely have to stay here anyway.

She did not tell Shraze of her new secret, if it was a secret at all. She had seen the vision in her sleep, but she wondered if it was a dream and she dismissed it. She would know for sure, soon enough.

"Do you know of her betrothed?" Zerasha asked the woman of her little girl.

"She will be the first generation in many to have one, but there are none for her now. Ran will check with the elders when we return to the island. We have decided that this is not a world to bring up a family in. There are too many times that she would have to work, and Ran wants her to grow as he did, no cares and plenty of time to play." Shraze was proud to be a part of the tribes that not even Ran knew much about.

He was the only surviving true ancestor of the Nehru tribe. His father had not talked to him about it, because he was sure after his younger son died so early in his life that the tribes would never unite again, at least not in Ran's time. Ran wished that his father could have seen the paradise.

The men returned in less than three days. They had met with Keiler and were prepared to leave this land. They would stay at Josh's house until the white was gone. It would be necessary, to see if the white held the nutrients the ground needed to survive again. There were a few more storms on the horizon, and even though they were small, Josh did not want to be caught out in them, not even in the temporary shelters they had constructed.

"Zerasha, will you help put the supplies in the sled while I take these hides off the poles? We will be going soon, back to the house." He stopped. He noticed that his wife did not look well. He wondered if the white had disease in it. He would never forgive himself if it did. "Is there something wrong, love?" He stopped what he was doing and sat beside her.

She could feel his concern. "I am just a little slow this morning. I will be fine as soon as I am finished with the hot plates and can sit for a minute." She did not dare tell him she was with child though he would suspect it soon enough.

"Zerasha, is there something that you are not telling me?" He sat in front of her with a quizzical childlike look on his face. He waited for her answer.

"There is." She stopped.

"Well, I think that you should tell me, so that I can finish putting this stuff on the sled and we can return to our warm house," he teased her. She could hear it in the tone in his voice.

"I think that it will wait until we get to our warm house. It's nothing, really." She tried to lie to him. It didn't work.

Ran could see that she was not as perky as her usual self. He questioned Josh about it, but did not get the answer that he suspected. Ran turned to Shraze and knew what the answer was without even asking her.

The sleds were packed and the place looked as if there had never been anyone there, except for the shoe prints in the white that the six of them left behind them. They returned to Josh's house. The white was nearly gone. The temperatures were still very warm in the height of the day. The white would be gone in no time and they would be able to see if it carried the nutrients to the land.

Zerasha went straight to the sleep floor upon their arrival at the house. She needed to rest. She was exhausted. The child inside of her already drained her of her energy. She would not be able to keep it from Josh any longer. He had followed shortly behind her. She would have to tell him.

"Are you okay, my wonderful woman?" He sat on the hides next to her.

"I am fine, really. It is just a natural thing that a woman goes through." She tried to hide the joy she had been hiding from him since he returned from the storekeeper's.

"What is this natural thing that we are talking about?" Josh could not stand the torment from her any longer.

"I will not be able to return to the island with you this time. I am not..., It will not..., I have..." she did not know how to tell this man that he would soon be a father, but he would not be here to witness the miracle of their unity.

"What are you talking about, Zerasha? I am not leaving you here alone. Whatever it is I will stay here until you are well enough to travel with me." He had become stubborn.

"I am with child." She did not say any more. She knew that there was no need.

"I'm going to be..." He was so astonished that he got up and ran to his friends on the other floor of the house.

He shouted from half way down the ladder, "I'm going to be a father!" Then he ran back to the woman of his desires. "I cannot leave you here alone." He waited for her to give him a solution.

"You must return to the island and tell the elders and your father that your mission is a success. When you have done that, then you can return here for me and our child. If you are fast, then you will get here before it does." She ruffled the hair on his head. She had never seen more joy in his face even when he found out that he was the lucky man to get to spend the rest of his seasons with her.

"I know that you will return. You always have. I will wait for you right here." She kissed him and lay down to rest.

Josh had sent Keiler, Jhemel, and Marleigh to Shurfate to wait for them there. He did not know that Zerasha would not be coming with them. She would truly be a stranger to the rest of the people that were left here, the ones who desired to stay. They waited one more day to be sure that the green plants had really returned to the once barren land. Josh was happy for one thing, that Zerasha would not have to stay here alone in the barrenness of this land. She would be able to see the plants flourish and fill the land with animals and birds. He kissed her and bid her farewell.

"I will return for you, my love. Do not ever, ever forget that!" He waved to her until he could no longer see her in the window of the sleep room where she stayed.

She only moved from the spot to eat and move around a little. The rest of the time she waited. She could be seen in the window by the children that came up the road in front of the big house. They always wondered "who is that stranger, where did she come from, why is she alone?" She just waited.

The time for Josh to return for her had long since passed, and the time was drawing near for the baby to come. It would be hard for her to give the child life all on her own, but she would do the best that she could. Zerasha could feel the pains coming faster and faster. She just wished that Josh had returned to her before the child's arrival.

No matter. She gathered what she would need to bring the child into this world and took all of the supplies to the sleep floor where she would stay until it was over.

Josh's Garden

After making one final trip to the cook floor for a pan of water, she climbed the ladder for the last time, alone.

CHAPTER FIFTEEN

Josh, Ran, Jhemel, Marleigh, and Keiler arrived safely in the island paradise with Shraze and baby Charli. The trip was uneventful and the dimensional path was easy for Josh to find now. He nearly had the spot memorized but he still used the 'communicator' to see his father and the elders showing him the way. His mind was so full of Zerasha and the report that he would soon have to give to his father and the rest of the elders.

Ran remained mostly quiet and sat with his family for most of the trip. He had joined Josh in the front of the transporter when they were close enough to the dimension path so that he could help guide Josh to their destination.

Several suns had passed and Josh was anxious to return to the harshland for his wife and their beautiful child. He had requested permission shortly after his arrival but the elders had forbid him to go back in the middle of the storm season. It was surely not a good time to be in a transport and though the Law had filtered out of the area and the safety of the people was secure the elders would not let him go during the time of storms. There would be little or nothing he could see until the white was gone and until it was gone nothing would grow or flourish; with or without Josh's presence.

"Father, I must go the ba.... Zerasha is waiting for me. It has been nearly a season and I want to make sure the plants and animals have returned. I must have Zerasha by my side. Please, Father! You must talk with the elders. I will be able to find my way back. Besides you will be here to guide me. My abilities have improved a great deal, and I know all of them well." Josh pleaded with his father for the elders to give him permission to leave. The paradise just had not been what it started out to be, since he had returned without his love and wife. And, he did not want his father or any of the other elders to know that she was with child.

"Josh, the legends forbid you to return to the homeland before you have completed your missions on all the other worlds. You cannot risk the Law finding us here. They will destroy everything this paradise has ever meant to the legends of the tribes. Why do you insist on a daily basis for me to change their minds?" Naihu was concerned about his son and his actions of late. "Besides, they are sure not to let you go alone. Zac did that so many seasons ago and he was unable to return to his family.

"Father, it is something that I can't tell you until Zerasha is by my side again. If you will not talk to the elders then I will." Josh stormed out of the palace hut and went to his own hut. He would need to clear his head and try to get a message to Zerasha. All the other times he had tried he failed. The different dimension made it very hard to contact someone in another dimension.

Josh lay on the furs of his bed and pictured his wife in his mind. He could see her clearly this time. It was as if she had him in her thoughts as well. "Zerasha, if you can hear me, please send me a sign." Josh watched the vision in his head.

"Josh, the ba...." The message ended.

Josh ran to the palace hut to meet with his father and a few of the elders. "Father, there is something that all of you need to know, then I am taking the transport and going to my beautiful wife." Josh waited long enough for Zac and his wife to arrive, and then he continued, "Zerasha did not return with me because she is with...,"

"I'm going to be a great father?" Zac could not contain his excitement. He had received a vision from Zerasha some months ago, and he knew what the young Josh was going through. He had not said anything to Josh, because of the elders' decision to hold him on the island.

"Zac, don't rush into things that you have no knowledge of," his wife spoke to quiet him.

"Yes, you will all be great parents, but not if I don't get to her. I have to be there, and from the last image I had of her, there is very little time left," Josh continued.

"Josh, did you know that she was with child when you left her? And, was it your decision or hers?" Naihu started interrogating his son. The legends forbid any man to leave his wife with child without knowledge of his return.

"Yes, Father, I knew she was with child. No, it was not my idea. I would surely have missed the end of the mission that I was sent on to be with her. But she insisted that I come back to the paradise and let you and the rest of the elders know that my mission was complete. However, I promised her that I would return as soon as the elders would allow. Now, I find that the elders have been sitting on my request and my child is due in the other world any day." Josh was furious. He had never spoken against the elders, but he did not like the idea that they held him here.

"Go, Josh. Be with your wife. She will need you to help her, and then you can bring your family to the paradise and have no more worries. I will make sure that a message gets to the mainland to have your transport ready for travel." The former Queen had intruded the thoughts of the elders and had given the young man permission.

She did not care what the elders thought of the idea of anyone finding the paradise. This man had been through enough in his lifetime. He did not need to miss the birth of his first child.

"Ma'am, please. I beg your permission to speak" Naihu did not like his royalty stepped on, nor did he like to have decisions made for his family.

"Permission granted." The Queen spoke coldly to the King.

"I misunderstood the intentions of my son to return to the other dimension for his wife. He did not share the information that he was waiting for the birth of his child. I am sure it was because the legends forbid it. I will make every effort to get him on the transport immediately and get him to his wife and child. Please forgive me, Madam Chair." King Naihu bowed to the former queen of the island.

"You are forgiven, but if you are still standing here when I open my eyes, I will forbid you the royal honor of picking the betrothed for your own grandchild." She spoke with her eyes shut.

Naihu charged out the door with his son following behind him. Josh had already prepared the things that he would need and had left them outside the palace hut door. Within minutes the two men were bidding each other fare well and good luck.

Josh would be by his wife's side in a few days. He hoped he would be in time. There was only one thing that he did not want to miss out on. That was the birth of his child.

He climbed into the small transport, radioed to take off, and was soon rounding the moon that would take him to the other dimension. Zerasha's image was clear and he had no trouble finding the old transport site behind the old house. He landed the transport in a clearing beyond the ridge. It would be more fun to surprise the joy of his life. He suspected she did not know he was here.

As he approached the large house of his childhood, he heard her screaming. He raced the last distance to the house and flung the door open. When he reached the top of the ladder to the sleep floor, he could see the beautiful woman he had left behind. Though she was covered in sweat and still screaming quietly, he still beheld her as the most wonderful thing that had ever happened to him.

She had not looked up when he came up the ladder, so he stood there for a few short minutes just watching her. When she screamed his name he answered her.

"Yes, my love. I am here with you now." Josh waited for her anguished expression to change. It did not. "What can I do to help, Zerasha?" He reached for her hand that was shaking from the strain.

"Josh! When did you...," A smile that put a glow in the room had crossed her face. "I knew that you would return. The baby is...," once again she was forced to not finish the sentence.

Josh could see the top of the baby's head between his wife's legs. He had learned enough from her mother that he knew it was time to help and comfort her. He bent down between her legs and reached for the tiny head. She pushed and cried one last time before the child cried its first sound. Josh took the towels from the side table and gently cleaned the small child before he handed him to his mother.

"Shall we call him Joshua of Naihu? Or Zachariah of Shahi?" Josh could not believe his eyes. The small life that lay in his wife's arms wriggled and squirmed at each of the suggestions. "What color are his eyes? Do you think he will have the abilities of the elders?" Josh started to laugh.

"You will call him Joshua Zachariah Naihu Shahi Nehra." The vision of Josh's father had appeared before the couple and their child. "He will be... Son, it will be your responsibility to find this young man a woman to marry when he is of the right age." The vision disappeared, and then reappeared briefly. "I am looking forward to seeing you both, all three in a few days, when you are healthy enough to travel, Zerasha."

"Josh, do the legends allow the mother to help in picking the betrothed for her children?" Zerasha had a glow about her that Josh had only seen one other time. It was when he had left her in the care of the old house, alone.

"Did you have someone else in mind, other than the beautiful Charli of Nehra?" Josh grinned.

"No." Zerasha wanted nothing more than to have their first born be wed to the first born of their friends Ran and Shraze. Shraze would be astonished with the news. "There have not been any other boy babies born on the island in the last few months, have there?" It was almost a statement though Zerasha felt like she had been cut off from the world of her ancestry.

"No, there have not been any other babies born. My brother is about to have one of his own, but it will be a few more months. My father told him if he had the heir to the throne, there may be consequences from the elders, namely our father." Josh could not hold onto his excitement any longer. He opened the window and bellowed at the top of his lungs, "I am the father of the heir to the throne of Naihu-Shahi-Nehra," though he knew no one would hear him.

The next few days were spent gathering enough supplies for the trip back through the dimensions. Josh boarded up all the windows on the large house and took the things they would not need and locked them in the secret room below the work floor. There would be a time when he would return to this land for them, but until then they would be safe from being found. When the last window was boarded up, Josh took the large lock and put it on the front door and locked it. There would not be anyone in the large house for many seasons and generations to come. This time Josh would leave it without fear of where he was going or when he would return. It was a time that he would never forget, and he would someday bring his son to the house where he and his father were born. Until that time, the house would remain untouched by any other hands.

The tribes of the legends would live on for many seasons and generations. J.Z. would learn all there was to life and the legends before he would be allowed to visit the house of his birth. Josh took the small child and held him up to see the house before the happy couple headed for the transport and the dimension that would take them home.

www.ingramcontent.com/pod-product-compliance
Lightning Source LLC
Chambersburg PA
CBHW051232260626
47162CB00002B/397